Gunman's Goal

A Western Story

MAX BRAND

Gunman's Goal

A Western Story

Thorndike Press • Chivers Press
Thorndike, Maine USA   Bath, England

This Large Print edition is published by Thorndike Press, USA
and by Chivers Press, England.

Published in 2000 in the U.S. by arrangement with
Golden West Literary Agency.

Published in 2000 in the U.K. by arrangement with
Golden West Literary Agency.

U.S. Hardcover 0-7862-1856-8   (Western Series Edition)
U.K. Hardcover 0-7540-4366-5   (Chivers Large Print)
U.K. Softcover 0-7540-4367-3   (Camden Large Print)

An earlier version of this story, "Three on the Trail" by Max Brand,
was serialized in Street & Smith's *Western Story Magazine*
(5/12/28–6/16/28). Copyright © 1928 by Street & Smith
Publications, Inc. Copyright © renewed 1955 by Dorothy Faust.
Copyright © 2000 for restored material by Jane Faust Easton and
Adriana Faust Bianchi. Acknowledgment is made to Condé Nast
Publications, Inc., for their co-operation.

The name Max Brand is trademarked by the U.S. Patent and
Trademark Office and cannot be used for any purpose without
express written permission.

The text of this Large Print edition is unabridged.
Other aspects of the book may vary from the original edition.

Set in 16 pt. Plantin by Minnie B. Raven.

Printed in the United States on permanent paper.

British Library Cataloguing-in-Publication Data available

Library of Congress Cataloging-in-Publication Data

Brand, Max, 1892–1944.
    [Jackson trail]
    Gunman's goal : a western story / Max Brand.
      p.   cm.
    Originally published: The Jackson trail. New York :
Dodd, Mead & Co., 1932.
    ISBN 0-7862-1856-8 (lg. print : hc : alk. paper)
    1. Large type books.   I. Title.
PS3511.A87 J3   2000
813´.52—dc21   00-044696

Editor's Note

Frederick Faust wrote a total of ten stories about James Geraldi, all of which appeared in various issues of Street & Smith's *Western Story Magazine* under the byline Max Brand. Two of the Geraldi stories were published as serials in a number of installments. "Three on the Trail" appeared as a six-part serial in *Western Story Magazine* (5/12/28–6/16/28) and was the first of the two serials to appear in book form as *The Killers* (Macaulay, 1931) by George Owen Baxter. "The Geraldi Trail" appeared as a four-part serial in *Western Story Magazine* (6/11/32–7/2/32), but its first book appearance was complicated by the fact that Dodd, Mead & Company, which was publishing Faust books at the time under the byline Max Brand, did not want to publish a Max Brand novel featuring a character that had already appeared previously in a George Owen Baxter novel issued by a competitor. Therefore, the character's name was changed from James Geraldi to Jesse Jackson, and the book published by Dodd, Mead in 1932 was accordingly titled *The Jackson Trail*.

Gunman's Goal — as the serial, "Three on the Trail," has now been titled — is the first story in the saga about James Geraldi. The James Geraldi stories will at last be published in book form in definitive texts so they can be read as a continuing saga — which was the author's intention in writing them.

Chapter One

A BIRD AND HIS FEATHERS

The landlord leaned in the doorway. He had not paused to knock, but, softly turning the knob, he had let the draft carry the door wide. Now he was able to observe his guest seated in shirt sleeves at the pine table between the cot and the window. He observed that the shirt was silk; also that it was so frayed that one elbow appeared in view, while James Geraldi, otherwise known as Slim Jim, manipulated a pack of cards.

Even the harsh eye of the landlord was enchanted by the skill of the youth. The fifty-two separate cards in his fingers became one liquid unit. His shuffling made no sound other than a light whispering, so dexterously could he mix the pack. Now he dealt, saying softly: "You lose . . . I lose . . . he wins."

The deal completed, he flipped the five-card hands face up, withdrew the useless ones, and then smoothly transformed a pair to a full house, three of a kind to four, and a

7

useless flush of four to a most useful flush of five. He gathered in the cards again, and again he shuffled with the same noiseless grace.

However, the landlord had seen enough: "You lose, kid!" he announced harshly.

Slim Jim moved neither head nor hands. But he tucked his feet quietly behind the front legs of his chair, so that he was prepared to spring up in any direction, in case of need. After this, he turned his head leisurely and surveyed his host with an inviting smile. He was a handsome fellow, this Geraldi, with blue eyes and blue-black hair and a flashing white smile. He possessed the lazy, feline beauty of a black leopard that looks vaguely through the bars of its cage. But suppose that the bars were down — what then?

The landlord thought of this as the calm, contented eyes of his guest turned upon him. But, on the other hand, he had some confidence in breadth of shoulders and downright weight, even if a vast deal of that weight was concentrated in the region of the stomach. Moreover, in case of need there was a hard lump in his right hip pocket, a pocket specially fashioned to accommodate a long-barreled, blue-nosed Colt revolver.

So he ventured into the room, but only a single step.

"Sit down, Mister Chalmers," said Slim Jim. "Sit down and take a little hand with me."

"Kid," said the big man, "I been watchin' your deal, and I see that you got the conscience of a buzzard, or a hungry coyote. But I would like to know, if you can do all of those things, why ain't you rich, instead of owing me three weeks for this room?"

"I'll tell you the answer," said Geraldi with a sigh, and in his velvet voice. "I've wasted most of the years of my life."

"You have? And doing what, kid?"

"Working," said Geraldi, and sighed again.

The landlord started to laugh, but he ended with a grunt that was almost a curse. "Wasted your time working, eh? Is that work, me son?"

"Ah," said the other, "but this is a recent discovery of mine. This is a talent which I never thought of using until I came to your charming old city, Mister Chalmers."

"You've had three weeks to work this charming old city," growled Chalmers, "but I ain't seen any rent paid down."

"That's because there is only one defect in this graceful old town," said Slim Jim.

"And what's that?"

"There are no suckers in this place," said

Geraldi. "There are no suckers, plain or flowering. Solomon was the grandpa of every man here. And certainly," he added, peering at the formidable bulk and the keen face of the big man, "he must have been yours, Mister Chalmers!"

The landlord admitted the effect of this compliment with a chuckle that shook his deep bosom. It rumbled like far-off thunder. However, it did not soften his mood for a moment. He immediately answered: "I've waited long enough. I never would have waited this long, except that the old woman has dunned you before, and you turned her fool head around. By God, if she didn't come to me this morning to try to get money to lend you!" He leered at Slim Jim, and then chuckled again. "Pay or jail, kid," he concluded.

"Very well," sighed Geraldi. "I'll arrange the payment this afternoon."

"You will not, me lad. You'll arrange it damn' *pronto,* now."

The sleepiness of Geraldi's eyes disappeared for a moment. He raised his head a little, and for an instant there was a yellow gleam as he looked at the big man. He banished that expression with care and made himself smile again. "You mustn't be too hard," he said. "You simply must remember that I've had a long streak of bad luck. The worst sort of bad fortune, you know!"

"Good fortune for the suckers, though," grinned the landlord.

"I could find the little fellows quickly enough," said Slim Jim. "But I don't want to catch minnows. I want full-size fish. One fills a basket. I don't want fools, either. But a hard-boiled sucker is the variety that I'm after, Mister Chalmers."

"You want to skin the sharpers, eh?" said Chalmers.

"I ain't a frigate bird, so to speak," said Slim Jim.

"And what the hell's that?" asked Chalmers, interested in spite of himself.

"A frigate bird," said the guest, "is a bird which hasn't much bulk, d'you see" — here he stretched himself, and then seemed to wave away the significance of his hundred and sixty or seventy pounds of supple muscle — "very little bulk, but chiefly wings and beak and talons."

"I get part of that," agreed the host, considering the boy narrowly.

"It lives constantly on the wing," said the boy.

"I guess you don't sit on the nest very often," commented Chalmers.

"It never rests on the waters, and yet it

lives on fish. Like me."

"How does it catch 'em?" said the landlord, highly intrigued. He had a deep-rooted interest in natural history, like most highly idle fellows.

"You must understand that in the part of the world where it lives there are many varieties of fishing hawks and other fishing birds. They make their catch and rise heavily with it. Then the frigate bird drops off a cloud and flashes his talons in their eyes. They drop their fish. The frigate bird dips down through the air and takes it again, one wriggle from the sea. And there he is with his dinner."

Mr. Chalmers scratched his skin. "You rate yourself that high?" he said.

Geraldi smiled his flashing smile, although his eyes remained as sleepily dull as ever. "I take my chances," he said.

"And wear out your shirt, eh?" concluded the other.

"Practice makes perfect," concluded the frigate bird.

"Young fella, me lad," said Mr. Chalmers, "there's some sharks due to come down here from the mines, any day, after they've lifted the month's pay off the miners. How would you come off with 'em?"

"I came into these waters," said the frigate

bird, "specially to meet them."

"There ain't a dirty trick of the card game that they don't know, and if they spotted you at anything, they'd shoot the smile off your face, kid!"

"There's danger in everything," replied Geraldi. "There's danger of blood poisoning from a pin prick, or a falling brick, or a stumble in the dark, or, for that matter, a mouthful of bread may choke me."

Chalmers chuckled. "Dog-gone me if that line don't make me ache for the old days," he said, "because I used to hear it slung, here and there." He added: "I've spent my time with the sharks, too, I don't mind saying. But I settled down. Bullets and the rope finished off too much brains, from what I saw. I settled down. And now, Slim Jim, I'll take that money."

"As a matter of fact," said Slim Jim, rising to argue the point — and wonderfully graceful were his motions, and wonderfully leisurely — "I could pay you double, as soon as the flood comes down from the hills."

Chalmers spread his legs and thrust his hands into his pockets, thereby revealing a soiled vest, decorated with a heavy gold chain.

"Pay, hell!" he said. "Don't take me for a fool or a sucker, kid. Not plain sucker, nor flowering!"

Slim Jim sighed. "Do you insist, then?" he asked.

"I'll cut the rapping short," declared Chalmers. "Just step over here to the window and look down in front of the hotel."

His guest complied. He leaned from the window and scanned the roofs of the town, for he was in the third story of the hotel. A whirlpool of dust formed down the street and swept furiously away. It caught a group of children coming back from school for lunch and threw them into a confusion of flying papers, shouts, laughter.

The frigate bird smiled gently upon them. "They have grandchildren in this town," he said.

"Does he look like a child?" asked the landlord, who had come to the window in turn. He called the attention of Slim Jim to a wide, thick man who sat on the edge of the watering trough, at that moment biting a chew from a plug of tobacco.

"That's Dick Wing," he explained. "He keeps this damn' town in order. D'you think that he could keep you?"

"He looks very rough," said the gentle Geraldi.

"Looks ain't nothin' to what he is," declared Chalmers. "On the side, he collects my bills . . . from deadbeats, frigate birds, and such." He chuckled at his jest.

The frigate bird sighed again. "How much do I owe you?"

"You know damn' well."

"I really don't."

"Three weeks at sixteen bucks a week is forty-eight, and twenty-seven for extras makes. . . ."

"Twenty-seven for extras," murmured Slim Jim, opening his lazy eyes a trifle.

"What the hell?" complained the land-lord. "Can you have extra steaks and roast chicken at a buck and a half a roast, and broiled ducks, and cream in your god-damn' coffee three times a day, and then kick at a measly extra twenty-seven?"

"I suppose not. I suppose not," mur-mured Slim Jim. "Well, I don't want to make any trouble about it. I detest argu-ments. So here you are!"

He took from his pocket several bills. The eyes of the landlord opened wide upon them. Into his fat hand was counted four twenty dollar greenbacks.

"Well . . . damn me," murmured Chalmers. Then he began to fumble vaguely. "I owe you five bucks, besides," he said.

"It's quite all right," answered the frigate

bird. "Keep that for the good service, the clean floors, and well-washed windows, and the respectable atmosphere of your hotel, Mister Chalmers. You're very welcome."

Chalmers recognized the irony, but he merely grunted. "Look here, kid," he said, "tell me why you held out so hard. Did you think that you could best me, in the finish? Did you think that you could talk me out of seventy-five iron men?"

"The fact is," said the frigate bird, "that I always hate to reduce my working capital below a certain figure."

"Sure," grinned the landlord. "A bird has got to have feathers, eh?"

And he turned from the room, while Slim Jim, stepping to the window, shied out of it a well-worn, pigskin wallet. It took the air beautifully, and skimmed to rest on the gutter of a roof across the street. After that, he glided to the door and locked it.

Chapter Two

A BIRD IN HIS FLIGHT

He hardly had accomplished this before there was a thunder at the door, and the handle rattled as it was turned frantically back and forth.

"You . . . hey! You yella dog!" shouted the landlord.

Geraldi went to the cupboard at the side of the room, opened it, and swept out an armful of clothes. These he sorted with speed, going through them with some slight attention to each garment.

"Hey, Geraldi!" yelled the landlord.

"Yes, yes!" said Geraldi cheerfully. "Is that you, Mister Chalmers?"

This polite inquiry seemed to madden the big man. "Is it me? Is it me?" he bellowed. "You god-damn' deadbeat . . . you sneak thief! Open that door and I'll show you if it's me!" He hurled his weight at the door.

Not another barrier in the hotel would have withstood that assault, but it so happened that this door was newly restored and

17

was of stout new wood. Even so it shook and gave under the battering.

The frigate bird watched the door with the calmest unconcern, but, when it seemed on the point of yielding, he took out from some part of his clothing — with a gesture far too fast to be followed — a full-size .45 caliber Colt and weighed it for a thoughtful instant in his hand.

In that instant a trained observer — such as the landlord, for instance — could have noted that there was neither rear nor front sight to blemish the smooth and polished barrel of the gun. The very hammer of the Colt had been filed and rubbed so that it would give the least friction to a rapid touch.

Slim Jim, noting that the door promised to hold out against the weight of the landlord, restored the gun to its former place, and again the speed of that motion baffled the eye. He continued to sort his clothes, while Chalmers boomed: "Are you gonna open this here door? If you don't, by the livin' God, I'll hang you in my back yard like a stray dog!"

"Tut, tut," murmured the youth. "Are stray dogs hanged in this town, Mister Chalmers?"

Another roar answered this pleasant remark, and then Chalmers was heard crashing down the hall. His voice thundered in the distance: "Here, you Mike and Pete! Watch that door till I can get help up here. I'm gonna jus' nacherally kill that damn' sneak!"

His footfall banged on the stairs, and the frigate bird, having gone through all his effects and apparently having decided that none of them was worth a delay or the care of transport, sauntered to the window and sat on the edge of the sill. There he rolled and lighted a cigarette, and saw his host dart out from the entrance to the hotel, seize on the bull-like man who waited at the watering trough, and with him reënter the building.

At the same time, his enormous voice had echoed throughout the neighborhood, and women and children and men began to run out from the dinner tables and stand gaping at windows or doors. Distinctly, Geraldi heard a frightened woman across the street wailing that there was going to be another murder in the hotel.

Still Geraldi retained his place on the sill.

He waited until the charge of the assailants was rolling down the upper hallway. Then he snapped the cigarette away through the window and sat up with his weight resting lightly on his hands. There was not a trace of lazy indifference about him now, and the misty blue of his eyes was shot with dangerous yellow.

He seemed to know exactly what all his surroundings were, and, when the moment came for action, he did not delay. He stood up on the sill of the window. Below him, dropped three sheer stories to the dusty ground. Above him, there was the small molding over the window head, and several feet higher the roof projected on untrimmed rafters. Between those rafters and the crossboards that supported the shingles was a slight gap — sufficient to admit the grip of a hand around the beams.

All of these things must have been noted long before by Geraldi, for he set to work at once. At one corner the molding of the window head was slightly warped away from the wall of the house. In this he fixed the grip of his left hand. With the spring of his legs and the thrust of his left arm, he drove himself suddenly high up and gripped his right hand around the projecting rafter. There he dangled while an hysterical yell rang up and down the street beneath him.

He had removed himself from the window, but his position seemed hopeless. He shifted his grip farther out, to the very end of the rafter. Then he swung his body to the side and twitched a leg over the gutter of the roof edge. He tested its strength with two convulsive jerks. When it held, he gave it his entire weight, and instantly he was over the rim of the gutter and lying along it at full length, while a wild cheer came from the watchers.

At the same instant the heads of the man of the law and the landlord were thrust out the window.

"Where is he?" roared Chalmers.

A wave of noise answered him, but, presently, pointing hands indicated the roof, and Chalmers snarled with satisfaction.

"I'm gonna shoot that god-damn' bird right off the roof, Bud," he said to the man of the law. "There ain't any place that he can go to!" And he turned to run down to the street level again.

In the meantime, young Geraldi stood erect, one foot on the slanting roof, one in the gutter. There, poised dizzily, he looked about him, dusting his hands, and then waving gracefully to the crowd in the street as though he accepted and acknowledged the applause.

He was on the highest summit of Sankeytown, and from it he could look over the roofs everywhere, and beyond to the hills north and west, and the shimmering

21

desert in both other directions with the bright gleam of the railroad tracks disappearing in the distance. He passed now along the roof to the side of it and halted there an instant to consider again. The next house was a story short of the hotel, and, therefore, the roof lay ten feet below the level at which he was standing. Moreover, there was a ten-foot gap between the two projecting edges. However, as he surveyed the gap, Geraldi nodded in content.

He retraced a few steps along the gutter and then turned and ran forward. Those who watched, gasping and chattering comments, now grew silent. Faces were strained, eyes bulged until Geraldi, reaching the side of the roof, bounded high from the gutter and dove through empty air. Then all throats were loosed. There was a cheer from the men who saw that feat; there was a scream from the women.

When he lost the momentum of his leap, he dropped the feet that he had carried tucked well up, and, with the legs dangling, his arms trailing above his head, he fell toward the lower roof.

All who watched expected surely that the shock would throw him, on the rebound, from the sharply slanted roof-line and down to the ground below, where only Providence could keep him from a broken neck. However, he fell loosely and lay in a limp heap for an instant. It seemed that he must have snapped every bone in his body, but the next moment he had risen again and was traveling rapidly, on all fours, up the slope until he topped the ridge of the house.

There he poised himself. Volleys of applause washed up to him, and Geraldi, removing his hat, bowed profoundly to either side, his hand over his heart, his feet perched precariously on the roof-tree of the building.

Here big Chalmers, running from the front entrance of the hotel and lurching far into the street, saw his quarry. "By God, he *is* a bird!" yelled Chalmers. "But here's where I bag him!"

He snapped up his gun for the shoot, but the other was dropping as the weapon exploded, and no one who watched could be sure that the pursued had slipped down to safety, or fallen with the shock of the .45 caliber slug that would roll him down the steep incline and send him hurtling to the ground in the back yard of the house.

Chapter Three

A LUCKY DAY

Ordinarily, no one could have been more sure of his marksmanship than was big Chalmers, of the hotel. However, in this case, the distance was a bit far for a revolver, and his heavy panting, after rushing up and down stairs several times, might well have thrown his shot out of line.

From the crowd he had little help. Chalmers was by no means popular, for everyone knew that his money had been gained, as he had confessed to Geraldi, among the sharks and the sharpers until fear of the law at last made him retire to quieter ways. He was a good deal of a bully, as well, and therefore, not knowing what crime could be laid against Slim Jim, the townsmen put their hearts behind his escape and stirred not a hand to help the pursuer. However, Chalmers had with him the man of the law, a practiced and relentless fighter. He had, moreover, a crew of waiters, stable men, and bartenders to follow at his heels.

This army he directed swiftly to proceed in two flying wings, one around one side of the neighboring house and one around the other.

"He's picked my pocket of a thousand bucks!" said Chalmers, frothing with rage. "I'm gonna pick his bones! Boys, I'll pay a hundred to the gent that drops him!"

They hardly needed that encouragement. There is something in a hunt that draws all men forward, whether the quarry be a fox or a human. They sprinted around the adjoining house. There was no sign of the fugitive either on the slanting roof on that side or writhing in the back yard.

"He got down onto the roof of that shed!" yelled Chalmers. "He's on a hoss, by now. Run, damn you, run!"

Run they did. But when they tore open the door of the horse shed, they found a startled horse in each of the four stalls. There was no Geraldi in the hay mow above. There was no Geraldi in the woodshed behind. There was no mark of his feet in the alley to the rear of the yard.

For Geraldi had found a skylight on the far side of the roof, to the rear. It was not a new discovery. For every good general, even on ground where he does not expect to fight a battle, is sure to consider means of retreat and proper lines thereof, just as he is sure to consider means of advance and attack upon the enemy.

He went straight to the skylight, and found it locked.

But from inside his coat he drew a short bar. It was neither thick nor heavy, but it was made of the finest steel money could buy, and one end was sharpened to a chisel edge. This edge he drove into the crack, and presently the skylight was turned back on its hinges. Geraldi peered down at a dusty ladder, and this he descended into a narrow attic room, piled at the sides with boxes and old trunks, all generously layered over with such dust as blew from the desert during a sandstorm, and had penetrated the cracks of the skylight above.

The door to this room was locked, as the skylight had been, but this time he did not draw the steel bar. He allowed the jimmy to remain in the lining of his coat and took from his pocket a narrow little blade of steel, tough and supple. This he passed into the lock, and worked for a moment, his eyes closed, his whole being concentrated in the sense of touch. After a brief moment the lock turned. It gave forth a rusty squeak, and young Geraldi stepped into a narrow hall, very dim even at midday.

He passed down its length, descended a flight of steps, and found himself on the second floor of the building. At the same moment, heavy footfalls beat up the stairs, and Geraldi noiselessly opened the first door behind him.

One glance assured him that it was empty, and he stepped inside and closed the door behind him. He touched the key, as though to lock it, but changed his mind and waited.

Several men had climbed into the hallway. He heard the loud bellow of Chalmers. "I'm gonna search every room of this god-damn' house. Beg pardon, Mister Asprey. I gotta find a low hound that picked my pocket of a thousand dollar roll!"

Geraldi, at that, conjured the revolver into his hand once more.

"I wouldn't use a gun," said the voice of a woman.

He whirled to the side, a very dangerous man, indeed, now, and that yellow glimmer was flickering back into his blue eyes. He saw that she was sitting in the farther corner of the room. Chintz curtains draped the two windows, and the dress she wore was of such a bright and cheerful pattern that it went with the curtain perfectly. He was not surprised that he had not noticed her when he first entered. Or else she might have been standing in the window niche, and stepped out to the chair while he was at the door, listening.

Two things seemed wonderful to Geraldi. The first was that, being a woman, she should be so composed. The second was that any creature on the soiled face of this man-stained world should be so fresh, so beautiful. He drank in all the picture with that first wild, threatening glance. Her hair was red-gold; her eyes were as blue as his own; and her slender hands, folded in her lap, seemed too transparent to be mere flesh.

She did not wince under his stare, and that could have been the third marvel to Geraldi, for, although in his short days he had wandered over most parts of this globe, he had only met two or three men who could bear the full weight of his glance. And those men had not lived to talk afterward of their daring and nerve.

"I wouldn't use that," she repeated.

"No," answered Geraldi in a voice as soft as her own, "you're quite right. He's not worth killing. Besides, it wouldn't do much good."

He fled across the room with a soundless step that a dancer would have envied. Out the window he glanced and noted a climbing vine that raised a strong stalk along the wall of the house. At that instant a hand beat on the door of the room. Geraldi in the split second revolved two thoughts in his mind. One was to leap through the window and go sailor-like down the vine. But before he reached the ground was it not far more than probable that a bullet would drive downward through his brain? It would be better to whirl about and dam up that doorway with the dead bodies of his pursuers. And yet instinct made him do neither. He slipped in behind the curtain and waited there, while the door was thrown wide.

A rush of three or four men poured in. He heard big Chalmers booming: "Fast but careful, boys. That bird will shoot your eyes out, if he's cornered! Hey, hello, Miss Asprey. I didn't see you. Did anything come in here . . . last couple of minutes?"

"I don't see what you mean," said the girl, with apparent wonder in her voice.

"A man . . . a slim-looking, handsome gent with black hair . . . slick and fast . . . did he come in here?"

"Oh, no," she answered.

"You been here right along?"

"Yes. I've been here reading."

"He couldn't've slipped in without you seeing?"

Miss Asprey laughed.

"I tell you, ma'am," cried Chalmers, "that gent can move like a shadow!"

"No shadow has come in here," she said with decision.

Geraldi heard the scrape of her chair, as she pushed it back — no doubt to rise.

It did not seem strange to him. Somehow he had known that she would shelter him, and he took what she said for granted. Her perfect poise, her calm indifference to the noise and the excitement of Chalmers and his bloodhounds seemed wonderful to Geraldi. He was almost tempted to peer out from behind the curtain to watch her face as she confronted the others.

"That's all!" said Chalmers suddenly. "Get out of here, boys. Sorry, Miss Asprey."

They retreated.

"Search every damn' corner. He's *got* to be here!" Chalmers was roaring in the hall.

It was the cue for Geraldi to step forth from his hiding place, but he kept in cover, instinct ruling him again.

Suddenly the door was cast open. The draft it let in fanned back the curtain into the face of Geraldi, and he knew that his feet must be showing beneath the edge of it.

"Well?" said the quiet voice of the girl.

"I'm sorry," snarled Chalmers. "But there ain't nothin' like makin' sure."

He withdrew, and the door banged this time with a definite decision.

So Geraldi moved from behind the curtain. He crossed the floor with no more noise than a blowing leaf, and as silently, cautiously, he turned the key in the lock. Then he turned to the girl. "That's that!" he said.

She was resting two rounded elbows on the polished surface of a little table, and watching him with her head turned a little on one side. But what amazed him was to see the faintest of smiles upon her lips.

"You're having a grand time of it, aren't you?" she asked him.

Slim Jim smiled broadly in turn. "It was rather a close thing," he admitted. "But a nose is as good as a length, isn't it?"

"Of course, it is," replied the girl, "if no one protests the winner."

He bit his lip.

"Won't you sit down?" she asked him. "You seem to be tired."

He took a chair close to her. He did not thank her. He did not ask her why she had spoken for him. Such questions seemed to be quite out of place at the moment.

She continued to look at him with interested and kindly eyes. "This is a lucky day for me," she said. "I've been watching you for days, and hoping I could talk to you."

Chapter Four

HOW THE BIRD LEARNED TO FLY

The frigate bird found himself at a stand. How she could have seen him while she remained invisible was to him a miracle, for there was little that escaped his eye, hardly more than escaped the glance of the bird whose character he claimed. So he made no answer, except that he bowed to her a little, and then waited. One could have said that it was a respectful distance which he kept from her. On the other hand, it might have been set down as the attitude of one who expects commands. But the girl interpreted this silence in neither of these ways.

She said with that faint smile of hers: "I peeped out the window and saw you one morning as you were sauntering downtown. And then I asked about you."

The frigate bird smiled in turn, a dry, ironical smile, which gave not the slightest hint of kindness to his eyes. It merely sharpened them to a more penetrating keenness.

"I couldn't learn very much," she went

on. "And I've been waiting and hoping that I could see you."

"I am glad," said Geraldi, "that you happened to be in when I called."

They even smiled together, now. He was sure that she was not so frank as she seemed; indeed, that she was letting out only so much as she had to say. Also, it was evident that she did tell the truth when she said that she wanted to see him. There was something both eager and critical in her glance; it reminded him of the face of a horse dealer at a fair, one about to buy, eager to buy, but kept in check by unknown reservations.

Geraldi grew more interested with the passing of every moment.

"I suppose you guess," she went on quietly, "that I wanted to see you because I had need of someone?"

He bowed to her again.

"We may not have much time," she continued. "You know that we may be interrupted . . . though really I hope that you're safe here. May I begin to ask questions?"

"Of course, you may," said Geraldi heartily.

"To begin with . . . you're not employed?"

"No, I'm not. Except in getting away from Chalmers . . . and you've taken that off my hands."

"You may not be through with him yet," she warned him. "I know a good deal about Mister Chalmers. If you are free, I am going to ask you if you would undertake some very hard work for me."

He closed his eyes as though the words gave him pain.

"What's the matter?" she asked.

"I have never worked in my life," said Geraldi plaintively.

She leaned back in her chair and laughed at him; not entirely in amusement, but in delight, for it seemed that for an unknown reason his answer had been just what she wanted. A wave of noise ran across the street; they could distinguish the bull voice of Chalmers roaring, and others answering him.

"He's going quite mad," said the girl. "What did you do to him?"

"I picked his pocket. Of a thousand dollars, he says. I haven't counted it."

In spite of her self-control, that answer made her flush and compress her lips a little; but Geraldi lifted his head higher and regarded her with perfect calm.

"You had something against him, however," she tried to explain.

"He was going to jail me for a three weeks' bill. That was all. I paid him with his own money."

The flush had died from her cheeks now, and she nodded a little; not that she agreed with the morality of this action, but it seemed to interest her and give her a certain amount of satisfaction.

"You've never worked," she said. "But still you've had to live."

"Yes, I've managed to do that."

"Do you mind a great many questions?"

"You have a right to ask 'em," said the frigate bird. "I'm glad to answer. For a while, at least."

"Well, if you've never worked, what *have* you done to live?"

"Picked pockets, for instance," said Geraldi, with a little lift of his head again.

"You're ashamed of that, though. I think I see that you're ashamed of that."

"Perhaps I am," he admitted. "But I learned young."

"How young?"

"Seven."

"Really at seven?"

"Yes."

"That's dreadful! I beg your pardon, I mean, it seems dreadful to me."

"You've read *Oliver Twist?*"

"Yes. Was it like that?"

"I found a Fagan. Otherwise, it wasn't a bit the same."

"Why do you say that?"

"Oliver was a good little boy. He cried when he had to pick pockets, I believe."

She nodded.

"I didn't cry," said the frigate bird. "I was perfectly at home. I loved it!" He chuckled a little. "I used to be a newsboy. I used to dress up in rags and tatters and work the afternoon crowd of businessmen and the evening crowd of theater-goers. Not going *to* the shows, but afterwards. That's the time to get 'em."

"Why should it be?"

"Everyone feels pretty good. The women because they've seen some pretty dresses or had a laugh or a cry. The men because they're better off than the poor devils they've seen on the stage."

"But how did their state of mind help you? Would they give you more . . . tips?"

Geraldi grew red. "I've never begged," he said shortly. Then he enlarged with perfect ease and good nature. "I've done everything else, I suppose. But I meant to point out that, when people are happy, they're blind. You want to keep a dog hungry to have the best out of his eyes or his nose."

She squinted a little, looking deeply into the truth of this. "But you found a good home, eventually?"

"Yes, I did."

"And then it was broken up?"

"I was an underbutler for two years . . . studying the ways and words of the upper set," said Geraldi.

Her eyes flashed — as though that explained a very great deal to her. "Yet," she said, "I suspect that you've seen a good deal more than the service side of . . . polite life?"

"Oh, yes!" said Geraldi, with an open-handed gesture. "Oh, yes, I've been a gentleman for months at a time, when I could afford it." He looked back into the past and nodded slowly. "I've hunted in Leicestershire, you know. And one winter on the Riviera I nearly married a rich countess. An Italian countess, I should say."

"Are they different?"

"Very!"

"But you didn't marry her, after all. Did you run out of funds?"

"No. As a matter of fact, I still had more than half of a very expensive diamond necklace."

"Why didn't you marry her, then?"

"She had a mustache," sighed Geraldi.

"Did someone give you that diamond necklace?"

"Someone's steel safe gave it to me," said Geraldi. "That was a grand night!" A sort of professional enthusiasm burned in him. "It was a triple safe," he said. "I drilled the first shell. I blew the second. And after the crash, there was the third lock looking me in the face." He shook his head and laughed with pleasure at the memory.

"No one had heard it, though?"

"Ah, yes," answered Geraldi. "That was the point. Doors began to slam, and stairs began to creak, while I was on my knees with my ear against the combination, trying to hear the tumblers fall."

"You *did* open it?"

"This was how I got the necklace. It was in the first drawer. I didn't have a chance to open any others."

Their talk halted for a moment.

"You've picked pockets and you've picked safes. Have you done a great many other things?"

"I'm a fair hand with a pen," said Geraldi. "And then I've fiddled about with smaller matters. I've even been in a circus."

"Really in a circus?"

"I was only a boy," said Geraldi. "As a matter of fact, I was with them four years, doing trick riding and shooting, with a few acrobatics and a little juggling on the side."

"Even juggling?" said the girl.

He took a narrow metal case from his

pocket, pressed a spring, and a long, delicate blade leaped into view. He spun the poniard into the air and caught it on the tip of a finger as it came down. "It's really much harder than it looks," said Geraldi. He threw it again. It spun up in such swift circles that it looked like a dim flash of silver, a silver shadow, a silver mist. Again he caught it on a finger tip and balanced it adroitly.

"You could make a very good living, doing such things," she said.

"Not a gentleman's living," he said. Then he summed up: "That's the story. I could give you a few proofs, if you cared to have them."

"Oh, not at all, thank you."

"Very well. Now that you know what I can do . . . tell me, how I can help you?" He added: "I haven't mentioned cards. They came rather late in my life."

"You mean . . . ?"

"Crooked cards, of course."

"Marked?"

"Yes, I can mark them, or run them up. Stack the pack, I mean. Do you understand?"

The girl looked down to the floor and sighed. Then: "You've had your hands on fortunes."

39

"Time and again."

"But here you are in a little Western town. And not very prosperous, it seems?"

"The fact is that I've never had a stake quite big enough to serve as principal . . . I've simply enjoyed very fat interest, from time to time. When that was spent . . . and I have expensive tastes . . . then I had to start again. But I was born in the West, and, therefore, I keep coming back to it. Besides, when one is constantly on the wing, one's trail begins to loop across a good deal of the world."

"You've been in a great many places?"

"Thousands. Yes, of course."

"England and France, it seems? And Italy, too."

"And Germany and Russia."

"Really?"

"And a dip into Africa. A time in India."

"What could you have been doing there?"

"Shooting tigers," said Geraldi, "and studying."

"What?"

"How to live without working."

"Like a Brahman, you mean?"

"No, just the opposite."

She chuckled. Her pleasure seemed greater than ever in this odd confession. "Other places, too?"

40

"I hunted a great mare in Arabia, and I hunted a great pearl in the South Sea Islands. Those are the main parts of my travels."

"You've crowded a great deal into a young life, it seems to me. Languages, too, I have no doubt?"

"Yes. Half a dozen. One of them dead, I'm proud to say."

"But how could you do it? Unless you have a photographic brain."

"Not a bit. But in my sort of life there's always a great deal of spare time. You know what kills the lives of most men?"

"Well?"

"Eight hours a day in an office. Two hours more, to go and come, another couple of hours doing nothing . . . or something foolish . . . in order to relax. That's twelve hours out of twenty-four. You see that they haven't much time left to live in."

"I never thought of that," admitted the girl.

"Whereas, every moment of my life is my own, unless I'm being hounded by the law."

"Has that happened very often?"

"A dozen times or so. I mean, a dozen times or so when the detectives hung to the trail a long time."

"But you always got away?"

"Always. I know the jungle."

"What does that mean?"

"The underworld. There's a Paris jungle, a London jungle, a Manhattan jungle. Then there's the jungle that runs back and forth across this country. Along the railroads one can disappear."

She sat up straight. "You've done a great deal of flying from pursuit. Did you ever do any pursuing?"

"Tons of it," he answered carelessly.

"Why should you? Were you taking the law on your own shoulders and helping it out?"

"I was enforcing my own private laws."

"I don't understand that."

"Usually I've worked alone. But now and again one has to take in a partner. And almost always the partner tries to double-cross one in the end."

"Do they really?"

"Of course, they do. Then one has to go on the trail to get one's own."

"I can understand that. It must be dreadfully difficult."

"It is. That's how I went to India, in the first place."

"On a trail?"

"Yes. It started from a little town in Saskatchewan. In two months that trail looped into South America, and toward Calcutta. It ended before Calcutta came."

She, watching him closely, thought that she saw a faint trace of dim, yellow, dangerous light in his eyes. She had seen it once before, when he had turned gun in hand toward the door of the room, and she recognized the motive. "Well," she said, "I thought at first that it wouldn't work out. But I begin to think that it may. That's what I've hoped for. I mean, that's what I'd want to ask you to do. To run down a trail for me."

He had no time to answer. There was a rapid, crisp knock at the door, and then the handle turned impatiently, as though there was someone in the hall who had a right to enter.

"That's mother," said the girl.

The frigate bird was already at the curtains.

"No . . . you'd better not," said Miss Asprey. "I want you to face it out, if you will."

He looked steadily at her. "Certainly," said Geraldi.

She went to unlock the door.

Chapter Five

A MAN WITHOUT FEAR

Mrs. Asprey came in, in a whirl. She was just the opposite of her daughter, who appeared to the frigate bird neither tall nor short, neither fat nor too slender; whereas her mother was decidedly short. She had the head and neck of a girl, except when the light showed the wrinkles of forty-two; but the rest of her was much too big, so that she gasped and had to talk short after the exertion of walking up the stairs. Upon the heaving bosom of Mrs. Asprey a necklace flashed, and, as she clasped her hands, jewels glittered on them.

"Louise!" she gasped. "Did you ever hear of such a thing? Did you ever hear? Did you ever dream? They came crashing right through our house! They didn't even ring the front door bell! I'm going to have Cousin Edgar simply . . . simply. . . . Did you ever hear of such a thing, Louise?"

"Mister Chalmers . . . ," began the girl.

"The . . . the creature," said Mrs. Asprey. "The . . . the unspeakable *thing!* As though anyone would dare to come into our house . . . except the lawless rabble themselves who. . . ."

"But someone did come," said the girl.

"Louise!"

"Yes."

"It can't be! How do you know? Where could he have gone in this house?"

"Will you promise not to scream?" asked the girl.

"Yes, yes, yes!"

"He came into my room."

"Ah-h-h!" shrilled her mother, immediately breaking her word. "Louise! Do you mean it? Here? In this room! How frightful! What did you do? Did you scream? Did you faint? Did he take anything? Child, where's your jewel box?"

"I don't know," said Louise.

"You don't know!"

"But there's the man," said Louise.

Mrs. Asprey turned. Her daughter had placed herself conveniently near, and, therefore, Mrs. Asprey was able to support herself by clutching the strong young shoulder of the girl.

"Gracious heavens! Gracious heavens! Gracious heavens!" said Mrs. Asprey. "What must we do, Louise? What must we do? Must we put up our hands? Will he shoot us?" She supported herself still with one hand on Louise; the other hand she raised as far as possible above her head.

A door closed downstairs.

"There's Cousin Edgar now," said the girl. "Hadn't you better call him in?"

"How dare I stir," moaned Mrs. Asprey.

"He won't hurt you at all," said her daughter. "But you might as well call in Cousin Edgar soon."

Mrs. Asprey, her eyes and her mouth parted wide, moved sidelong toward the door, and, when she was close to it, she toppled through, half leaping and half falling. At once her scream diminished down the hall, down the stairs, as she cried: "Cousin Edgar! Cousin Edgar!"

"I'm sorry," said the girl. "But there was no better way of having her meet you. It would have been just as much of a shock, no matter how I'd managed it. You'll find Cousin Edgar . . . different."

She said that with a significant little pause after the name; but what the pause meant, the frigate bird could not make out. He was growing a little nervous, under his cool exterior, for it seemed to him that the screams of Mrs. Asprey were loud enough to rouse the entire household.

Presently Mrs. Asprey's voice was heard

moaning and gasping and chattering up the hall again, and a deep, smooth bass voice was reassuring her.

"Well, well, well! We'll see about it! We'll see all about it! Dear Cousin Olivetta, trust it to me. My shoulders are broad enough to carry greater burdens than this, I trust."

"Oh, Edgar!" cried Mrs. Asprey in a passion of relief and gratitude. "How could we live without you? How could we exist at all without you? How could I live without you?"

They came into the room, and Geraldi saw a big, smooth, pale man, not fleshy enough to be encumbered by weight, but sufficiently fat to banish wrinkles. He had a little pink spot low down on either jowl, and in times of excitement or of any emotion that pink spot waned and diminished, or increased in size and brightness. His eyes seemed rather small and bright, but that might have been because of the fullness of his face. Nothing about him fixed the eyes of Geraldi so much, however, as his hands. They were remarkably large, and very white and soft, so that when Edgar Asprey pressed his hands together, as he often did while speaking, it seemed to Geraldi as though there were no bones in the fingers.

"And this is the man?" said Cousin Edgar,

as he entered the room.

"Don't go near him, Edgar, dear!" pleaded Mrs. Asprey.

Cousin Edgar paid little attention to the interruption. "A very young man, too," he went on. "An exceedingly young man. What is your name, young man?"

"James Geraldi," said the frigate bird, growing very sleepy-eyed, indeed.

"James Geraldi! A foreign-sounding name, isn't it? But, in these cases, there is usually a foreign-sounding name, and foreign blood as well, I dare say."

He stood in the corner of the room and smiled on the shrinking form of Mrs. Asprey who clung to him more violently than ever; he smiled upon Louise Asprey; he smiled upon the frigate bird himself, and now Geraldi began to grow very interested, for he saw that for the first time in his life he had met a man without fear.

Chapter Six

IN A FRIENDLY WAY

It is an easy thing to bandy about the word "fearless." The nerves of James Geraldi himself were just a trifle stronger than steel cable, but he understood at once that there was a difference between himself and this big, soft man. Now that Cousin Edgar had come well into the light, there was no mistaking him. His soft thick voice, his genial smile, his pulpy body, his graceful gestures were all saying one thing; but his eyes were another matter. As though the soul of an eagle had slipped into the body of a minister of the gospel, living fat and snug in the secure harbor of a rich parish.

It would not be fair to say that Geraldi was frightened as he confronted this man, but a swarm of disagreeable pictures or comparisons started across his mind, and the one that stuck was the thought of a white-bodied octopus floating at ease in the water, with cruel tentacles and deadly eyes to match.

This melodramatic idea made Geraldi

shrug his shoulders and smile a little. He was determined to be wide awake.

"Now let us begin at the beginning," said Cousin Edgar.

"He's a thief," said Mrs. Asprey. "He's stolen money from. . . . Do call out the window, Cousin Edgar. Louise, do something! My nerves are giving way."

"Lean on me, my dear," said the hypnotically smooth voice of Cousin Edgar. "Lean on me . . . trust in your cousin. I will soon put everything right. And by the beginning I did not mean the beginning of this young man's crimes. That might be a long story . . . or a short one. Am I right, Mister Geraldi?" He went right on, unctuously, never pausing for answer: "I mean the beginning as it affects this house."

"How simple you make everything, dear Edgar," said Mrs. Asprey.

"Only by going logically and quietly about things, my dear Cousin Olivetta," said the fat man. "And so, Mister Geraldi, will you tell us how you came into our lives, if I may be allowed to put it that way?"

From the corner of his eye, Geraldi saw the girl glance down to the floor, and he guessed that she was much annoyed. For that reason, he made himself cheerful.

"Through the roof," said Geraldi.

"Through the roof!" screamed Mrs. Asprey. "Gracious heaven! Edgar! Dear Edgar! What are we going to do?"

"We are going to be patient," said the big man, and his soft hand squashed over her frantically gripping fingers. "We have made a little beginning. He came, it appears, through the roof. So far, so good. Now let us proceed."

It sounded to Geraldi like the talk of a self-complacent fool, but all the time he was most keenly aware that this man was neither complacent nor a fool. His was a strong, athletic, swiftly moving brain that simply went about its work in a way that differed from the ways of other men.

"Let us go a little further. Having broken through the roof . . . the skylight, if I dare suggest . . . ?"

"The skylight," admitted Geraldi.

"Do I dream?" Cousin Edgar said gently. "Or did I really at one time suggest that an iron frame was much better for a skylight? An iron frame, and a chain and padlock?"

"You did. You did suggest it," moaned Mrs. Asprey. "Oh, heavens! Oh, gracious heavens, why do I ever stand out against any of your ideas?"

"Your own are very good. Your own ideas are admirable, dear Cousin Olivetta," said the fat man. "But by taking thought . . . by patience . . . one marches ahead. One develops. What would Napoléon have been without his marshals? A brain without hands. That is what I want to be, Cousin Olivetta. A hand to you, to help you, and to sustain you."

"You are, Edgar," she said, her eyes filling with tears as she looked up to him. "You are all of that and much more, much, much more!"

Louise Asprey looked upon the pair, and Geraldi saw that her blue eyes had turned as gray as steel.

"Then we must learn how Mister Geraldi happened to take shelter in this room," continued Cousin Edgar. "And how could it have been, my dear young friend, my dear young misguided friend? I trust I may be allowed to say misguided?"

"The thief," breathed Mrs. Asprey.

"Ah, my dear," said the big man, "who among us is without sin?"

"I simply opened the first door," said Geraldi.

"But it isn't the first door," said Cousin Edgar. "It isn't the first door at all. It's quite in the middle of the hall, if I may be allowed to say so. So suppose that you tell us frankly what brought you to this particular door, when there were so *many* doors which you might have opened?" Here his glance wavered for the subtle fraction of a second toward the girl.

Another would have failed to notice it; but the frigate bird saw all things, even from afar.

"I don't know what you're driving at," he answered carelessly, although he was beginning to guess very well. "I only know that, as I came down from the top floor, I heard steps coming up from below, and I turned in at this door. I didn't see anyone in the room, until I was well inside," he added carefully.

"He didn't see anyone," said Cousin Edgar, shaking his head, while the fat fold shook in sympathy beneath his chin, also. "He didn't see anyone! Not even my dear Louise, my sweet Louise, who is such a light among girls? He did not even see Louise, in her gay dress? Come, come, Mister Geraldi, you must be more candid!" And he shook a large, soft, white forefinger at the frigate bird.

The latter grew a little restive. His own smile flashed bright, but there was no mirth in it. "I can't give you a new set of facts," he suggested.

"Perhaps you are right," said Cousin Edgar gently. "Yes, perhaps you are right. It is usually better to stay with one story. It gives one a sense of confidence. I have been a lawyer. Oh, yes, I understand a great many of these little things."

"You understand everything, Edgar!" cried Mrs. Asprey, so filled with admiration that she forgot everything else, even her fear of the moment before.

"But here we are," went on Cousin Edgar. "We have him safely, after a troubled voyage, in the room of our dear Louise. And then? And then? Did I understand that this room was searched, Louise, my child?"

"Yes. It was searched."

"And yet he was not found? But no doubt, since he came in without seeing you, he came in without being seen in turn. Soft as a shadow he flitted, let us say, and hid himself under the bed?" He beamed upon the girl.

Her answer came back like the clinking of metal. "I saw him the instant the door was ajar. And when the search came, of course, I sheltered him."

"Ah . . . ah . . . ah," murmured Cousin Edgar. "Is that it? Is that it?" Again the dewlap wagged beneath his chin. "My wise, bright, clever Louise. Sometimes I forget that you are in the romantic age. May I be permitted to say the romantic age, Louise?"

The girl caught her breath, sorely tried.

Geraldi, with hot rage in his heart, controlled himself sternly and maintained his careless smile.

"That's not a fair thing to say," said Louise Asprey. "Of course, I couldn't turn him over to the head-hunters."

"Of course, you couldn't, my dear. Of course, you couldn't," said Cousin Edgar. He put back his head, and his smile covered his eyes until nothing except a single bead of light was visible. "You observe, dear Olivetta," continued Cousin Edgar, "that she could not, of course, give him over to the head-hunters. And I don't blame her. Of course, I don't blame her. If I were a young girl and saw such a handsome young rascal . . . I hope I may be forgiven even by you, Louise, for saying rascal?"

"Cousin Edgar, you are making me very angry," said Louise Asprey.

"Louise!" exclaimed Mrs. Asprey. "I never have heard such a speech in all the days of my life! Louise! Can I believe my ears? To your dear Cousin Edgar? My gracious! My gracious heavens!"

"Oh, don't make a mountain of a mole hill," Cousin Edgar said gently. "The young are thoughtless, Cousin Olivetta. But it would take far more than a thoughtless speech from a girl . . . a dear girl whom I love

. . . to make me forget my duty. And my duty is to serve you with all my heart and all my mind. I trust I may be permitted to say that?"

"Edgar, I can't speak," said Mrs. Asprey. "I'm . . . I'm overcome. Louise, apologize this moment! Louise, I never. . . ."

"Please . . . please . . . please!" said Cousin Edgar. "That there should be trouble in this house on my account. A great many things, I dare to say, that I have borne . . . forgive me. But that I could not bear. I never could endure it."

"See, Louise?" cried Mrs. Asprey. "See what you've done. Our dear, noble Edgar . . . with never a thought for himself . . . I could simply cry." Tears, in fact, made her eyes wet, and one rolled slowly down her cheek while she looked upward to Cousin Edgar.

He did not seem to see it, but with a cheerful voice he continued: "But let us get on . . . let us finish this little matter. How small it will seem in a few months. Time is the great physician. Even for romantic hearts, I dare hope. I do dare to hope that, Louise, dear girl."

She had stood more than she could bear, and now she cried angrily: "I won't be badgered any longer. I've told you the exact facts.

I sheltered him. I'd do it a thousand times again. My father taught me what hospitality should be in the West. You were raised in the East, you know. That makes a difference!"

"Louise!" cried Mrs. Asprey, outraged again.

"Girls are young, both east and west," smiled Cousin Edgar. "East and west, and north and south, they are young, young, young. God bless them . . . and keep them safe."

"Edgar!" gasped Mrs. Asprey, in what was meant to be an aside. "*What* do you mean? Call the police! Get the sheriff. . . ."

"Hush, dear," said Cousin Edgar. "Everything slowly . . . the sudden strain breaks the rope. Humor her, Cousin Olivetta. Youth has foolish fancies." He added aloud, for the rest had been a plainly audible whisper: "Perhaps you are right, Louise. And the very best thing is for us to keep the young gentleman for dinner . . . so that we can talk everything over in a friendly way."

Chapter Seven

BIG GAME HUNTERS

So the frigate bird was carried away by Cousin Edgar. He could not make out whether that gentleman had from the first intended to keep him over in the house until dinner, or whether it was a last minute change of tactics, when he saw that he had infuriated the girl to such a degree. Mrs. Asprey was left behind in the room of her daughter, and the last Geraldi heard was the high tremolo of the lady assailing her daughter. However, he had no doubt as to how a duel between the two of them would come out.

Cousin Edgar did not allow any embarrassing silences. He began to talk as they went along the hall and down the stairs, putting in his words slowly, so that they covered a good deal of space. "So here we have him again," said the big man. "Here we have the young adventurer . . . the gentleman adventurer," he added. He had changed his tune most decidedly since they left the

58

room; there was a rich good-fellowship in his voice. "We'll go down to my study and have a bit of a chat, unless you prefer a *siesta*."

The frigate bird did not prefer a *siesta*, so he was ushered into a room on the ground floor, not a very large room, and one that seemed yet smaller because of what was within it. The skin of a black-maned lion hung on one wall. The stripes of a black-maned Bengal tiger decorated another. A wild boar champed his tusks in a corner, and above the fireplace the dreadful mask of a leopard grinned at them.

"You're a collector," suggested the frigate bird, perfectly willing to maintain pleasant relations with everyone in this house until the coming of night should give him an opportunity to escape from the place and the whole town.

"In a small way I've been a collector, in the days of my youth when I, also, was an adventurer," smiled Cousin Edgar. "But not with money, my dear young man. Never with money. These are the pick, each in its own way, of all the trophies which have fallen under my rifle."

"I see," said the frigate bird, "that you give the place of honor to a leopard."

"Does that surprise you, my friend?"

59

"Not a bit," answered Geraldi. "The devils will kill you as easily as a lion or a tiger, and they're twice as brainy and three times as fast."

The eye of Cousin Edgar grew luminous with sympathetic agreement. He seemed inspired to talk by this opening, and for a long time he breezed gently through a narrative of hunting exploits. Sooner or later, nearly every wild thing that may happen to a hunter was embraced by the discourse of Cousin Edgar, and the frigate bird, listening with his pleasant smile and his dull, sleepy eyes, made sure that it was a pure fiction of the mind. It appeared that Cousin Edgar wished to make an impression upon him.

"But," he said, when the narrator paused, "you don't say anything about the leopard?"

"That was an ugly thing," murmured Cousin Edgar. "I rarely speak about it. It was an ugly thing. I was hunting with a young *maharajah.* . . ."

The frigate bird looked down. *Maharajahs,* no matter how often they appear in hunting tales, do not ordinarily take on every chance adventurer to add to their shooting parties. He looked up again as Cousin Edgar continued: "He was a beautiful young prince, slender as a sapling, as the saying goes, and strong as a spring of steel. He really was. We found ourselves together in the midst of a hunt. The servants and the other hunters were out of sight when I wounded a leopard. It was growing dusk. I wanted to turn back, but the *maharajah* insisted that the dead leopard would be found behind the very next bush . . . and then the next. We got deep in the woods. I stumbled and wrenched my knee, and by the time I had got up and was starting to walk again, my companion was far ahead. I hurried to catch up with him. He grew from a glimmer to a man, ahead of me. And then I saw a black shadow drop on him from a tree.

"It was the leopard, of course. I tried my rifle. It missed fire. There was nothing to do but to close with that snarling devil. By the luck, the greater stroke of the luck that I carried with me, the point of my knife drove through the eye of the leopard and reached his brain!"

The frigate bird looked his host fairly in the face. "That was a wonderfully brave thing to do," he said, and in his heart he told himself that this was a peculiarly gross lie. Cousin Edgar should polish up his sorties, for some of them were too old-fashioned.

"It does sound brave," said Cousin Edgar. "As a matter of fact, this thing happened in

61

such a flurry that all of my actions were instinctive. I didn't have time to think. It's in the pauses, I dare say, that fear gets hold of us. I expected to find the prince ripped to shreds, but, as a matter of fact, he was almost uninjured. I had occupied enough of the attention of the leopard, and there were only two deep gashes down the face of the *maharajah*. A dreadful pity, I have always thought, that such a handsome fellow should have been spoiled. But then he was rash, I dare say, rushing ahead like that into the dusk of the jungle."

The frigate bird flipped back the pages of his memory. He, too, could remember a *maharajah* who had been struck down by a leopard. He was neither young nor beautiful, but rather resembled a fat, crouching spider with a hideous sallow smile, and half of his face was writhed to the side, horribly drawn by two jagged scars. He remembered the story that been told, of the prince in the rashness of his youth, and a gigantic white man who had gone in heroically and killed the leopard with a simple hunting knife.

The unctuous recitations of the host no longer seemed to Geraldi unimaginative lies. They were true. All were true! He looked upon Cousin Edgar with new eyes. But, after all, from the first glance at that

62

smooth face and the hawk-like, active little eyes, he had been prepared for almost anything. Suddenly the talk was no longer about the hunting exploits of Cousin Edgar. It concerned another subject — Geraldi himself.

"I take it that you are out of employment?" suggested Cousin Edgar.

"I am," said the frigate bird.

"And I dare to say that as for the work that comes your way, you hardly care whether it is safe or dangerous. For I see that you are of the true metal, my young friend."

Geraldi honored the compliment with a smile. And the other continued with an odd narrative. A friend, a good friend, was persecuted by a malignant scoundrel. The friend was desperate. Owing to peculiar circumstances, it was impossible to reach the offender by the law. Matters had come to such a pass that it was essential to find the culprit, and, in short, put an end to him. With the same quiet unction with which he had told of his hunting exploits, Cousin Edgar joined his soft, white hands and looked above them at Geraldi.

"I think not," said Geraldi with an equal quiet.

"It would mean no small sum. It would mean ten thousand dollars in cash . . . and half of that paid in advance."

"You are very kind to trust me," said Geraldi, "but I never have killed a man . . . except in self-defense. I don't intend to begin. Furthermore, I rarely act as a hired man."

Cousin Edgar did not press the point for an instant. "I understand exactly," he said. "A sort of knight errant, riding in an unlucky century."

Geraldi knew that the fat man was disappointed. He knew, in fact, that he had been taken down to the study for the special purpose of working him up to this point, to this handsome offer of ten thousand dollars blood money for a murder done. No matter how lightly Cousin Edgar turned from the subject, it was a shock to the fat man to have his offer refused.

Shortly afterward, he excused himself. The frigate bird was to make himself comfortable in the study; there were plenty of books to read. Cousin Edgar had other matters to attend to. Geraldi would stay that night to dinner, and afterward, having performed the duties of a good host, Cousin Edgar would show him from the house and bid him Godspeed on his journey.

With that he left the room, and the frigate bird lay down on the sofa under the window with his hands behind his head and tried to piece the matter together. This was a household that seemed to enjoy plenty of money. The jewels of Mrs. Asprey and the dress of her daughter were eloquent on that point, but it seemed odd that such an apparent fortune should be lodged in such a small Western town, shouldering a noisy, brawling hotel. That was not the only singular thing. Mrs. Asprey could be put down merely as a nervous and rather foolish woman. But Cousin Edgar was unique, and so was the girl. Moreover, it could not pass for anything but queer that the girl, at the very first meeting with him, had proposed that he go on an adventurous trail to do certain work, he knew not what. And on the heels of that, Cousin Edgar suggested ten thousand dollars for a murder. However smooth he might be, it was nonsense to imagine that the fat man was representing any friend. This was work of his own, to be paid for out of his own pocket.

Yes, it was an interesting household. And the frigate bird began to smile grimly.

However, there was time to be spent. He took from his pocket a small pack of cards, and, sitting down to the little center table, he began to deal the latest of his cards. For one never could tell with what implements one would have to work. It might be with soiled, edge-thickened cards in a lumber camp; it might be with a miniature pack like this in a boxcar. And the frigate bird believed in being prepared, in all the possible circumstances of war. This was his moment of peace.

But between shufflings and dealings of the cards, his mind harked back to Cousin Edgar. He never had met the like of that man before. He doubted that he would ever meet his like again, and to the very marrow of his bones he was possessed by a thrilling sense of danger to come.

The afternoon wore away. He heard cheerful voices. And venturing a glance out the window, he saw that in the tennis court at the rear of the house and to the side, Mrs. Asprey and her daughter were playing tennis — Mrs. Asprey with gaspings and puffings and shrill cries of despair, and her daughter left handed and, even so, unable to play down to the level of her parent.

A very odd household, indeed!

Chapter Eight

NOT FOR ANY PRICE

It was a singular dinner, when at last the four of them assembled at one table. Geraldi was disappointed because he had not had a chance to talk with the girl again, but doubtless Cousin Edgar and Mrs. Asprey, between them, had arranged to keep Louise occupied every moment. After dinner there might be another chance. He was reasonably sure that she would not rest contented unless she were able to speak with him again before his departure.

At the table, too, Mrs. Asprey attempted to be the bright hostess — no matter under what disadvantages — but he could not help being aware that she was constantly casting side glances of horror and disdain at him.

Her daughter, on the other hand, was quietly pleasant, and Cousin Edgar pointedly included the frigate bird in the talk. It began to be a dialogue between them, with a word from Louise, from time to time. It was to be noted that Cousin Edgar was willing to let

67

the conversation turn on the accomplishments of the singular guest.

"I have been up to the skylight," he said, "and I saw that you had some sort of lever to work on it."

"A little steel bar," said the frigate bird. He produced it in his hand from the inside of his coat.

"A jimmy, in other words," said Cousin Edgar.

"Cousin Edgar, how wonderful," said Mrs. Asprey. "You really know about everything."

He hardly could speak without bringing down her bright, uncomprehending admiration upon his head.

"One travels about the world," he admitted. "One picks up a few ideas, here and there, Cousin Olivetta. Now, Mister Geraldi, after the skylight was pried up in that clever manner, when you came down the stairs from the attic, there you found a locked door at the end of the passage, did you not?"

"Yes. It was locked."

The two women attended with interest — that of Mrs. Asprey being tinged with horror.

"And how did you manage that? I saw no signs of a jimmy." He added: "Not that I wish to draw any what might be termed professional secrets. No, that is far from my mind."

"You're quite welcome to know," said the frigate bird. He produced a little sliver of bright steel. "That was my pass key," he said.

"A very simple device," said Cousin Edgar.

"We'll all be murdered in our beds, some night!" cried Mrs. Asprey, wringing her jeweled hands.

"Mother, dear!" protested Louise.

"I don't mean by Mister . . . ah . . . Geraldi. But by somebody else with jimmies and pass keys. . . ."

"But it isn't a key at all," said the girl.

"Then how did he get in?"

"One can learn locks," said the frigate bird genially, as he smiled upon them all.

Cousin Edgar smiled richly back upon him. "But what patience, what care, what constant thought and practice," he suggested admiringly.

"I had six months with a locksmith," said the frigate bird. He had an astonishing way of opening his mind and telling everything, or what seemed to be everything.

"Six months," said Cousin Edgar.

"He was a genius," reflected Geraldi. "He

made locks of all kinds. He could read the mind of a lock, I think."

"But what a long time to invest in that sort of a study. Six whole months?" commented Louise Asprey.

"We had nothing else to do," said Geraldi. "We were on a little island."

"A desert island?" gasped Mrs. Asprey. "How dreadful!"

"It wasn't a desert," replied Geraldi. "As a matter of fact it was a lovely spot with a few high hills, and palms, and a few little rivulets."

"How did you live?" cried the hostess.

"On shellfish and roast birds, and eggs and fruit, raw or cooked. We really lived like kings."

"How extraordinary!" said Mrs. Asprey. "Isn't it extraordinary, Cousin Edgar? I mean, to live like kings on a desert island?"

"Of course," said Cousin Edgar deeply, "but then you see that your young friend is an extraordinary man."

"But he isn't my . . . ," began Mrs. Asprey, and checked herself just in time. She grew a little red, and urged: "Do go on."

"I don't know what else I should say," said the frigate bird. "I simply was explaining how I happened to study locks."

"But . . . gracious me! . . . you haven't told

us how you happened to get to the island, at all."

"The locksmith and I rowed to it in a gig."

"Rowed to it? Heavens above, Cousin Edgar, they rowed to it . . . clear out on the ocean!"

"It was in the South Seas," Geraldi instructed her patiently. "We didn't have far to row, though. You see, we went most of the way in a sailing ship."

"How perfectly unusual, Edgar," breathed Mrs. Asprey. "I mean, that they should have gone off to a desert island like that, just to study locks."

"Perhaps they had no choice, my dear?" said Cousin Edgar.

"That was it," said Geraldi. "The captain of the ship put us off. Marooned us, you know."

"Heavens, how dreadful!"

Louise cast an impatient glance at her mother. "Do let him get on," she urged.

"He was very fair," said Geraldi. "He gave us some biscuits and a rifle and some ammunition. He let us take most of our things, too. Including my friend's case, which had his locks in it. As a matter of fact, the ship's captain was dealing with us better than he knew. When he hove to, the island was only a blue smudge, and he was sure that it was a naked rock."

"The dreadful creature!" said Mrs. Asprey. "Oh, dear, think what people there are in the world!"

"Hove to, did you say? Was it a sailing vessel?"

"Yes, an Arab."

"Ah, and yet he wasted a boat and a gun and such matters on you?"

"It wasn't entirely his choice," admitted Geraldi. "We were occupying the cabin, and we'd made a fort of it, keeping watch for eight days."

"Ah, ah, ah!" said Cousin Edgar. "That must have been very jolly, eh?"

Geraldi merely smiled.

"So you spent the six months studying locks?"

"Every day and even by firelight. It was fascinating work. Delightful! He was very old and very wise. He had made locks since he was a child. His mind was crowded with facts . . . all about locks. It was filled with stories, too. Perhaps you have no idea how many stories hinge on locks, their making and their unmaking?"

His eye was bland and innocent as he regarded Mrs. Asprey, and she shook her head violently: "I don't see how there could be," she declared. "They're simply iron . . . or steel . . . or some such thing, aren't they?"

"So is a sword, you know," said Geraldi gently. "It's simply steel."

"Gracious me," said Mrs. Asprey, "how did we get to the subject of swords?" She shivered a little.

"You learned to take them apart and put them together?" This from the girl.

"And to listen to the tumblers fall . . . to listen to the tumblers fall!" Geraldi said, half closing his eyes, dreamily. He held forth his right hand, the finger tips close together as though they were surrounding a small knob. Those supple fingers seemed vibrating with an electric sensitiveness.

"Is it so hard to do?" asked Mrs. Asprey.

"It's half in the ear, and half in the touch," said Geraldi. "Or perhaps most in the touch, would you say, Mister Asprey?"

"In the touch, of course," said Cousin Edgar instantly.

"Gracious, Edgar," said Mrs. Asprey. "Do you know about these things, also?"

The glance of Cousin Edgar gleamed wildly at the innocent, too innocent face of Geraldi. "I did not study on a desert island," he murmured.

Louise hastily put in: "But how did you get away from the island? Did you try a voyage in the little boat?"

"It was a rotten little boat," said Geraldi.

73

"One could have punched one's fist through the bottom. We only got to shore in it by dint of much bailing."

"Then how in the world did you leave? Did the Arab captain repent and come back for you?"

"He never repented . . . not until a year or so later, when we happened to meet," said Geraldi, with his flashing smile. "But in the meantime, at the end of our six months of hard study and delightful practice, a big native boat arrived with a crew of half a dozen."

"And they saved you. How delightful," murmured Mrs. Asprey. "Oh, it's civilization that corrupts the world, isn't it, Cousin Edgar?"

"A very good thought . . . a very deep thought, I dare say," replied Cousin Edgar. "And a very new one," he added.

He looked full at Louise, and she looked steadily back at him. Geraldi could guess that they knew one another well. The detestation in which the girl held him was too apparent, and certainly he had no love for her.

"But the dear, kind natives?" said Louise dryly.

"They were very friendly for a while, but in the night they rushed us. And so the end of it was we had to sail off in their boat alone."

"Alone? But I don't understand," said Mrs. Asprey.

"You forget," said Geraldi with that same flashing smile, "that we had a rifle and ammunition."

"I don't see what that explains," said Mrs. Asprey.

"I should have added it was a moonlight night, and it was a repeating rifle," said Geraldi.

"And what became of the locksmith?" asked the girl suddenly.

"He has retired," said Geraldi, picking his words. "He no longer works at his trade. In fact, the state recognized his talents at last, and now it takes care of him."

"How really wonderful and beautiful," breathed Mrs. Asprey. "You should write down that lovely story, Mister Geraldi . . . I mean, about the dear, good old locksmith."

"Dear Cousin Olivetta," said the fat man, "may I suggest that perhaps Mister Geraldi means that the locksmith is now in prison?"

"Heavens!" she cried. "Is it possible?"

"He was very ambitious," said Geraldi, "but, after all, the Bank of London is the Bank of London. He will never have to worry again about his living. But what a genius was removed from the active world."

Mrs. Asprey took her daughter into the library. Cousin Edgar lingered at the table for coffee with his guest. He seemed highly pleased.

"You have much understanding," he said. "That is a great thing. Understanding. And patience. One needs patience. I mean with women, particularly. Poor, dear Missus Asprey. An extraordinary person."

He rubbed his large, white hands together, but there was a cold gleam in his eye, and Geraldi could guess that the fat man had not quite expressed his full thought concerning his giddy cousin.

They finished their coffee; cigarettes were lighted. And then, as they rose, Cousin Edgar laid a hand on the arm of Geraldi.

"I have seen my poor friend again this afternoon," he said. "He is becoming desperate. Poor fellow! A really fine man . . . intelligent, educated, a cultured soul. And yet in danger of wreck by the machinations of a scoundrel and a fool! The criminal is armed doubly by his scorn of the law, Geraldi. But let me suggest to you again . . . ten thousand dollars as a price might be improved upon, eh? Advanced a little?"

Geraldi faced him. "You'd trust me with an advance payment?"

"Exactly! Exactly! Of five thousand, say."

"Then you think there is something honest in me?"

"My dear young man!"

"Then believe me," said Geraldi, "the honest taint in me never would let me kill for any price."

Chapter Nine

WANTED, A KILLER

Cousin Edgar, at this second rebuff, spread out both hands. "My poor friend," he said. "How desperate he is."

"Look here," said Geraldi bluntly, "if you want a killer, it isn't hard to find them. And in this town. Chalmers's hotel is full of them."

"Bullies and stupid brutes!" said Cousin Edgar, some of the richness leaving his tone, and a ring of metal coming into them.

"Dick Renney isn't a brute or a bully," said Geraldi. "He ought to suit you."

"Renney? Renney? Is he there?"

"He's expected, I think."

"Ah," said Cousin Edgar.

He made no effort to conceal his satisfaction, and Geraldi wondered that the big man should show so little tact. Unless, indeed, it really was the business of another man that he was transacting as an agent. A foul business, at any rate. But it was not the first time that men had lowered the bars to

Geraldi and showed him the glimpses of the devil inside. They felt that they spoke to a blood brother in the trade; they could not realize that to him crime was a fine art.

They passed on into the library. Mrs. Asprey had taken up some needlepoint; Louise was watching the fire, chin in hand. Cousin Edgar paced up and down through the shadows. Presently he excused himself. He would be back in a few minutes.

And, as he left, Geraldi wondered if the errand might take him to Chalmers's hotel in search of Dick Renney. In sooth, stranger things than this had been. *They would make an admirable partnership,* thought Geraldi. Cousin Edgar, bland and smooth, and Dick Renney all fire — a very ferret in his love of blood.

Louise Asprey suddenly raised her head and glanced across at him; then he saw that her mother was asleep above the needle-point. She made a furtive gesture. Geraldi rose at once and retreated obediently to a chair nearer to the door, and there, presently, she followed him.

She did not whisper, but her voice was wonderfully guarded and soft. "It's almost too lucky," she said. "Cousin Edgar gone and mother asleep. I have to talk to you."

"Are you sure that your mother is asleep?"

"She isn't capable of deception," said the girl frankly. "In the first place, Cousin Edgar wants you to do something for him?"

"I've refused."

"Ah . . . I wish that you'd simply put him off. You can't tell me what it was?"

"He spoke to me in confidence."

She looked curiously at Geraldi, wondering at the broad streak of inviolable honor in this professional, this readily confessed criminal.

"I started to talk to you this afternoon."

"Yes," said Geraldi. "I hoped to hear the rest of it."

"It's easier for me to talk, now," said the girl. "Otherwise, the story would seem too strange. But, to begin with, I must tell you that, though my father is not here, he's not dead. At least, we have no proof that he's dead. And recently I had a suspicion that he must be alive."

Geraldi waited.

"I have to talk very frankly to you, or else not at all."

He nodded.

"Now, then, there's always been a wild streak in the Asprey blood. I have to tell you that to explain my father. There never was a kinder man. He was clever, too, in business. He grew quite rich. Then some of his investments turned out badly. We became almost poor. Father used to worry about it, and the worry brought out that wild streak I was speaking of. He began to gamble to make up for losses. Honest gambling, but for high stakes. And that gambling, of course, cost him still more money. Then one day he had a brawl with a professional gambler. I think that the man had done something dishonest with the cards. My father killed him."

Geraldi leaned forward a little in his chair. He was not greatly surprised by the news.

"That was five years ago. At the trial, a number of Father's enemies . . . he was an outspoken man who made more enemies than friends, I'm afraid . . . his enemies used all their influence against him. I think that he would have been acquitted, but in the middle of the trial he grew nervous, escaped from jail, and since then we've never seen him. His guilt was taken for granted when he ran away. He's an outlawed man. . . . That's the first part of the story.

"Then our affairs began to grow better. There were two or three investments of Father's . . . one was in a Mexican silver mine, in Chihuahua . . . which began to pay richly. We grew very prosperous, but there was never a word from Father.

"Then Cousin Edgar arrived. We never

81

had known him very well. He'd been a great wanderer, you must understand. You've seen his hunting trophies? Mother told him her troubles. He was very sympathetic. He's as strong and hard as steel, but he can seem as soft as a baby. He was so sympathetic and understanding that mother began to ask his advice. She begged him to stay on with us. In a single month he had all our business running through his hands. And he's never left us from that day to this. All the accounts, all the descriptions of stocks, bonds, everything goes through Cousin Edgar. You understand?"

"I understand perfectly," said Geraldi.

"I think he's very intelligent about business. I don't doubt that he's invested all the money well. But I can't help wondering if he isn't working more for himself than for us. Because . . . I have to tell you even this . . . he wants to marry Mother, and last week she promised that she would, if we had no word from Father before the month is out."

Geraldi drew in a long breath. He had guessed at this. But, nevertheless, his anger grew as he listened.

"The governor came through the town the next day after they reached that agreement. I went to see him. He talked over my father's case with me. He was very kind. He told me that he was sure it had been an entirely excusable killing, if a shooting affair ever is excusable. He said that if my father would come and talk to him as I had done, he had no doubt that a pardon could be arranged. When I came home, I found that Cousin Edgar was in a great state of excitement. He can control everything except the pink spots in his cheeks. And they were flaming. He always had been *too* kind to me before. Suddenly he began to be as hard as steel. He let me see that he detested me. And I'm sure it was because he knew of my talk with the governor."

"Naturally. He didn't want your father to have the least chance to come back."

"Of course not. If my father should return, then who can tell? It might be found that Cousin Edgar's accounts are not so perfectly straight as they should be. If my father does *not* return, then everything goes directly into the hands of Cousin Edgar. And in one week after the marriage, I'm sure that everything would be so arranged that, even if my father did come back, there would be very little for him to get his hands on. Is that clear?"

"Perfectly."

"Now the excitement of Edgar was too great. After a five years' absence one would take it for granted that a man was dead. Edgar was so worked up that I'm fairly sure he knows that my father is living, and *where* he's living! And now I'm living in terrible fear lest he should . . . should . . . I don't dare to say what I'm afraid of."

Geraldi could not help putting two and two together. That killing which Cousin Edgar would pay for so richly.

"I needed," went on the girl, "a brave, keen, clever man who would try to unravel the clues and find my father. The law couldn't help me. But. . . ." She hesitated.

"Someone on the other side of the fence would have a better chance," he helped her. "I entirely agree with you. You'll have to tell me something more about him, though. His habits, and such things."

"I'll describe him. He isn't very big . . . but he looks big. His face has a battered appearance. He looks as if he'd been through a good many storms. And he has . . . of his own making. He always loved excitement and danger. He's fearless. Sometimes I'm afraid he's almost fierce. But there's nothing faithless, treacherous, or cruel about him. I know him, and I love him! So would you. Would you try to find such a man for me?"

"Would I try? I'd give blood to find him," said the frigate bird with a sudden enthusiasm. "I would. . . ."

He broke and laid a finger on his lips. Then, gliding to the door just behind them, he turned the knob swiftly, silently, and jerked the door open. The tall form of Cousin Edgar was revealed against the shadows of the hallway.

Chapter Ten

IRON CREATURES

Cousin Edgar advanced at once. "Ah, thank you, thank you!" he said genially to Geraldi. "*B-r-r-r!* It's turned chilly out! We have our breaths of wind from the snows, you understand. But then, you're familiar with the climate here? One always must be on the watch for sudden changes. This climate requires a philosopher. A stoic, I should say."

He came into the room on the current of his own conversation, softened at once when he saw Mrs. Asprey asleep. "Poor soul. Time tells. Time tells," said Cousin Edgar gently.

Geraldi neither moved nor spoke, but the girl followed Cousin Edgar to the fireplace and looked at him with stony eyes.

"Did you walk far, Cousin Edgar?" she asked.

"Around and about," he said, "around and about. There is nothing so good as a little walk after dinner. But that's an old fashioned custom, and you youngsters . . .

iron creatures! . . . can do without it." He smiled on them tolerantly, his rich voice a murmur of envy.

"I must go," said Geraldi. "It's well after dark. You've all been very kind to me. I don't want to waken Missus Asprey. Will you give her my thanks?"

"Ah, but wait," said Cousin Edgar. "I have something in my room for you. Wait here a moment, Mister Geraldi. It may take me a moment or two. I'll have to rummage through a trunk."

"Thank you," said Geraldi, and Cousin Edgar left the room.

They heard his footstep in the hall, on the stairs, creaking higher and higher. Geraldi beckoned to the girl.

"That's a fake," he said.

"Of course, it is," she answered hotly. "He was listening at the door. After this, it's simply war!"

"Come with me," said Geraldi. "I'm going to show you something."

He stepped into the hall with her. It was very dark just outside the library door, and at one side stood a wide-spreading palm. Behind this he drew the girl. "Now don't make a sound," he whispered at her ear, and she nodded.

In fact, they heard nothing. It was only a

shadow that loomed suddenly before them, and then the tall silhouette turned the corner at the bottom of the stairs and hurried to the front door. He opened it swiftly and yet without the slightest noise, and he closed it again behind him in equal silence. There was no noise of a footfall on the stairs outside.

"He had to go outside to get his present for me, you see," said Geraldi. "I thought that he would."

"He never left the house after dinner," said the girl through her teeth. "Did you notice? There was no dust, even on the heels of his shoes."

"You should be a detective," smiled Geraldi. "I must go, or else he'll come back with the present. Have you any marching orders for me?"

"I haven't," said the girl.

"Have you any hint where he may be? This United States is a fairly large place to start a blind hunt for a man."

"I haven't got the slightest thought. He may be living as a cowpuncher on the range. Or he may be in New York City playing the market. He's liable to try almost anything."

"It's a dark trail," sighed Geraldi, "but I'll try it." He added: "Who was the man he killed?"

"Frank Lopaz. Oh, if I only could give you

a starting point for the trail. Because, after tonight, if you get away, I'm afraid that Cousin Edgar will be desperate and try desperate measures."

"Perhaps he will," answered Geraldi. "There's a handicap. But many a long chance comes home. There's that to remember."

"One last thing . . . your reward. I have money of my own that even Cousin Edgar doesn't touch. You'll have whatever you want. Ten . . . twenty . . . thirty thousand dollars. Whatever you want. If you can trust me to give you what you ask?"

Perhaps there was a streak of foreign blood in Geraldi. Certainly there was a touch of foreign manners. He kissed her hand. "We'll talk of that afterward," said Geraldi. "Good bye. Only one last thing . . . if I were you, I'd carry a gun in this house. Something small that you can keep about you . . . and a steady hand to use it. Good bye again." He vanished down the hall, and through the front door.

He was no sooner outside it than he stepped sidewise, then leaped from the edge of the porch. Within the front fence of the yard a high border of geraniums grew, trained up on dead branches so that it grew tall and thick. In the shadow of this, Geraldi crouched and waited. He had hardly a moment to pause there. Then half a dozen shadows trooped through the front gate and shut it behind them without a click.

He heard the whisper of Cousin Edgar distinctly: "You . . . and you . . . into the back yard. Don't give a warning. If you see a man who moves like a cat, start shooting. Do you hear? It's five thousand to the boy who downs him. Five-thousand spot cash! You . . . and you, take the front yard. All of you keep alive. He's liable to do anything. Pop out of a window and drop on your heads. You take that side. You take the other."

"The hell I will!" Chalmers murmured. "I'll stand in back. That's the way he'll run. And I'm gonna wring his god-damn' neck, I tell you. I feel in my bones that I'm gonna have the wringing of it!"

They departed to their separate posts. One man remained.

"Renney, I count most on you. Go wherever you choose!"

That was the final order. Cousin Edgar went softly up the steps of the porch. The door opened and closed silently upon him. At the same time the shadow of Dick Renney stepped into the gloom of the geranium hedge and crouched not two yards from Geraldi.

Geraldi recognized instinctively the touch of the master — the sixth sense of Renney had brought him, even without his knowledge, perilously close to his quarry. Still Geraldi could afford to smile as he kept his covert. But he had a gun in his hand. It might be that someone would grow desperate and use a flashlight. In that case he would have to shoot, and, first of all, God help Dick Renney!

Now, from inside the house, he heard the squeaking of steps. Cousin Edgar was coming down from his room, noisily. He had found his present, at last.

The light from the open window of the library fell not ten feet from Geraldi. He heard the opening of the library door. He even made out the cheerful voice of Cousin Edgar.

"Well, Louise, where's our young friend, the adventurer?"

He could not hear the answer of Louise. He waited, almost expecting a noisy outburst. But, after all, that was not the way of Cousin Edgar.

Presently the shadow of the front door yawned wide. Cousin Edgar stood on the front path, and Dick Renney was instantly beside him. There was a sort of crouched eagerness and readiness about that fellow.

"He's gone," said Cousin Edgar in a whisper, but such a whisper as Geraldi never had heard before. There was more than even the hissing venom of a rattler in it. "He's faded."

"We'll hunt, then," answered Renney.

"No, no, listen to me, Renney. You have different work than that to do for me. Go around and dismiss the rest of them. Let them know that he's gone, but tell every man of them that my offer stands. Five thousand for the death of him, and I don't give a damn how he's killed!"

"That's liberal," said Renney.

"Liberal? Man, if you can manage it, I'll give you a crown of gold! But listen to me."

"Governor, I'm markin' you like a pointer."

"Do you see that first window to the left above the front porch?"

"I see it."

"Could you climb up to that window?"

"In about five seconds."

"Then, after you've sent them away, climb up there. I'll be in my room, and I want to see you."

"It's done."

Cousin Edgar disappeared into the house. The hired men, whom he had fetched, presently came trooping — still silent shadows

— and thronged out the front gate, and only Chalmers paused for a moment's conversation with Renney. His voice was a bass rumble, barely heard.

"You dirty dog, Renney, you've spotted him, and you're saving him for yourself! But, if I find that you've double-crossed me, I'll have your throat cut, you swine!"

Renney laughed — a mere catch of breath. He seemed to take this violent language as a mere pleasantry. And, after big Chalmers had gone, the gunman waited for a moment, leaning on the gate. He was a slight figure. It seemed odd to Geraldi that so much fame should be locked up in so small a form, but certainly his was a name to conjure with. Usually the deeds of men in the West only became noised abroad after their death, but Renney already had made much newspaper copy. There was something about the fellow that was like a flame. It consumed the imagination. And like fire was his touch. No one had stood before him, and yet it was said that eighteen men — white and gunfighters themselves — had gone down before him. As for Mexicans, they, of course, were not counted.

So Geraldi kneeled in the shadow of the geraniums and asked himself, gravely, whether he or Renney would conquer when they met. He had a shrewd idea that the shorter course for him would be to put a bullet through that agile body, then and there, but he forebore. The creed of Geraldi was not long, but it was as binding as adamant.

Presently, when the last of the men of Chalmers were gone, Renney turned back toward the house. He stood for a moment under the front porch, looking so small, so slight, that Geraldi almost thought that he would abandon his attempt. However, that was not in the mind of the other.

He was simply determining the best course, and, having decided on it, he scaled up the left-hand post of the porch and got onto its roof like a cat. Then up he went, and presently disappeared through the dark window that big Edgar Asprey had indicated.

The room no longer remained dark. A light gleamed in it. Already they were at their conference, and Geraldi, with a slight shake of his head, as though to throw off hesitation, laid his hand on the same pillar that Renney had chosen, and followed that man of blood.

Chapter Eleven

INTERESTING CONVERSATION

What had been easy for Renney was still simpler for the acrobatic skill of the frigate bird. He did not "swarm" up the height like a sailor; he went up it like a man up a ladder, at his ease.

Several feet below the window through which Renney had disappeared there was the top of the outer frame of the window of a room beneath; that top made a firm base for the foot of the frigate bird. His head came just above the level of the sill of the upper casement, and, therefore, he was ideally placed for spying on those within the room.

He found Renney and Cousin Edgar seated at a center table. The latter had lost no time in beginning his business. Already there was a map spread out on the table. With all his might, the frigate bird strained his eyes at the map and tried to make out the spot that the fat man was now pointing out with the pressure of a pale, soft finger. But the angle was too flat. He could see nothing surely.

"Then you have the place in mind, Mister Renney?"

"Sure, I have," said Renney.

"The next subject we should discuss is remuneration."

"You gave me a description of this gent . . . but what's his name?" asked Renney.

"That isn't important, Mister Renney."

"Ain't it?" said the gunman softly. "To me it is, though."

Cousin Edgar smiled blandly upon his companion.

"Suppose that I take a flying guess?" suggested Renney.

Cousin Edgar was tapping the edge of the table, making no noise with the tips of his fingers.

"Suppose that I say his name is Asprey?" snapped Renney. "Robert Asprey, eh, and your cousin?"

The white hand of Cousin Edgar no longer tapped the table. Otherwise, he showed no emotion.

"And what's in a name?" asked Cousin Edgar gently.

"Price is in a name," answered Renney. He grinned with a venomous pleasure, and then added thoughtfully: "You gimme a job to go out and soak some common bum. What do I ask? Maybe a thousand. I dunno.

Maybe I do it for fun. But here you hand me a fighting man. Well, that'll cost you something, friend."

Renney felt so sure of himself that he thrust his hands in the side pockets of his trousers and tilted back in his chair, grinning steadily into the face of Cousin Edgar. The estimation in which the frigate bird held the gunman mounted high at once. He knew what it meant to sustain the weight of Cousin Edgar's attention. But Renney was as steady as stone.

"I'm a reasonable man," said Edgar Asprey. "So what's your price?"

"Twenty-five thousand bucks will about cover the bill," said Renney.

Cousin Edgar permitted himself to smile. He made no other rejoinder.

"Are you gonna talk turkey?" demanded the gunman sharply.

"You've named your price . . . and it seems to me that you've answered yourself," replied Cousin Edgar.

Renney pushed back his chair and rose. "It don't sound to you, then?" he asked abruptly.

Cousin Edgar shook his head, and the flap beneath his chin wagged solemnly.

"Then good night, Mister Asprey. There ain't any use in us wasting time."

He started for the window, but the frigate bird did not move. He was quite certain that the conversation would not end at that point, and he was right. Halfway to the window, Renney whirled about on his heel. All his motions were as light and quick as the movements of a bird.

"Hold on," he said. "Suppose that I find out what you wanted to gimme for this job?"

"Ten thousand dollars," said Cousin Edgar.

"It ain't enough!"

"And yet," replied Cousin Edgar, "for all the work that you've done in the past, you've never had such a price before."

"Tell me, bo," asked Renney, advancing to the table and resting his fist upon it. "Tell me what you know about the work that I've done in the past?"

"I know everything," answered Cousin Edgar, as gently as ever.

"Aw, the hell you do. Nobody does!"

"Do you want instances?"

"Come on. You can't bluff me! Come on with your instances. What was the first job I ever done?"

"That was a charity job," said Cousin Edgar. "You did it for nothing."

"You're guessing," answered Renney instantly. "Gimme some particulars, if you can."

"Certainly. You were a young boy . . . barely fourteen. You were fond of a sixteen-year-old girl whose name was. . . ."

"Oh, damn the name," said Renney, with a touch of emotion. "Get on to the story."

"A young cowpuncher also was fond of her. She cut a dance with you in favor of him, and then the heart of youth turned to fire in the breast of young Dick Renney. He waited for the cowpuncher outside the hall and, when he came through the door, shot him securely from the dark."

Renney paused. "It's a lie!" he announced.

Cousin Edgar had begun to pat the table with his soft hand again. He made no answer.

"Well, what next?" asked Renney viciously.

"That shooting wasn't traced to you. You were too young to be suspected. Nevertheless, it gave you confidence. And when two Mexicans shouldered you in the street, you tackled the pair of them. One of them died the next day of his wounds. The other was crippled for life."

"Everybody loves that story," said Renney with satisfaction.

"Do you want me only to deal with the secret chapters of your life?" asked Cousin Edgar genially.

"Yep. Lemme have some of them," said Renney.

"Like many an errant knight," said Cousin Edgar, "you always have had a weakness for the fairer sex. Pretty girls upset your mind, my friend. Now it so happened that one day you were traveling through a mountain pass with the blood of a fresh wound congealing on your side, and presently your horse, worn out by the spur and the work, died under you. In its fall you were pinned down to the ground. You were too weak to work yourself through. The wind was very cold . . . snow began to drift around you. Your leg was numb. The pain in your side grew more and more severe, and finally the drowsiness that precedes death by exposure began to pass over you. Is that enough?"

"Go on," said Renney through his teeth.

"You were found there by a hardy fellow, a trapper who worked through those high mountains. He did not ask whether you were worthy of help. He simply told himself that he saw a man dying, and, therefore, he got you from beneath the horse and carried you on his back . . . he was a tall, strong man . . . down to his shack, more than a mile away. There you were nursed back to strength by the trapper and his daughter. And as the warm spring of the year came on, with the blossoming of the flowers . . . shall I say? . . . love came to the two of you. The trapper was blind for some time. At last, he asked you to leave the house. You left, but came back by night. It happened that the trapper was on the watch. He challenged you and asked you to leave. Your answer was a bullet through the brain. After that, you took his best horse and fled on it."

"And who's been telling you that pack of lies?" growled Renney hoarsely.

"You asked me for some secret chapters from your life, and I've obeyed. Will you have any more?"

"Go on, then!"

"The next noteworthy occasion occurred on the Río Grande. There was a Mexican who kept a little irrigated patch of alfalfa on the bank of the river. He was a poor man with half a dozen goats, a donkey, and a mule. Also, he had a daughter who was just beginning to smile at men, and who. . . ."

"Leave it be, will you?" snarled Renney.

Cousin Edgar was silent, and Renney, after a moment, began to walk up and down the room. His foot made not the slightest sound, and Slim Jim watched with a more

101

intense interest. He, too, was a master of that art, and he knew the training of the natural gift that is required.

Renney halted. "Who the hell gave you all that dope on me?" he asked.

"I didn't find it in a newspaper," smiled Cousin Edgar.

Renney paused. His nostrils were flaring, and his face was an ugly study. There was no decency in the man. The cruelty of a barbarian shone at his eyes.

"We'll get back to the business again," he said. "You would give ten thousand for this bird. You say it's more than I ever got. Well, that's true. But here I ought to get a fatter slice."

"I'll wait for you to explain that," suggested Cousin Edgar.

"In the first place," expanded Renney, "it's a dirty job. A gent that kills a cousin had ought to pay higher. A gent that gets his cousin killed by a hired man ought to pay still higher."

"You grow philosophic," smiled Cousin Edgar.

"You live fat and easy in his house," went on Renney. "You got his money sticking to your fingers. . . ."

"Will you tell me why you say that?" asked Cousin Edgar simply.

"You handle all his stuff, don't you? And you run all the Asprey business, don't you? Everybody knows what that timber land paid you the last couple of years. I say, when you bump your cousin off, you get the whole cheese. Well . . . I want a bigger slice, that's all. Besides, it ain't an easy job. Asprey's a fighting man. Hell, I knew him right here in town. I want twenty-five thousand. That's my figger."

"I'm sorry," said bland Cousin Edgar.

"You're sorry, are you? Suppose that I go and sell what I know to Asprey? You've told me where to find him."

"You couldn't do it," said Cousin Edgar. "Because I have ways of warning him from a distance. You wouldn't find him when you arrived at the place."

"You're slick," admitted Renney. "Look here, chief. I got a liking and an admiration for you. We'll call it twenty thousand flat and shake hands!"

To the astonishment of Slim Jim, the other replied instantly: "That figure is high, but I like to find a man who realizes his own worth. We'll call it twenty thousand, Renney."

The small, bony hand of Renney was stretched forth. That of Cousin Edgar closed over it.

"Another matter," said Cousin Edgar. "You've heard about the young vagrant who picked the pocket of Chalmers's?"

"I ain't heard nothin' but, at the hotel," chuckled Renney. "Aw, gawd, Chalmers is wild. He'd give his soul for a whack at that kid."

"That same young man," said Cousin Edgar, "is mixed in this affair. He, also, will be trying to find . . . your man."

Renney grinned with a malicious curiosity. "You don't like to name him, do you?" he said. "Well, damned if I wonder at it."

"About the boy . . . Geraldi," went on Cousin Edgar, not noticing the comment, "if you should meet him. . . ."

"I'll send him back to Chalmers by parcel post."

Cousin Edgar smiled and shook his head. "My dear, young friend," he said. "My clever, active, brave, and patient young friend. I don't want you to make a mistake. This boy is very dangerous."

"He run like a rabbit from Chalmers. How come, then, if he's a hot one?"

"He hates unnecessary risks. Being very intelligent, he never kills merely for the pleasure of killing, but only when an absolute necessity comes to him. Such men are always to be feared, because they never act except with forethought."

"All right," said Renney. "I know him. I thought that he was only a fancy card-shark. But if I meet him, I'll bump him off."

"Do so," said the other gravely. "Do so, because, otherwise, he may give you great trouble."

"I'll pass a chunk of lead through him," said Renney with assurance.

"Just one moment," said Cousin Edgar. "I love your enthusiasm, Renney. I love the whole-hearted abandon with which you go about these affairs. It's the sign of the artist . . . working out of a full heart. But this young Geraldi . . . if that's his name. . . ."

"Well, go on. What about him?"

"You've killed your men, in your day, Renney."

"I've had my share," nodded Renney, and shrugged his shoulders.

"The share of young Geraldi, you may be interested to know, has been even larger."

Renney frowned. "That's a lie on the face of it. Somebody's been filling you up."

"No one ever fills me up, as you adroitly phrase it. Furthermore, all his men were killed face to face, Renney."

"Meaning what?" snarled Renney.

"Meaning that, if he comes on your trail, you'll earn your twenty thousand dollars, my dear, young friend. And that, I believe, ends our talk." And he rose placidly from his chair as he spoke.

Chapter Twelve

ONE AFTER ANOTHER

Geraldi melted down the face of the house, reached the front yard, and dropped in the shadow of the geraniums. He was hardly there before Renney in turn emerged from the window, descended with noiseless agility, and passed out from the yard by means of the gate.

He turned down the street, and the frigate bird moved behind him, having leaped lightly over geranium hedge and fence to gain the sidewalk. It was a difficult task to stalk Renney in such a place, for although the sidewalk was shaded and set off from the street by a row of pepper trees, yet the trunks of those trees were so slender that a man easily could have been detected passing behind them. Moreover, shafts of lamplight streamed out through open doors and windows, for the night was warm and the town was still awake.

Still, he managed to keep Renney in sight, until the latter came to the railroad yard.

There he disappeared in the shadows among the piles of recently unloaded timber, but the frigate bird felt that he understood the meaning of this new direction. Renney was determined to take a train out of the town and proceed with his work at once. He was, as Cousin Edgar had said, admirably fervid in the performance of his work.

The frigate bird, from the gloom to the lee of a timber pile, watched the freight train thunder in, with flashes from the wheels, and a hot glow from the firebox. He waited until it started on again, saw the brakeman with his lantern swing aboard the caboose, and then he watched a figure run from the side and bound up against the iron ladder that ran up the steps of the third boxcar from the front. He imitated that example on the car next to the rear of the train.

Flattened on the roof, he took note of his surroundings. Then he stretched on his back to rest. The stars all were out. There was not a cloud blown across them, but only those deep wells of infinite shadow that show here and there across the face of the heavens on the brightest of nights. So he studied those familiar constellations, that traveled serenely with him far above, no matter how swiftly the train thundered through the night with clanking of trucks and with rattling of cars.

He was glad of the open again, glad of the speed of the train. It was as though he absorbed some of its resistless energy. But so, driven across the night, all his faculties worked more smoothly, more keenly. He had on his hands as difficult a task as he could have asked for. Merely to deal with Cousin Edgar might have been hard enough, but now he was handicapped with the weight of Renney, and a great weight he knew that rascal might prove in the final battle. But follow Renney he must. It was the trail of Renney that lead him to the final goal, with a vague prayer that, having come to the goal, he might strike down Renney before that bloodhound could strike down Robert Asprey.

In addition, he was wanted by the law, and, if Renney found him on the trail, the gunman did not need to take the work into his own hands. He simply could inform the police that a pickpocket, wanted by the law officers of Sankeytown, was present in the person of Geraldi. That would be enough. Chalmers alone could be depended upon to make his share of trouble.

The frigate bird smiled into the mysterious depths of the skies. He had been in situations fully as bad — worse. But always before he could drop out of sight, take wing, and disappear beyond the horizon, even in this century where the wireless has stretched horizons to an indefinite width. Now, however, it was different. He worked with an anchor — a weight of lead dependent from his neck, and that was the obligation to find Asprey for the girl.

The train struck a grade, slowed to it, and then began to pant and struggle with all its might, slowly heaving up the steep incline. It was time to be wary. To the left, a cliff wall rose sheer, close by. To the right, there was the space for the second track, and, therefore, to that side he gave his attention, and only in time to see a shadow drop from far forward and, running to the side, disappear in the brush that grew there.

The frigate bird hesitated. It might well be that this was some vagrant. There was hardly better than one chance in two that it was Renney. And if he dropped off in pursuit, he would certainly be seen by the gunman, if it were, indeed, he.

He determined to get off the train, but he waited until it had swung around the next turn. Then he climbed down the ladder, and, as the grade flattened and the engine gathered speed, he dropped to the ground.

His foot slipped on a round stone. He rolled head over heels and came to his feet again, rather dazed. But there is an art in falling, a fine art that he had learned long ago from tumblers in the circus. He was shaken, but hardly bruised, and he ran at once for the brush.

Crouched there, he watched the train roar past, with the tail light dimmed by the swirl of dust that the suction beneath the cars had raised. Then the light itself was jerked out of sight beyond the next turn of the winding way. Then the noise grew dim and far off at once, but as the engine beat around distant cliffs, fresh waves of sound came loudly back to him.

He was alone, except for that other shadow, somewhere in the brush behind him. And, if it were not Renney, by now he had totally lost the trail of Robert Asprey. If it were Renney, two things might have moved the gunman to leave the train. The first might have been that he knew a pursuer was on it. The second might be that he had wished to make a false start and double back, not sure that he was followed, but simply making security doubly secure. He himself, in a similar situation, would have done the same thing, he felt.

He began to make his way back around

the curve, keeping well within the brush, sharpening his senses, but moving swiftly. He had served his time as a woodsman; the uncanny lightness of his feet was a vast help to him; but he felt that there were many others more at home in this craft than he.

When he came to that point at which the track straightened on the long downgrade, he ventured to the verge of the brush and there crouched and watched. Lying low as he did, the eastern stars twinkled up the polished tops of the rails, and whatever moved across the way would be seen at any reasonable distance. It might be that the tramp, however, had turned straight back into the brush, intent on camping out for the night on some known spot. From Renney that would not be expected.

He hardly had turned these thoughts in his mind, when a man stepped noiselessly out of the brush and stood at the edge of the track. His hands were in his pockets. His cap was pulled low on his head. Something in the meager outline of his shoulders and the forward jutting of his head told the frigate bird that this was Renney again. The man was whistling softly, as if in thorough content. Then he turned down the track and began walking the ties back toward Sankeytown.

Chapter Thirteen

SIX-FIFTEEN

Toward Sankeytown the stranger wended, and Geraldi followed cautiously, feeling all the while that there must be something to be gained from patience.

He had been over an hour on the train, therefore, thirty miles separated him from the town, or perhaps more. But just at the foot of the slope down which he was going at the present time, the train had whirled through a small blur of lights, and Geraldi was fairly sure that his quarry would use that town as a starting place for his next stage of the journey.

The moon came up. It made the eastern mountains seem wonderfully near and as steep as sheer cliffs of black rock, but to the west over his shoulder the country dissolved in misty waves. However, there was enough light to make him fear lest Renney should become aware of his pursuer. He dropped back until Renney's form, ahead of him, was a glimmer that faded and grew again, guessed at rather than seen.

The tracks curved a little to the right, in a wide and sweeping bend, and now they entered the squat shadows of the village. It was about the dimensions of Sankeytown, he guessed, and he was glad of that. It provided a bigger background in which he could lose himself while he waited for the next train.

By the railroad, he was sure, Renney would travel. A horse was apt to be far too slow for him. He had an idea that Robert Asprey must be at a great distance from the house where his family lived. Otherwise, he would be sure to make a desperate effort to visit his wife and daughter. But the conviction being strong in Geraldi that his quarry would travel by the train alone, he was at ease. He could do what he chose, so long as he was on hand to watch the trains.

Close up to the station went Renney, and Geraldi saw him disappear into a little all-night lunch counter, one of those places which are apt to be open in a town where numerous railroad men gather. Through the smoky glass of the swinging door, he saw Renney settle himself before the counter and order rapidly and at some length.

Then, contented, Geraldi crossed the street, where the very fellow of this lunch counter was established. In fact, it seemed to be the older brother of the pair. Its counter was covered with oilcloth that had been scrubbed or elbow-worn to tatters. Its array of cans was not so imposing, and the cook-waiter looked up with an air of irritation from his newspaper when he saw Geraldi enter.

Nothing can be cooked more quickly than a hamburger steak. This and bread and coffee and a wedge of soggy, apple pie Geraldi ordered and paid for. The "steak," when he received it, was composed more of bread crumbs and onions than of meat, but he ate it with the patience of one who has had to put up with much worse fare. He ate it with greediness, even. For he felt that this might be his last chance in a long, long time before he would be able to eat again.

When he was halfway through the meal, he was aware that the cook was staring past him. The little shack quivered with a soft but heavy footfall. Geraldi looked over his shoulder and saw a sawed-off shotgun approaching with two vast, ugly black mouths pointed toward him. Accompanying the shotgun was as big a man as Geraldi had seen in many a day. He was no lumbering hulk, but, rather, the hard-boiled essence of fighting strength.

"All right, bo," he said, "I want you!"

"You want me for what?" asked Geraldi mildly.

"For picking the pocket of Chalmers in Sankeytown. That's all."

Geraldi turned a little farther in his chair.

"Shove up your hands."

"Willingly," said Geraldi.

Now, from the corner of his eye, he was aware of a shadow that had flitted from the rear door of the lunch counter. And he had just time in that glance to note the slight hump of the shoulders and the forward thrust of the head. Renney!

Working under a handicap, with all the cards in favor of his enemy, Renney had played the game and won it easily. Geraldi made that admission to himself, and then stood up at the order of the deputy sheriff and allowed his hands to be fastened behind his back by the cook, at the direction of the man of the law.

"Pull them cords tight," said the deputy. "This here is a bird that's all oil and feathers, they tell me. Now, kid, you walk ahead of me. You can spend the night in jail, or in the cemetery, whichever you pick. Understand?"

"I know a man when I see one," said Geraldi, and walked obediently, straight from the shack and then down the center of the street. It was too late for a crowd to follow them. They went to the jail, and Geraldi, to his great disappointment, found a little up-to-date building of heavy stone. The cells were gathered in one intricate network of tool-proof steel.

The jailer came to the office of the sheriff and helped to search Geraldi. There were many exclamations of professional delight as they drew out from his pockets first the bar of strong steel, and then, one by one, other small implements.

"Picking pockets! Hell, he could pick a bank," said the jailer.

The deputy watched with sparkling eyes. He saw political recognition in such a capture as this. He saw that the search proceeded with care. Geraldi was forced to strip and stand, shivering, while every inch of his clothes was probed and worked over by hand. Then he was permitted to don the clothes again. The deputy picked out a cell in the middle of the cellroom and departed with a final warning to the jailer: "Keep your eye on him. He's slippery. I got the tip from one that knows."

The jailer, accordingly, stood outside the cell for some time, lantern in hand.

"Where'd you learn the trade?" he asked.

"I grew up with it," Geraldi assured him.

"Always the same line?" asked the jailer. Then he answered his own question: "Sure, it's always that way. One line, always the same. That's what makes you crooks so easy to tumble to. What you do once, you'll do again. You got no variety. Hell, I should think you'd branch out a little."

Geraldi looked down at his feet. They were securely ironed. His hands were held by powerful handcuffs.

"My friend," he said, "if you don't mind, I'll go to sleep. I want to get the first train out."

The jailer was willing to chuckle. "That'll be six-fifteen," he said. "Maybe I'd better give you a call a few minutes before?"

"Thank you," smiled Geraldi. "Good night."

"Good night, kid. The six-fifteen!" He went off, still chuckling, and settled himself in a chair in a corner of the cellroom. There he yawned noisily a few times. The chair creaked as he settled down in it. In half an hour, he was snoring.

A clock struck the hour, beating out six heavy strokes that sent the alarm circling out in slow waves through the heavy, damp air of the night. Geraldi, half in a stupor on his cot, seemed to be roused by this sound.

He straightened, listening to the snoring

of the guard for a moment, and then worked gently at his handcuffs, Supple hands will fold in at the palm and grow smaller than the wrists. Any child can do the trick. It is simple even for grown men, if they keep their muscles sleek enough. Now Geraldi pulled his hands through the steel rings with ease and deposited the handcuffs on the cot.

His feet were still fast. And between him and liberty remained three locked doors: that of his cell, that into the deputy sheriff's office, and that from the office to the outside of the building. From the inside of the sole of his right shoe, he drew out a small, flat blade of steel, and with this he worked diligently at the lock of his foot irons. The mechanism was perfectly oiled. In an instant it gave way noiselessly, and Geraldi stood up, free in person, at least.

He stretched himself deliberately, limb by limb. Then he attacked the lock of his cell door. He had to reach over and work at it from the outside, but in this manner he made some progress. At last he reached the crucial bolt. It stirred. The bolt itself shoved easily back, and Geraldi walked through the door into the aisle.

He found the jailer nodding heavily in his chair, a relaxed and helpless bulk, with the light from his own lantern flooding up toward him. Behind that chair, Geraldi had to walk to get at the door of the sheriff's office, but, as he reached it, he heard the long hoot of a train's whistle, dim and dreary with distance.

The sleeper roused with a jerk. He sat up, swaying a little in his chair, and Geraldi grew tense, waiting.

"Six-fifteen," murmured the jailer, and sank again into torpor.

Geraldi opened the door, and passed into the office. There he found all that had been taken from him laid out on the desk of the deputy, even the bulging wad of money that once had been the possession of Chalmers in Sankeytown. There was a safe in the corner of the room, but the big deputy evidently trusted so completely to the efficiency of his fine little jail that he did not bother with extra cautions. Geraldi lined his pockets as they had been lined before. The key stood in the outer door; in another moment he was in the fresh outer air, and the scream of the train's whistle pierced his ears.

He hurried. It was apt to be a short stop at such a station. Finding his way to the yard, in the gray of the morning, he heard the engine begin to snort while he was still at a distance. He had to sprint to make it. The long, lofty wall of a number of boxcars shot past him. He saw the glimmer of an iron ladder, and, leaping at the guess, he missed with both feet and his right hand. Only the left caught a hold, but that was enough. He regained the ladder with an effort, swarmed up to the top of the car — and found just above him a figure dimly drawn against the night, and the familiar outline of a Colt revolver leveled at his head. A small man, feet planted to the sway of the boxcar.

Renney?

"All right, bo," said the voice of the brakeman. "A dollar down on account, and you ride my division. Otherwise, I'll roll you, by God!"

Chapter Fourteen

ALL ABOARD!

Geraldi paid. "Anything else on board?" he asked.

"There's a nigger in Number Seven. That's an empty. You can work the door."

Geraldi went back to Number Seven and "worked the door." It was not the simplest trick in the world to open the sliding door of a boxcar and then swing down into it from the top, but Geraldi managed it with the ease of long experience. He heard an exclamation from the darkness of the empty.

"It's all right, bo," said Geraldi.

A match lighted. A pair of gray-black hands cupped the flame and shone it upon him.

"Tramp royal!" announced the Negro. "All right, bo. Sit down and tell me what's been doing down the line."

"Give me your hand. Here's a dollar. Go back to the door and watch there. I'm going to sleep. Mind you, I sleep as light as a cat, but I don't want to be disturbed."

The Negro chuckled. "Turn in," he said. "I'll watch the door for you. I'll give you a call, if anybody else drops in."

Geraldi contentedly stretched himself on the dancing boards of the old boxcar. The light was beginning to grow. Silver streaks of it broke the darkness in the car. There was much danger that, if this were the only empty on the train, Renney might show up in the car. However, it was a part of the philosophy of young Geraldi that a certain percentage of risk must be taken. He was very tired. Sleep he must have to remain efficient through the day. Therefore, he closed his eyes.

For three hours he was as the dead. Then he wakened and knew that someone was kneeling over him. He hardly dared to peer up through his eyelashes, but, when he did, he saw the face of the Negro, the eyes glittering with curiosity and greed and fear combined, as he bent over the sleeper. In his left hand he carried a knife. The right hand was stretched out toward the coat of Geraldi.

Curiosity had been too much for the black man. Geraldi groaned and stirred; instantly the other withdrew; Geraldi sat up in safety.

"Thought you was gonna have your head jigged off by this road bed," said the Negro amiably. "You are sure one of them champeen sleepers, bo!"

"Yes," said Geraldi, "but I usually wake up just in time."

The guilty eyes of the Negro flickered to this side and that. Then he grinned, and Geraldi grinned back. One ounce of understanding was better with people than tons of sham.

He offered a cigarette. It was accepted. They smoked in amiable silence, regarding one another with a frank interest. Two seconds more of his slumber and Geraldi would have been dead with that knife through his heart, for the sake of the bulge of bills that swelled his vest pocket. But the worst had not happened. Therefore, he was able to smile.

"No stops yet?" he asked as a matter of course.

The Negro shook his head.

"Who closed the door?"

"The shack gimme the high sign."

"Why?"

"Ah dunno, boss. I never asked no shack to tell me what he was thinkin'. I jus' done what he said."

Geraldi tried the door. It was fast locked.

"He'll sure open it up at the first station," said the Negro.

"You black hound!" said Geraldi with a soft unction in his voice.

The Negro stared. His face turned savage, and his eyes went small. "Who you callin' a houn'?" he asked in a voice that was high and thin. "Who you callin' houn'? Ah don' take that from nobody, bo!"

He had pitched himself to his knees, his hands deep in his coat pockets, certainly fumbling at weapons of some sort. But Geraldi moved his hand openly, yet so swiftly that it seemed to disappear. He held the leveled gun braced over his up-jutting knees.

"Take 'em out," advised Geraldi, and smiled down the shining barrel of his gun.

The Negro did not hesitate. He drew forth his hands and thrust them well above his head.

"Now, we'll talk," said Geraldi. "We'll begin with the doors. Who told you to close them?"

"The shack . . . the brakie," said the black man, blinking his eyes rapidly. "I told you that before, governor."

"You lying snake," said Geraldi, guessing at random.

"Ah dunno then who he was," groaned the tramp. "Never seen him before."

"He came down and saw me?"

"Boss, he sure did."

"What did he slip you?"

"He give me. . . ."

"Five dollars."

"Five bucks it was," sighed the Negro. "You know everything anyway, boss. There wasn't no harm in what I done, was there?"

"You had him promise to open the door for you?"

"He sure did promise."

"You black fool, when the door *is* opened, you'll be jailed along with me. Have you a knife?"

"A sort of little penknife, boss."

"Look at the board behind you. Isn't that old, half-rotten wood?"

The Negro knocked the plank with his knuckles. "It is, boss."

"Start working on that, then. Carve with that knife of yours."

The black man took out the same long and heavy weapon that Geraldi had seen when he wakened from his sleep. He seemed as much frightened on his own account, now, as he had been before when the gun first covered him, and he cut strongly into the wood. It gave readily under the knife edge. In a mere moment he had slashed out a trough and threatened to drive the knife straight through the plank. But this was not wanted by Geraldi. He directed operations until two boards had been cut through so that they were hanging by mere splinters. They could be knocked out or drawn in, at the will of the captives. And they had about finished this work, when the engine hooted for a stop.

It might be that Renney had left the train when he discovered that his persistent pursuer was with him again. It might be that he had remained with it, and Geraldi inclined to the latter opinion. It was unlike such an efficient worker as Renney to make too many delays. Therefore, he was on this train still, and would be watching the car that held his pursuer. Watching it like a hawk, now that the freight was drawing into the station.

They broke out the boards, therefore, and drew them into the car. If they were cast outside, Renney was too apt to see them fall and know that the birds were ready to fly.

The brakes were beginning to grind. Looking out cautiously, Geraldi saw that they were entering a large yard. A maze of steel rails flashed under his eyes, blurred together with speed, then detaching and forming a steady pattern as the speed of the train decreased. He stepped into the opening.

"Don't you do it!" said the Negro, closing his eyes in a panic. "You'll smash yourself to a pulp!"

But Geraldi had made up his mind. He swung out suddenly through the aperture, prepared himself, and dropped. He hit the ground running at full speed, and that, of course, diminished the shock. Even so he went staggering, as though a vast load were heaped on his shoulders, unstringing his legs at the knees.

He could hardly endure that weight, and then, glancing up, he saw Renney on the ladder of the car immediately preceding his. Renney was facing straight out, prepared for the drop. He apparently was willing to trust the wooden prison to hold his enemy. He dropped to the ground and began running as Geraldi had done. In the meantime, the latter had regained control of his limbs. He was able to slow up. Veering sharply to the right, he cut in around the tail of a long passenger train that stood before the station.

He did not hesitate. He climbed up the first few steps, paused an instant to brush off the dust that covered him, and then walked down the line of the cars, found an empty seat in the smoker, and dropped into it.

He was very willing to wager that his

128

quarry would use the wings of this same train to help on his way. The engine began to labor. The train heeled and swayed around a curve, and then gathered speed. Was Renney aboard? He would have to gamble on that.

He remained in his seat. He had taken the corner one in front, that looked down the double row of chairs, and, picking up a newspaper that lay on the floor, he screened himself behind this, only allowing himself a glimpse, now and again, as though the vibration of the train and its swaying were driving his hands to the side.

By those glimpses, at first, he saw nothing whatever except that conglomeration of men of all sorts such as one usually finds on a local passenger train. But, half an hour after the start, he was aware of a small man, his clothes very dusty, who came in and dropped into the first vacant place. He walked with a singular perfection of poise and lightness, with his head thrust out a little, in an aggressive manner. It was Renney.

Geraldi rose at once and walked to the platform at the front of the car. He trusted that he had not been seen, but, when he ventured a glance back through the glass of the door, he noted that Renney was looking fixedly in his direction, with brows gathered to a shadow of thought.

He could guess, then, that Renney had seen his back as he went out, and, if he had not recognized him, Geraldi had been sufficiently familiar to trouble the mind of that arch criminal. If that were the case, then surely Renney would come to investigate. He had hardly determined that when he saw Renney rise from his place and come lightly up the aisle, swaying easily with the heave and pitch of the car.

Chapter Fifteen

WHO FOLLOWS?

There was only one way to escape the coming of Renney. Geraldi took it by gripping the overhanging edge of the car's roof, and so clambering onto the roof. Nothing in the world is so little framed to be sat upon as the roof of a passenger car. There are no flat places. And every jerk, every jar, thrusts one almost irresistibly toward the edge, the fall from which is death.

Yet Geraldi stood up and ran back along the train — actually ran, the swift drive of the train making the roof seem to rise to meet his feet. He sped back along two cars, and then he dropped flat and watched.

What Renney would do he was unable to guess. But he knew that the little man would understand, when he stepped out onto the platform and found that the owner of the suspicious back had disappeared. He would know that it was Geraldi, of course. But what would he do about it? Would he undertake the difficult task of getting off the train unobserved and changing to another, at the great risk of having all of his labor for nothing? Or would he attempt to have Geraldi thrown from the cars, and thus solve the problem at once? One answer came immediately.

Suddenly a man stood erect on the top of the pitching, swaying train. He stood lightly, undisturbed, and, drawing a revolver, he fired straight down at Geraldi.

The latter heard the crash of the gun, almost stifled by the roaring of the train that was swaying and heaving over a very rough section of the track, and the noise was echoed out from the face of a mountain wall at the left, to pass on the right out over the empty, unechoing void of a great valley. Geraldi, then, strove to swing away from the second shot, and he succeeded, but that very success nearly cost him his life. For he lost his fingerhold and rolled suddenly over the edge of the car roof. He had one almighty glimpse of the valley profundities beneath him, huge and still as eternity, and then his left arm, up to the elbow, hooked inside of a window.

The wrench almost tore the arm from its socket, but it checked the fall. In another moment Geraldi had wriggled through the window into the lavatory. There he remained for a time, massaging his shoulder until the strained ligaments seemed more normal. He then washed his face and hands, and brushed the layers of dust from his clothes, for he was beginning to look like a hopeless vagabond by this time. Although the dust could be brushed off, the grease spots would not come off.

But he could not remain in the lavatory indefinitely. He had to be out watching the movements of Renney. That active genius might well have taken it for granted that the fall of Geraldi had been caused by the impact of his bullet. And if he had peered over the edge of the train and failed to note the body of Geraldi along the track, that might have been taken for granted, too. As a matter of fact, the boulders stood close to the track, and at the first roll a fallen man might have crashed down among them.

So there were great possibilities that Renney, contented, had gone back into the smoker, to sit down at ease and finish his trip. Or, if he were not sure, he would make a rapid tour through the train. Such a tour by this time must be completed.

So Geraldi complacently left the lavatory and wandered back to the rear car. A scowling conductor was pacified with a five dollar bill slipped covertly into his hand,

133

and Geraldi sat down in the last seat and watched the mountains turning red and black as the afternoon sun lit up the western faces and left the eastern slopes in thick shadow. He regarded this grandeur and listened comfortably to the rattling of the tracks as the train hurried on.

At such a speed, even the great Renney could not very well dismount. The way led through a pass with lofty walls on either side. This opened again suddenly, in the dusk of the day, and the train hooted for a stop. The halt came in a sprawling mountain town, and, slipping low in his seat, Geraldi studied the group that dismounted.

Last of all was his man, Renney himself, sauntering carelessly over to the corner of the platform and surveying the group that had left the train, like one who has no real suspicion, and, therefore, keeps look-out with only half an eye.

A savage thrill of satisfaction leaped through the body of Geraldi. Even Renney would not be half so dangerous, now that complacent self-satisfaction came to him. Then, stooping low, Geraldi hurried forward in the train and passed to the front coach as the engine once more began to puff and pant. On the steps farthest from the station, he studied his time, and, as they drove past a line of freight cars on the siding, he dropped off and sprinted around behind them. By the time the passenger coaches had roared past, Geraldi was ensconced between two boxcars, peering carefully forth, and he could see the unmistakable outline of Renney's body and forward jutting head as that little warrior still leaned against the corner of the station house.

Even in his time of triumph, Renney seemed capable of taking a good deal of precaution. But at last he turned away, and Geraldi did not hesitate. He streaked across the intervening tracks, and rounded the station house on the run, in time to see Renney sauntering idly up the main street of the town. Geraldi followed.

Three times the uneasy Renney whirled and looked back. Three times Geraldi was a slouching idler leaning against a tree, or the side of a building. At length the quarry turned in at the door of the hotel, and Geraldi boldly followed.

Glancing in, he was able to see the desk, with Renney in earnest conversation with the clerk. That conversation lasted some minutes, and, when it ended, Geraldi faded back behind a group of loud-voiced idlers on the verandah.

Renney came out at once, hung an instant

on the verge of the steps, and then trotted down the street at an active gait. Geraldi left the verandah, also. He had an idea that the chase was drawing so close to its goal that shadowing no longer would serve in the case of so keen a fellow as Renney. He ran around the hotel at full speed and rushed into it, panting. Up to the clerk's desk he pushed and leaned on it, struggling, apparently, for his wind.

"Friend of mine here a moment ago. Asking for an old pal. He left word where he was going. Did he leave it with you?"

The clerk squinted at Geraldi. But a man red-faced with work never looks a suspicious character. "Asking after Toomey?" he inquired.

"That's it," nodded Geraldi.

For, of course, Robert Asprey would not be known by his own name.

"He didn't leave any message for you."

"You think a minute. He must have."

"No."

"Well, then, where's Toomey? I'll go to him."

"You'll have to have a horse," grinned the clerk, and looked at the battered, dusty clothes of Geraldi.

"I have Shank's pony."

"You try walking the Lawson Trail," said

the clerk with a serious nod.

"Well?"

"It's eight miles. Two hours by daylight."

He glanced toward the door, where the blue dusk was piled, darker than night in contrast with the yellow lamplight inside. "Where does the trail begin?"

"Back of the town. Turn up the left side of the creek. There's only one trail all the way. Toomey has his shack about eight miles back. What's the rush of news for Toomey? Had a rich brother die?"

Geraldi left at once.

All Westerners were apt to look upon foot travel as a dreadful torture, but Geraldi knew many a trail where a man would leave in the distance the neatest-footed horse that ever stepped over mountain ways. By the tone of the clerk he judged this to be one, and, therefore, he did not wait to secure a horse. Doubtless Renney would be doing that, and the lost moments might put him ahead of the killer on the way.

He walked briskly down the main street, reached the creek, listened for a moment to the foaming rush of its waters, and then turned up the bank as he had been directed. He broke into a dog-trot. Long ago he had learned the trick from Mexican Indians — the trick of that shambling pace that wears

137

out the miles with a patient endurance, calling least upon the wind of the runner.

In a moment the way began to pitch upwards. Still he maintained that steady pace, only shortening his stride, and lifting, lifting constantly through the darkness. Difficult going it was. He could understand why the clerk had said two hours — by day. For he had to feel for every footfall, and twice he stumbled and almost fell, tripped by jutting rocks. Some hurrying mountain goat must have laid out the line of the road. There was nothing man-made or man-conceived about it. It sheered up. It jerked down.

His wind began to give way. He had to fall back to a rapid walk. He began to climb what seemed almost a sheer wall, and finally, climbing along this, he reached a dizzy summit.

Standing in the blackness, he wondered how any horse could live on such ground, and, steady though his nerves were, he could not help a little shudder at the thought of striving to ride that way through the darkness. Behind him lay the vast dark trough of the valley with the scattering yellow lights blossoming in its heart. Before him more tumbled wilderness of mountains, jutting up against the stars.

He went on again down a sheer pitch,

then the trail wound out more easily, and he could run once more. He judged that he had gone at least six or seven miles from the town, and he paused to take his breath. As he did so, he heard behind him the ring of the hoofs of a horse upon the rocks. He looked back, and saw flashes of fire struck from the stones. Someone was following. Renney?

Chapter Sixteen

FROM BEHIND

He sank upon one knee, to breathe more easily, and to think. He could not conceive of any other human being taking the desperate chances of that night work — no one other than Renney, the professional desperado. And yet what made Renney use such speed, except his natural ferocity?

In the mind of the head-hunter, there must have been comparative peace. Surely, he would go forward with leisure. On the other hand, some stalwart mountaineer, young enough to be foolishly rash, might have ridden this perilous way so often that he was capable of dashing forward at that reckless gait even through the darkness.

Geraldi was in a quandary. If he could be sure that it was Renney, he could draw a gun and shoot him down and be as free from remorse as though the fellow were a mad dog, for no longer did he need the guidance of Renney to take him to Robert Asprey. Yet, he could not be sure. He thought of sending a bullet through the horse. But that would be perilous work in the darkness, and to the left the ground pitched down in almost a sheer cliff. If the horse fell, the rider would be bound to go down with it. So, drawing great breaths, shaking his head in confusion, Geraldi watched the rider coming by the sparks that flew from the hoofs of the horse.

Almost instantly the pair were upon him and driving past as Geraldi crouched low. They reached the edge of a grove.

"Damn you, get on!" yelled the rider to his horse.

Geraldi leaped up. For it was the voice of Renney.

Horse and rider were gone, but their echoes flew behind them, and Geraldi ran in pursuit. Now that it was a second guess, it seemed clear enough that he should have known from the first. However, there was nothing for it except to use all his strength and hope that he would not be too utterly distanced.

Never before had he put forth such an effort except for one terrible bleak night, many a year before, in the throat of an Alpine pass, struggling for his own life, as he now struggled for the life of another. But pride and a stern resolution such as rises out

141

of the hearts of brave men made him keep on.

He went up another steep rise in the winding way. Then a little plateau spread before him, and on that tableland he saw a gleam of light, and, running on, he came on the outline of a small mountain shack, leaning its back against a lofty rock. He drew still closer. He saw the lamplight streaming through the open door, and in that light Renney was dismounting. Yes, there stood a tall man holding out his hand and welcoming the head-hunter. Was that Robert Asprey?

It came sharply home to Geraldi that perhaps Toomey was by no means Asprey, but simply a link on the way — a man, perhaps, who knew where the quarry was to be found, or an ally for the work of destruction. Otherwise, it seemed certain to Geraldi that Renney would simply have drawn a gun and shot the big fellow down.

At any rate, this was his cue to go on more slowly, regaining his breath. For he who goes into action when he is racked by shortness of breath is apt to be a dead man when the next morning dawns. He made a slow circuit of the shack. There were two apertures in the walls. One was a little slit that could serve as a window. One was the door.

Both were open to the air of the night, that was strangely balmy, in spite of the altitude, for a south wind was blowing gently from the hot regions of the desert.

At the narrow window Geraldi posted himself and looked in on the back of the mountaineer, Toomey, at his work at the stove. He had long, gray hair that brushed his shoulders, and those shoulders would have commanded respect in any prize ring. He was dressed in overalls and a flannel shirt, rolled up to the brawny elbows. Renney, the killer, sat on a stool cocked back against the wall, and his unnaturally bright eyes were constantly fixed upon his host. The latter was dropping thick slices of venison into a frying pan and then adding coffee to a black pot.

"You'll eat tonight, my friend," he threw over his shoulder to Renney. "What you running from?"

"A pair of damned dicks that have been trailing me for a month," lied Renney with convincing emotion.

"They'll never follow you over this trail by night. How did you manage to make it?"

"I took a chance. I was scared to death."

It occurred to Geraldi that this was bad acting, for, if the man at the stove had cast a single glance at the face of his guest, he might have known that fear was no familiar of the little gunfighter.

"What you do?" asked the host, still busy at his cookery.

There was a pause. In it, Geraldi surveyed the cabin. It was very poor. Only a rifle here, an axe leaning there, a belt of cartridges hanging on the wall. But yonder was a shelf loaded down with books.

An odd taste in a poverty-stricken mountaineer. The interest of Geraldi grew more intense, and he yearned for a glance at the face of the big man.

"You don't have to answer," said Toomey. "I can guess for you, I think."

"You guess, then, partner," suggested Renney.

"You dropped somebody," said the host without emotion.

Renney tipped forward on his stool. "I shot somebody, eh?"

"I suppose so."

"How d'you come by that?"

"You have the look of a handy boy with your guns. I know the eye of a man, pretty well."

The host chuckled as he spoke, and his great shoulders quivered. It sent a chill up the spine of Geraldi to hear that speech, and to watch the venomous writhing back of the lips of the gunman.

"I look pretty bad, eh?" said Renney.

There was that in his voice which made Toomey turn around. Toomey? Not a bit of it. Drawn on broader, rougher lines, like the rudely blocked-in sketch of a finished statue, this was the very face of the girl who had sent Geraldi on the quest.

He wasted not an instant, but softly, swiftly, as he well knew how to move, he passed around the shack and gained the door, his Colt quivering in the eager grip of his fingers.

"Bad?" the fearless giant was saying. "You don't look bad or good. You simply look like what I said. I've known gunfighters of all kinds. I've fired a few shots myself. But no matter what I thought of you, you're safe here, my lad. I've never turned a man from my door, and I never will. And once inside you own as much of the house as I do."

It was a hearty speech; it warmed Geraldi to hear it; but again the chill shot up his spine as he saw big Robert Asprey turn back to the stove.

No matter what the world held against him, he, Geraldi, would be willing to swear to his total innocence of any base or cowardly action. He was such a father from which such a daughter must have sprung.

"I own as much of the house as you do?" echoed Renney. "And maybe, partner, I own a little bit more."

A Colt hung dangling from his fingers, and Geraldi raised his own for the kill. Yet, he hesitated. He could act in the hundredth part of a second, while Renney would need at least twice that long. A sufficient interval for Geraldi to make all safe.

Asprey had turned, but without haste. He looked down at the gun, and he looked down at the man who held it. "You've come for me, have you?" he asked gravely.

Renney shook his left forefinger at the big man in triumph.

"I ain't touched as much as a crumb of bread or a glass of water from your hand, Asprey. I ain't touched a thing. You got nothing on me!"

"Except that you sat here like a sneak and pulled a gun on me."

"You picked my business for me, a minute ago," said Renney with a shrug of his shoulders. How his head thrust out, like a bird of prey. And what a glow of unholy joy was in his eyes.

"By Jove," murmured the big man, in more wonder than fear, "you're proud of this job, I really think."

"I am," admitted Renney instantly. "I've

146

done some slick jobs in my life, but this is the slickest."

"Tell me how," asked the older curiously. "Because it seems to me that this will be one of the easiest murders on record. I had a gun when I met you at the door. I hung it up after you came in. What makes your work hard?"

"Not you, Asprey," snapped Renney. "You've been a fool. You're gonna die on account of it. But there was another. I've dodged wise ones and fast ones, but he was the wisest and the fastest. By God, there was a time when I thought that he'd beat me."

"Beat you here?"

"Aye. He was your girl's man."

"*She* sent someone?"

"Oh, she sent him. And she picked a good one. But I settled him as I'm going to settle you. I shot him off the top of a train, and the pulp that's left of him the buzzards are picking right now in the rocks of Channing Pass."

"Well . . . God rest his soul," said the big man slowly. "But my girl knew I was in danger?"

"She knew. She guessed. I dunno. Women can guess a good deal. Asprey, you got a second to live. Want to say anything?"

"Why," said the other thoughtfully, "I believe that there's nothing to say. You can finish your job, my friend." And he stood fearless, looking at the death which worked into a snarl on the lips of Renney.

"Damned if I don't almost hate to do it," said Renney. "I'm almost sorry for you, Asprey. You look like a man to me. But you ain't the first man I've sent to hell before me. Asprey, good bye!"

And the revolver raised in his hand.

Chapter Seventeen

CONFESSION OF FAITH

The finger of Geraldi quivered on his gun, but still he waited that last shaving of a second.

"Just a moment," interrupted big Asprey, raising his hand.

"All right," answered Renney. "Is your nerve busting a little, partner?"

He asked that with almost an affectionate interest, as a man would ask after the welfare of a friend. And Geraldi, watching from the outer darkness, well could understand, for it was not merely to kill that Renney lived. It was to see his victims beholding death before its arrival. It was to watch the anguish of their faces and the horror of their souls that this man of evil performed his crimes.

Under that question, Asprey smiled. His courage was as perfect as that of Cousin Edgar.

"I think that my nerve holds out fairly well, so far," he answered. "But I would like to ask you a few questions about affairs in general. You can answer freely, I suppose?"

"Sure," said Renney, and pinched his shoulders together. "I've always thought that there was nothin' more interestin' than to see how a gent could watch hell risin' at his face. I never had no better chance than I got now."

He pitched himself back sharply on the stool and braced himself, dogging his heels at the floor, and propping them in a convenient crack. All the while he studied Asprey hungrily. And yet, now and again, his glances flashed uneasily from side to side. He was worried. Spasms of nervousness overcame him, and left him shaking and almost helpless with excess of nerve force tied up within him.

He interrupted Robert Asprey before the latter could speak and ask his questions.

"Make your chatter quick, though. Make it short."

"You have to start on your return trip so soon?" Asprey asked, steady as a rock.

"I dunno . . . you can't tell. He was like a snake . . . quick and easy in everything that he done," declared the killer.

"Who was?"

"Who've I been tellin' you about?" screamed Renney in a sudden perverse rage.

"I been telling you about him, ain't I? About that slippery snake, that smooth-workin' devil, Geraldi!"

"You said that you shot him off the top of a train. That ought to end him pretty effectually."

"Maybe you'd think so," remarked Renney. "I thought so myself, but right from the first I had a doubt. I killed him. I drove a bullet right through the top of his skull. I knocked him off the top of that train at fifty miles an hour. And he had a whole precipice to fall down. There's plenty of reasons why he should be dead, but still I don't *feel* him dead. He ain't dead and buried. He's still hangin' in the back of my brain!"

Geraldi was stirred with interest. Never before had he seen a clearer proof of mental telepathy. Undoubtedly, Renney was something more than a mere brute. He was a highly organized and sensitive spirit — a hair-trigger brain — an electric spirit of apprehension.

Big Asprey made note, in his turn. "You're too keen ever to be happy," he said. "Isn't that true, my friend? You haven't told me your name."

The other grinned slowly. It was unlike the white flash of Geraldi's smile. It began stretching in the corners, and curling, and

151

the glints of yellow teeth showed through one by one, like a watchdog beginning to gather anger against an intruder.

"I'm Renney."

"Ah, you're Renney," said Asprey. "That explains everything, I suppose. And you're Renney. I thought that Renney was a bigger man."

"Did you? Well, he ain't! He's my size. He's me. And I tell you what," added the killer venomously, "if I was only half my size, I'd still be big enough."

"Of course, you would," answered Asprey. "All that you have to do is be able to draw a gun. Even a child has enough strength for that!"

"Is that all I have to do?" sneered the criminal. "Well, anyway, I'm man enough for the work that I have to do."

"But tell me, Renney, have you always done this sort of work?"

"Ask your cousin," answered Renney darkly. "He knows my life. When you meet him . . . around the corner" — again with that sinister smile — "ask him, and he'll tell you."

"Cousin Edgar?" echoed Robert Asprey.

"Yes, him."

"And what has he to do with you . . . and with me?"

"Now how'n hell can I tell?" answered Renney. "Except that he sent me."

"He sent you?" cried Asprey. "Did Edgar send you?"

Renney crouched a little lower, and his head thrust still farther forward. "That fetches you, does it?" he said. "That's your sore point, is it?"

Robert Asprey reached out a long arm and braced himself against the wall of the house. He supported himself, breathing hard, and dragged the other hand across his forehead.

"Edgar has always been . . . why, man, I've befriended him. He's been . . . it's not possible!"

"Them's the things that you always gotta count on," said the other gravely. "Them's the things that I always count on. It ain't what you see that's worthwhile knowing, but it's what lies behind the wall, around the corner, up in the air . . . that's what you gotta keep feeling and guessing at and tryin' to know. That's why I ain't satisfied with my dead Geraldi. I'm gonna go back and see him lyin' in the rocks with the face of him clawed up by the buzzards. Then I'll be satisfied."

"Edgar . . . Edgar . . . ," murmured Robert Asprey. "But why? What could he gain?"

"Hey," snapped Renney, "don't you know that your wife's richer'n hell?"

"Rich!"

"Aw, tell me, man, where you been buried all this time . . . all these years?"

"Rich? Rich," echoed Asprey, more and more troubled. "But my wife has been writing to me constantly about the dreadful poverty . . . and I've been working like a slave to make what money I could to send. . . ."

"You talk like a sap," declared Renney shortly. "Your wife dunno that you're alive, even."

Asprey frowned and said nothing at all.

"Why, if she guessed that you was really alive, would she be thinking of marrying . . . him?"

"Who?" cried Asprey.

"You know . . . the fat man . . . your cousin."

Robert Asprey drove his heavy knuckles against his forehead. "Edgar again! But my letters. . . ."

"He's a handy gent with a pen."

"He is!" cried Asprey. "He is . . . he is! I remember that from when he was a boy. Ah, God!" He paused, stunned with grief and astonishment. "Renney," he said suddenly, "you've been paid for this work?"

154

"Not a bean," said Renney. "But I'm gonna be. Oh, I'm gonna be."

"You are," said Asprey. "But let me tell you this . . . you say that my wife is rich . . . ?"

"Sure. Everything that had failed with you has turned into gold ever since. That's what everybody says about it."

"Then that wealth is mine."

"That wealth belongs to your ghost, not to you."

"Renney, do you believe that my word could be trusted?"

"You? Sure, I guess you're honest."

"Then let me tell you . . . every penny that I have on earth will go to you. I'll see that every penny is put into your hands, if you'll turn about-face and help me through with this work. Or without help . . . simply leave me free . . . to find him . . . to. . . ." He paused, choked with emotion.

Renney, listening with admiration and bright eyes, nodded in understanding. "I foller that," he said.

"You hear me, Renney? I mean what I say. If I'm rich, I'll swear to pass it all over to you. Edgar . . . God, God." The dreadful nature of the news that he had heard seemed to strike him with fresh force, and he groaned aloud.

"Damn my soul," murmured Renney,

"I'm sorry for you. But this game won't work with me."

"Game?"

"I know that you mean to go square with it. But I got my points of honor. I ain't a Sunday school pupil. I never pretend to be. All the same, I'd like to have you know that I stick straight to my line of work. Now, Asprey, I'm sorry for you. You got the nerve. I'd like to see you win, any other time. But your cousin hired me for this job, and I'll stick to it, on the terms that I laid down with him, as long as I got a drop of blood inside of me." He paused, breathing hard.

Geraldi, crouched in the dark, fascinated, realized that he was hearing this man's confession of faith.

"If he give me nothing but a nickel," croaked Renney, "and you had a mountain of god-damn' diamonds piled up here to hand me instead, I'd tell you to go to hell with your diamonds. I'd take the price that I'd agreed to work for."

"That's fixed," nodded Asprey, understanding that further argument was totally useless. "That's fixed then. Finish your job."

"Are you ready?"

"I'm ready."

"Then . . . here you are." And the gun gleamed at the level.

Geraldi drew his bead on the working muscle in the temple of the killer. And then his aim wavered down. Never before had he shot from behind, not even to slay a murderer — still that was not battle after his liking. At the last minute he changed, and he fired at the glint of the weapon in Renney's hand.

Chapter Eighteen

A LAW-ABIDING CITIZEN

Clean and true that shot found its target. There was a double explosion. For the Colt, knocked from the hand of Renney, struck the floor near the wall, was fired by the shock, in turn, and by the recoil was kicked almost to the center of the floor.

Asprey seized that moment's respite as well as he could. He caught up the axe that stood against the wall, nearest to the stove. It was such a weapon as even a woodsman of standing would have found load enough for both his arms. But Asprey made it tremble in the grip of one hand.

"It ain't any use," remarked Renney. "Drop the axe, partner. I could shoot the liver out of you before you had the time to swing that once. But what's the good? He's got me."

He sat exactly as he had been before — prepared for firing the bullet that was to end Asprey's life. That is to say, he was leaning forward on the stool, and the right hand which had supported the gun was still stretched forth. He had not changed color in the slightest, and Geraldi noted curiously that a peculiar smile, unlike his fighting snarl, was on his lips.

He was not at all like a man about to die. He was rather like one vastly amused and interested in something that he saw — some little drama on the opposite wall — some jest, some deep and biting criticism of life.

"Who is he?" shouted Robert Asprey, facing the dark of the doorway.

"Oh, it's Geraldi," answered Renney, taking the response on himself. "It's him . . . and I should have trusted the jump in my nerves and the ache in my bones. Damn me for a fool!"

Geraldi leaned in the doorway. "Hello, Renney," he said. "Evening, Mister Asprey."

Renney turned his head with deliberation. "Not even a scratch on you, I suppose?" he asked.

"On my clothes, yes," Geraldi said cheerfully.

Renney looked at him gravely. "Sure," he said, "I might've known that I was right. Take the jump in your nerves. That's better than an article in a newspaper. All right, kid. You beat me. And it's the first time that's been done. Shake on it."

"Put up your hands and face the wall," answered Geraldi. "Asprey, have that axe ready to brain him."

"Ah, I see," sighed Renney. "You wouldn't trust me, Geraldi. You'd think that I'd try to double-cross you?"

"Man, man," said Geraldi, "do you think that I'm wasting time on you, except that there may be a bargain we can strike with you? Otherwise, I'd never have shot for the gun."

"Ah, that was near," said Renney. "That was what I call clever shooting. That was what I call perfect shooting. But you say face the wall . . . and face the wall it is." He turned obediently, but the leisurely movement turned into a lightning twist. Jerking around, under his left shoulder appeared the miracle of a revolver that he had conjured forth from the thinnest air apparently.

It was very fast. It could not have been a quicker move, or a better conceived one, and more than one man, before that evening, had died because of it. But for all that, it did not play a bullet from his gun. But a straight left was the matter-of-fact magic that he used. His knuckles caught Renney's cheekbone as the latter whirled, opened the flesh deeply, and crashed him against the wall.

He fell in a heap, but, even as he fell, his semi-conscious right hand was at work, as though it could keep on functioning after a half paralysis, like the unconscious brain during sleep. Three times he fired, and three bullets hissed through the open door of the shack.

Robert Asprey, his face contorted with fear, disgust, and surprise, heaved the axe up and stood closer, looking very much like a man about to step upon a spider, and not at all sure that the soles of his boots are thick enough to keep out the tarantula's bite.

"He's done for a moment," said Geraldi, in answer to this silently proffered help. "He's asleep for a minute or two. His head banged the wall before he flopped."

He took Renney by the shoulder and stretched him face up.

Beyond a doubt the smaller man was totally unconscious, but the instant that the hand was removed from his shoulder, he began slowly to curl back into his former position, twisting on his right side.

"Look," smiled Geraldi. "Like a snail."

"I'll throw some water on him and try to bring him to," suggested Asprey.

"Wait till I've searched him."

"But we have his two guns."

"We have. Maybe we'll have some more."

They did have more. Two snub-nosed guns came out of the loosely fitted clothing of the killer, and finally, from up his sleeve where it was held in place by a rubber band, Geraldi drew out a little two-barreled pistol. It was very small, indeed, but as Geraldi assured his host, that gun would kill at ten paces, which is as great a distance as intervenes in most bar-room battles. That was not the total armament of the accomplished Renney. There was also a long Bowie knife, running diagonally down the inside of the cartridge belt that looped his hips. And under one arm they plucked out a typical Italian stiletto — one of those weapons that cause strong men to die suddenly, without pain, without a cry.

Robert Asprey touched the assembled guns and knives with the toe of his boot and shook his head. "All fangs," he said.

"And a little poison," murmured Geraldi, taking out the pocketbook of the fallen man. He opened it and revealed a thin layer of cells, each covered over with semi-transparent oiled silk. Geraldi examined each cell delicately, carefully.

"Arsenic, morphia, strychnine . . . oh, he has quite a list. He could, as they say, work in the dark, Mister Asprey. Have you any doubt about him, now?"

Asprey looked at the assembled poisons with open mouth. "Are you sure of all of those?" he asked.

"Not quite all," answered Geraldi. "I know a little bit about this game, but only for purposes of defense. I've never used them. I hope to God that I never will. But Renney is an expert. You see that he's an all-around genius."

"An absolute devil!" shuddered Asprey.

Geraldi looked up at his host curiously, his head canted a little to one side.

"Why do you say that?"

"What else should I say? What else is there to call this fellow, Geraldi? You are Geraldi, I suppose?"

"I am Geraldi."

"I want to shake your hand, Geraldi."

"Thank you. First we'll tie this spider hand and foot and lay him against the wall."

"But he's helpless without his weapons."

"These are all the weapons we can see. That's all."

"Now, what do you mean by that?"

"It's clear enough."

"I don't think so."

"I mean, Asprey, that these fellows have weapons in their minds. We don't want those weapons to be turned loose against us, do we? We never can tell. There are all sorts

163

of subtle tricks that we never have a chance to admire until they are killing us."

Asprey argued no longer, but began to help tie Renney, hand and foot.

"You haven't killed him?" he asked, alarmed.

"Would you care?" asked Geraldi, curious again.

"Care! Good God, man, he's a human being, isn't he? You wouldn't want to take his life?"

"Human? Well . . . I suppose so," replied Geraldi, biting his lip a little.

"He's lain unconscious for a long time. Let me listen to his heart."

"He's not unconscious now," answered Geraldi. "He's been awake for a couple of minutes, listening, and hearing what he can." He tapped the shoulder of his victim. "Renney!"

There was no response.

"Renney, wake up. I want to talk to you."

The eyes of Renney opened wide and clear. They shone with a rat-like brightness at Geraldi.

"Hello, kid," he said. "You'll do."

"Thank you," answered Geraldi. "I'm sorry that I had to tie you up like this."

"Don't mention it," answered Renney politely. He writhed into a sitting position.

"You got my circulation stopped with these ropes," he complained.

"They *are* too tight," said Robert Asprey. "Look there! His hands are turning blue."

"They'll be turning green, however, before the birds eat him," said Geraldi calmly.

"Murder, you see?" said the killer to Robert Asprey. "You see what he wants? Murder is the only thing that'll satisfy him . . . the bloodsucker."

Robert Asprey smiled at his would-be executioner. "We'll talk about that at our ease," he suggested.

"Have it your own way," snapped Renney. But even he allowed a faint light of amusement to come into his eyes.

There was neither dignity nor sympathy in Renney, but certainly there was an infinite amount of understanding of everything, and of everyone.

"Sit down, sit down, boys," he said. "Gimme a cup of coffee while you talk things over, and remember that you're gonna hang for it, if you murder me. I'm a law abidin' citizen, god-damn me, if I ain't!"

Chapter Nineteen

TIED BY THE TRAIL

Like a lion and a leopard and a wolf they sat in the shack of Robert Asprey, the big man intent upon the word that had been brought to him, and seemingly indifferent to the danger through which he had passed, or to the final disposition of the killer who was now helpless before him. But the attention of Geraldi and Renney turned keenly upon one another.

In their attitudes there was something as old as hate itself. There was also something as new as the rivalry between two boys in a school yard. They looked at each other curiously. Each had tested the other's mettle. Neither had been found wanting according to a certain grim standard.

Suddenly the host remembered that food was prepared. He placed it on the table and insisted that Renney should join them with free hands at the meal. Geraldi observed quietly: "You had the nose of that fellow's gun in your face a moment ago. If you let him free of his hands, you may have a gun on

166

you again, before long. But you own this house, and I suppose that you ought to be free to control what happens in it." Accordingly he freed Renney.

The latter stood up, rubbed his hands and arms, teetered up and down to restore the circulation to his legs, and then sat down at the table without a word.

They ate, and still in silence they looked at one another and on their own thoughts.

"Geraldi," said Asprey, suddenly taking himself away from his gloomy reflections, "I owe you my life tonight. I haven't thanked you. There is no way to thank a man for such a thing. But tell me what sent you on this trail?"

Geraldi pondered a moment. Then, looking straight at Asprey, he said: "I picked the pocket of Chalmers, the hotel keeper, so that I could pay his bill. He discovered what he had lost and came back with the sheriff. I got across the roof to your house, and down through the skylight. Chalmers and the rest were boiling up below like hornets, by that time. I dodged into the first room, and there your daughter sheltered me from them. Afterward . . . well, she talked a little, I saw a little, and . . . I've always been tempted to put my money at long odds, if you can understand that."

This condensed and frank confession caused Asprey to narrow his eyes a little, but at length he smiled. Yet Geraldi felt in the man a sort of iron honesty that refused to understand such a speech entirely.

"You heard what Renney told me?"

"I heard it."

"Was it true?"

"Every word. Have you been trying to get in touch with your family?"

"I've written to them regularly after I once got on my feet. Of course, I wouldn't abandon them."

"How have you helped them, then?"

"I've worked with my hands, man, and sent them every penny. Do you think I'd be here, otherwise, leading the life of a dog?"

"You've had regular letters from them?"

"From my wife and my girl. Certainly! And exactly as they would have expressed themselves."

The wind had been rising for some time; now a gust wailed across the peaks and came humming and singing around the cabin so that Renney shivered as though with cold, and cast an anxious look at the open door.

Once through it, and he would be free. But he knew that he could never get that far. There was no gun in the hand of Geraldi,

168

and it would be one leap to the door. But in a hundredth part of the time that the passage to the door would require, the hand of Geraldi would be armed. And never in an instant was the killer out of the eye of Geraldi. Never for a moment as he talked with Asprey did he keep his keen attention from Renney. So the latter fiddled at his food, and filled his coffee cup a second time, and fingered a knife on the table, hungrily. One fatal blow he might strike with it — but never two.

"Your cousin, Edgar, is a clever fellow," said Geraldi. "And you yourself said that he was a penman."

Asprey locked his hands on the edge of the table. "If he's done such things through all these years," he said slowly, "then God never put a more consummate villain on the earth."

"For my part," answered Geraldi, "I don't think that he ever has." He added: "There's a fairly simple solution."

"For me?" asked Asprey bitterly. "My hands are tied by the law. I'm a hunted man."

"Your daughter has seen the governor. He's promised that, if you will come and talk to him, there is more than a chance that you can have a free pardon to clear you."

"Has he promised that?" Asprey repeated, rising a little from the table. "Has he promised that? Then I'm off to him. Now, by heaven! I'll start now. And afterward . . . my dear Cousin Edgar. . . ." He muttered it softly through his teeth, and little Renney grinned in malicious appreciation.

"There's this man to dispose of," said Geraldi. He nodded at Renney.

"There's this man to dispose of," admitted the big fellow gloomily. He scowled at Renney.

"What have you to say for yourself?" he asked grimly.

"Friends," answered Renney calmly, "you know me. I've showed my hand, and I'm damned if I try to sneak out of the hole now. I've tried to get the pair of you. Now you've got me."

That was frank enough, and its frankness opened the eyes of the giant.

"Very well," said Asprey. "But what can we do? Can we take him along with us?"

"Not very well."

"Can we afford to turn him loose?"

"I'd rather turn loose the devil," said Geraldi.

"Certainly we can't kill him in cold blood."

Renney looked sharply up, unbelieving.

"We can't," agreed Geraldi.

They made a pause.

"There's another way," suggested Geraldi. "Renney, you don't deserve a man's chance, but I've never taken advantage of a fellow whose hands were tied. If I give you a gun, will you stand up and fight it out like a man?"

"Hold on!" broke in Asprey. "This Renney . . . why, Geraldi, he's a natural genius . . . or devil . . . with a gun."

"I'll take my chance with him," persisted the other. "Renney, what do you say to it?"

Renney closed his eyes with a strong pressure. "Partner," he answered softly, "it's the best thing that I've heard in years, and the squarest and the most sporting."

"I won't have it," said Asprey shortly. "If there's such a fight, I would have to take the place opposite him. And I'm not a trickster with a revolver. Now, this trail past the house is traveled not too often, just once or twice a day travelers go by. They head for town in the morning. They come drifting back in the afternoon. I say that in the morning we'll tie Renney to a tree near the road. Let him take his chances on the first man who comes past. I think that's fair."

"That's fair as can be," said Renney. "That's white man's talk."

171

"Be quiet," broke in Geraldi. "What do you know of white men, except in books?"

Renney chuckled in the most perfect good nature. "You got the right to talk," he admitted. "I've lost. You take the pot."

So the thing was settled. Geraldi himself tied Renney hand and foot again. They laid him on a blanket in a corner of the shack, far from knife or gun. Then the other two turned in — Geraldi, at the insistence of the host, on the bunk, Asprey himself on the bare floor near the stove. The door was barred, the lamp put out, and they lay in quiet, listening to the loud voice of the night.

Geraldi turned his face to the wall and slept at once. He was by no means sure of their prisoner, but he trusted that sheer weight of bad tidings would be sufficient to keep Asprey awake until the morning, and in that fashion they would be maintaining a watch over the captive.

Not until the full morning did he waken. The sun was not up, but the cold, clear light was streaming through the small window, and the cracks of the door were lined with rosy fire. Then Geraldi rose and found Asprey seated by the cold stove, his chin resting on his hand. Renney, blue and shivering, crouched in a corner, trying to huddle the blanket closer around his bones.

Now that Geraldi was awake at last, the fire was built up, a breakfast of bacon, cold bread, and coffee prepared and eaten, and then they led Renney out from the shack.

In the near distance, his horse, its saddle twisted to one side as proof that it had tried to roll, was grazing cheerfully on the dew-wet grass. A lump-headed brute it looked, and Geraldi could not help wondering, when he remembered what a fire-breathing Pegasus the animal had seemed when it plunged through the darkness of the night before over the perilous trail.

They selected a young fir sapling not fifty yards back from the trail and bound Renney to it, using a whole length of rope to do the job. His cheerfulness had departed in the cold of the morning.

"If I ain't frozen by mid-morning," he said, "the wolves'll have me by night, and damn you both. Geraldi, you said that you'd give me a chance at you with a gun. Have you turned yellow, man?"

They were deaf both to appeals and to taunts. They had a long trail before them on that day.

Geraldi took the killer's mount. The mountaineer brought forth a powerful, stocky mule, and, making up a hasty pack of food and ammunition for the journey, they started at once across the mountains on the back trail.

Chapter Twenty

"DEAR COUSIN EDGAR"

In the garden behind the house of Robert Asprey in Sankeytown, Cousin Edgar walked with Louise Asprey. It was a very bright morning, but she, with an old-fashioned sun-bonnet to shade her eyes, had been working busily with a trowel, her arms and hands guarded with long, ragged gauntlets. A shadow had fallen across her, and she had looked up to find the big man between her and the sun. He had come silently, as always. Sometimes she felt that honesty possesses a solid weight that could not have been reduced to such a feathery lightness of step. However, she stood up, and she walked with him around the garden. She wanted a pergola built, and he was suggesting ways and means, should the columns be hollow wood or solid wood, or should they be of concrete, or courses of heavy stone, rough-edged. And what if a little pool were made within the semicircle of the columns?

She could guess that he had not come to

talk of such things as these alone. And presently he added: "And your mother has something to say to you, Louise. Shall we go in to her?"

"Perhaps I'd better go alone," said the girl.

"We had better let your mother decide that," smiled Cousin Edgar, and he followed her through the doorway.

Mrs. Asprey was in the library, sitting half in sun and half in shadow. She had done her hair close about her head, her dress was very simple and young, and Louise was most of all surprised to see that, although she was not wearing her glasses, there was an open book in her hand.

Louise was quite sure that her mother had not been able to read print without glasses for several years. Her mother turned the book face down in her lap and nodded at her daughter.

"Sit down, Louise. We must have a little chat."

"I'd better leave you alone," suggested Cousin Edgar.

"Leave us alone?" cried Mrs. Asprey. "Oh, by no means! This is just the sort of time when I need to lean on you, Edgar."

"I hope you'll forgive me for staying, then?" he said to the girl as she sat down.

Louise made a little gesture, hardly looking at him. She detested him so thoroughly that she often schemed to keep her eyes from falling on his bland face.

"What are you reading?" she asked.

"*Diana of the Crossways,*" said Mrs. Asprey.

"Oh," said Louise.

"And now, child," said Mrs. Asprey nervously, "I have to tell you something that will surprise you . . . but you'll see the good sense behind it at once, I do hope and pray."

"How humble you are, dear Cousin Olivetta," broke in Cousin Edgar.

"I hope not too humble," she said anxiously. "After all, Louise has a right to know."

"How could anyone be too humble?" said Cousin Edgar. "It's the first Christian virtue, I've always felt. But I'm sure that Louise must be touched. Are you not, my dear child?"

Louise looked at the floor. She did not wish to show any emotion, but she joined her hands and locked them hard. She knew that a blow had been prepared for her, but she would not let herself use her imagination.

"We begin . . . we begin . . . ," faltered Mrs. Asprey. "Where do we begin, Edgar?"

"I don't know, I'm sure," he said. "Perhaps you wish to talk about the future of Louise? I can't read your mind, dear Cousin Olivetta."

"Oh, no, of course not. Of course not. I feel rather in a flutter. We begin with. . . ."

"A future which seems to be concerned with so large a fortune, perhaps," suggested the oily voice of Cousin Edgar.

"Ah," sighed Mrs. Asprey, settling back a little in her chair with relief. "Once I have a starting point, I'm all right. I can go right on. Fortune . . . yes. You see, Louise, that the estate has been growing, thanks to the *wonderful* way that Cousin Edgar has done everything for us."

She beamed on Cousin Edgar. He waved the compliment away into the thinnest air.

"I thought that my father had left a great deal of money," said Louise calmly. But her heart was beginning to beat very fast.

"Ah, yes, he left some property," nodded Cousin Edgar. "He left property . . . of a sort."

"I don't know what you mean," said Louise.

"My dear child," said Cousin Edgar, "of course, you don't know what we mean. One doesn't expect a young girl with her head full of delightful life to be able to understand what business means."

"I should like to know the facts," said Louise.

"So should I," agreed her mother heartily, "but though I've tried . . . and though Cousin Edgar has showed me sheets and sheets of figures . . . haven't you, Edgar?"

"Ah, yes, naturally. Of course, I show everything to my principal. I'm only a servant in this matter, Louise."

"Do hear the man!" cried Mrs. Asprey. "A servant! Dear, *dear* Edgar, what a thing to say. As if . . . but the fact seems to be that though everything was in the most dreadful confusion when your poor father died. . . ."

"Died?" echoed Louise suddenly. "Died?"

"Oh, heavens!" cried Mrs. Asprey. "I knew that it would be like this. Louise, Louise, will you be reasonable?" She stretched out her hands imploringly. She was so excited that she rose a little from her chair, and the book slid from her lap to the floor.

Louise hurried to pick it up. She was very glad of the chance to leave her chair and compose her nerves by some sort of action. She saw that the volume was not *Diana*, but Soule's *Dictionary of English Synonyms* which her mother had apparently been reading with such an absorbed interest.

She was not greatly surprised. But before she passed back to her place, she looked once, long and earnestly, into the dim, uncertain eyes of her mother. Where the bridge of the glasses usually rested, the crimson streak had been covered carefully with powder, but the indentation of the years was plainly visible, and the wrinkles of strain at the corners of the eyes.

"Of course, Louise will be reasonable," Cousin Edgar said gently. "She's too logical not to admit facts when she sees them. She's had too good and expensive an education not to be convinced by logic, haven't you, my dear child?"

"I don't know what logic you mean to use," said Louise, trying hard to keep her voice up, "but I know that there isn't any proof that he's . . . that he's. . . ."

"Poor child," said Cousin Edgar. "What a sweet sight, Cousin Olivetta. Doesn't your heart swell? Poor child . . . poor, tender-hearted child. Alas, Olivetta, that the cruelty of life should be shown to her so young, so gentle, so. . . ." He drew a deep breath and dropped his head so that his finger tips sank into one fat cheek.

"*I'll* say it!" exclaimed Mrs. Asprey. "It's

too much for poor Cousin Edgar . . . poor, gentle, tender soul. But the truth is, dear Louise . . . the truth is that the estate is big, too heavy a weight for me to handle. I must have help . . . and there is Cousin Edgar, giving his life. Don't you think, Louise, that he should have some reward?"

"I do, indeed," answered the girl, feeling herself grow pale. "I do, indeed, think that he should have a handsome salary. Or a percentage, say."

"I hadn't thought of that," said Mrs. Asprey blankly. "Edgar, had you thought of that?"

Cousin Edgar had covered his eyes with his hands. But now he managed to say hoarsely: "Money! Salary! Percentage? To me?" He drew himself upright in his chair and sighed. "I thought," he said with dignity, "that I had deserved a little better than to be looked on as a hired man."

"Heavens!" screamed Mrs. Asprey. "Hired man! Whoever heard of such a thing? Louise, Louise, will you apologize this instant? Hired man! Oh, Edgar, do forgive us . . . her, I mean to say. Good gracious, I'm so confused I don't know what I'm saying."

"Dear, dear Olivetta," said Cousin Edgar, "I hope that I don't praise humility without possessing a little share of it myself. I _do_ forgive dear Louise. She's very young. Besides . . . dare I say it? . . . I fear she never has quite understood me."

"You've hurt your dear Cousin Edgar terribly," Mrs. Asprey said, growing red and breathing hard.

"I didn't mean to," said the girl. "We were talking business. I thought that I had made a business suggestion."

"The thoughts of the young," murmured Cousin Edgar. "Ah, well, like drifting, idle leaves, bright or brown, bright or brown. No matter."

"But what do you want, then?" asked Louise.

"I? I ask for nothing," said Cousin Edgar. "What a painful question, really."

"Really!" gasped Mrs. Asprey. "One would think, Louise, that you lacked fine sensibilities, to hear you. What does he ask for, indeed! Nothing. But I have thought of a way . . . you'd never guess what way." She was triumphant, her eyes shining.

Louise sat in silence. She knew clearly how the blow was to fall, and she did not wince from it. There was too much of her father in her, for that.

"I've suggested to Edgar that, since my poor, darling Robert undoubtedly has . . . has left this unhappy world. . . ."

182

"Undoubtedly?" asked Louise.

"Louise," said Cousin Edgar, shaking his head, "tell me . . . was your father a good man?"

"The best man I've ever known," said the girl heartily.

"I do hope so," said Edgar, turning up his eyes. "And would he be true to those he loved?"

"To the last drop of his blood!" she cried.

"I know he would," Cousin Edgar said. "There is a certain strain in us Aspreys, all of us. But then, child, considering that he was such a man, can you imagine that he would let five years pass without communicating with you in some way? At the risk of his very life, even?"

She was not convinced, but she was silenced.

"You're *much* cleverer than I," said the mother hurriedly. "Even I can see that, Louise. You don't hold out against such facts as that, I know."

"Youth will be stubborn," smiled Cousin Edgar. "Ah, well, it will be stubborn, but time is the greatest teacher of all, and time will teach even Louise, I dare trust and pray."

"Louise," said Mrs. Asprey, "the thing that I've thought of . . . I know you'll agree, because it's the only way we can make

183

Cousin Edgar a part of us . . . is that he and I should marry. Don't you admit that's a wonderful solution?"

She had expected it. She even had guessed exactly how the words would come, but still she was glad that her hands were locked together so that by sheer physical effort she could counterbalance the shock. She could not look at the face of her mother, childishly pleased and expectant and half frightened, too. But she turned her head to Cousin Edgar, and, through the smile with which he regarded her, she saw the steel-bright gleaming of his triumph. Then, bitterly, to her own heart she admitted her weakness against him.

Cousin Edgar stood up. "It is rather a shock, such a sudden bit of news," he said, "and we must give our dear Louise time to think it over. Shall we leave her alone, dear Cousin Olivetta?"

"Yes, yes!" exclaimed Mrs. Asprey, apparently glad to flee.

Cousin Edgar drew nearer. On the head of Louise he laid his soft hand. "My daily prayer, dear child," he murmured, "shall be that I may become a second father to you."

"Oh, Edgar," breathed Mrs. Asprey, "how beautiful." And she left the room upon his arm.

Chapter Twenty-One

THINK TWICE!

Like one surrounded by inevitable disasters, Louise Asprey remained in her chair. She felt an hysterical impulse to cry and strike her hands against her forehead, but she kept her fingers interlocked and by a great effort made her mind clear. Against the surety of this impending blow — and very soon it must fall — she had no hope to balance except the slender one attached to that handsome young adventurer who had taken up the trail to her father so lightly. As lightly, she told herself, he would abandon it, and she never would see him again. No doubt there was strength in him, but it was the strength of a thief, a pickpocket, a robber, a fighter. All hopes built on him were founded on shifting sands, surely.

There was a sound as of a sigh in the room. She almost thought that her mother had come back to sentimentalize over her, and over the future. Therefore, she kept her head down, arming herself with resolution. But in another moment she felt a light draft, and she looked up to see one of the closet doors closing, and James Geraldi standing before it, his head high and that familiar, flashing smile turned upon her.

Her first thought jumped from her lips. "You've never left Sankeytown at all, Mister Geraldi?"

"That's not the faith that moves mountains, is it?" asked Geraldi, coming closer.

And as he passed out of the shadow into the fuller light, nearer the windows, she saw that the clothes he wore were those in which she had last seen him. But they were much altered. Before, they had been at least clean. Now, although they had been brushed, great grease spots showed on them, and she counted a dozen rents. Those clothes looked as though they had been through the center of a cyclone.

He could not have come back with that smile, and a complete failure. The thought drew her up from her chair.

He did not leave her an instant in doubt: "I've seen him," he said. "He's alive and well. Is that too much of a shock?" he added, seeing her turn white.

"I'll sit here by the open window a moment," she whispered.

He helped her to the chair. Behind the chair he stood and talked, speaking swiftly in answer to every question.

"And the five years?" she murmured, when her brain cleared a little.

"He's written to you constantly . . . you and your mother."

"I don't understand."

"Don't you? But he's sent you money. He's worked hard to . . . keep you out of poverty."

"I knew he would. I knew . . . God bless him. But still I don't understand."

"Of course, you don't. He sent you letters and money. You both wrote back letters, telling him what a struggle you were having with poverty."

"Cousin Edgar!"

"He's a clever fellow," agreed Geraldi. "You see, your father didn't dare to come back to see you with his eyes. He had to stay far away, eating his heart out. If he dared to come back, and were caught and imprisoned, then, you see, there'd be no support for your mother and for you. You see the trap he was in. He didn't even dare to ask questions about you from people who might have been in Sankeytown. He was terribly afraid, always, that, if he showed any interest, it would lead to his discovery. He's been working in a net."

"He's coming now?"

"No, of course not. He's going to try to get to the governor first."

"I understand. But I don't understand how you found him."

"Cousin Edgar thought it was time to bring things to a climax, and, therefore, he sent Renney to kill your father. You're strong enough to hear the facts."

"I am."

"Well, I followed Renney. And Renney led me to the place."

She was herself again. She rose from the chair. She began to read his face as well as his speech. "It was a terrible trail!" she urged.

"It was a lucky trail."

"But if he led you to my father . . . what did he do?"

"Renney wasted time talking, you see. Finally, we left him tied up, near a trail where he'll be seen. He won't be a day behind me."

"Why did you do that?"

"I couldn't think of another way. It was that, or kill him in cold blood."

"Then . . . ," she began, with a cold gleam in her eyes, but immediately she flushed. "I'm ashamed," she said.

"No way but the clean way goes with your father," said Geraldi.

"I know. I remember." Her eyes filled with

tears. "How does he look?"

"You can see the pain on his face. But he's still strong and hard. His hair is gray."

"How did he stand the news?"

"Like a rock. But God help Cousin Edgar. Now I have to talk fast."

"Oh, James Geraldi, what have you done for me?"

"Nothing! I'd do ten times more for the sake of finding another man like him. But there is no other. Now listen."

"I'll remember every word."

"Dear Cousin Edgar will have the complete story from Renney tonight or tomorrow morning. Then what will he do?"

"At least, he can't marry my mother. I thank God. I thank God."

"Are you sure?"

"Knowing that my father is alive?"

"People can be married in a few minutes . . . before the judge. Very well, if he were married to her, he'd have a new grip on Robert Asprey. For the sake of all of you, there'd have to be an arrangement, an understanding."

She groaned. "What can be done, then?"

"We could tell your mother."

"Cousin Edgar could make her think black is white. He's able to talk her out of anything."

"Perhaps. But the talking might take time. And time is what we want, what we pray for. You see that?"

"I do. I do. If he can get to the governor. . . ."

"It won't be easy. Cousin Edgar's hands are filled with money."

"The governor is an honest man."

"No doubt. But there are friends of his who, perhaps, are not so honest. The instant Renney arrives and tells his story, Cousin Edgar will send a flood of money to the capital of the state, and he'll know what crooked politicians to send it to. They'll try to block this pardon. They'll try desperately hard to block it. Cousin Edgar will spend anything to block that pardon, because as long as it's denied, your father has to live like a wild wolf."

"I understand." She pressed her lips hard together and locked her hands. No whit of emotion should trouble the completeness of her understanding.

"You're not to use this unless you have to. Take it."

He gave her an unsealed envelope that she opened and read in a swift, strong hand:

Olivetta, have a little patience. For five years I have been trying to find a messenger whom I could send safely to you. At last I have found him. I am sending you word that, in a few days, I expect to be able to take my place among the lawful citizens of the land. That instant I come back to you. I am sending you this note because I know of Edgar and his schemes. Believe me, dear, when I say that in spite of them, nothing can make me stop caring for you and for my dear girl. *Adieu* in great haste.

Robert

"But why can't I show it to her now?" asked the girl, trembling violently. "Even Cousin Edgar couldn't talk down this letter."

"He'd find a way, we're afraid. Keep it for the last moment, and, in the meantime, never let your mother out of your sight, day or dark."

"I'll do it!"

"Haunt her like a shadow."

"Yes, yes. I'll find ways."

"You might seem to Cousin Edgar to be reconciled."

"I can try that, too. But he's very shrewd. And you?"

"I'm going back to your father. He may need me. Cousin Edgar's money will be working before he possibly can get to the governor, we're afraid. In the meantime, we have to leave the fight at this end to you. Everything lies in your hands."

"I'll never flinch."

"Be brave, be steady, and always think twice. Good bye for a day or two."

"How will you leave?"

"I'll try to go as I came in."

"How?"

"Through the cellar, and then across into the hotel cellar. And so back through the sheds."

Her eyes opened with a gleam of admiration. That light turned to terror at a sound in the hall. She hurried toward the door to bolt it, if necessary, but, before she reached it, she turned and glanced back.

Geraldi already was gone.

She went to the window, therefore, and hung for a moment, drawing in great breaths of air, telling herself that she must be "brave, steady, and think twice." Then she left the room. The hall was empty. So she went out into the front garden and walked a few turns up and down it.

When she came back, she found that she had left the front door unlatched, and, therefore, it opened noiselessly before her, and noiselessly fell her step on the hall carpet.

The library door was a trifle ajar, and so, glancing casually through it, she happened to see Cousin Edgar, crouched almost on his knees, and moving slowly across the library floor until he came to a closet door. That door he jerked suddenly open. She saw the gleam of a gun in his hand. But within the closet was blank darkness.

Still she lingered. She could remember, now, that it was from that door that James Geraldi had appeared to give her a new hope. And she knew that Cousin Edgar, in some manner, had detected strange footsteps on the floor. All the danger which that discovery might bring down on the household came flooding through the heart of the girl and left her frozen in her place.

Cousin Edgar, after a moment, closed the door and turned away from it so that she could see his face. For the first time she saw the full truth of him revealed. For it was like a face of white iron. The nostrils flared. In the eyes there was a look half desperate and all evil. It seemed to the girl that his glance must have found her in the hall, and the dreadful shock of that fear moved her at last. She was able slowly to climb the stairs to the second floor of the house, clinging to the banister, for her knees were giving beneath her.

When she reached the upper hall, she had a nightmare feeling that soft, padding steps were flying up the stairs in pursuit, but still she could not hasten, for her legs were numb and would not respond. Ten seconds of horror lay between her and the door of her room, but at last it was closed behind her, the key turned in her fingers, and she tried to reach the bed. Blackness whirled across her eyes. She reached the rug beside the bed. She fumbled for it with her outstretched hand, and then fell face downward in a faint.

Chapter Twenty-Two

GERALDI SLIPS IN

In the very center of Sankeytown, where the pressure of business and the value of land was pushing up buildings to a considerable height, there still remained a few of the smaller shops and the smaller dwellings. The streets, too, retained their original meandering courses, and the blocks of buildings were cut across by a tangle of little alleys whose origins had been, perhaps, trails of cattle driven out to pasture from the first little village.

In the most tangled heart of the town stood a small shop. It did not open on a main street, and, in fact, one would have thought that it could not have been more poorly placed for business of any kind, least of all for the business of a pawnshop, with the display of cheap jewelry, second-hand watches, golden or silver spurs, even fine saddles and bridles inlaid with metal or pearl, to say nothing of costly guns, mounted to grace the hand of a royal prince.

Yet the three golden balls above that show window could only catch the eye of a person who succeeded in finding the most obscure alley in Sankeytown, the narrowest alley, the darkest alley. There was no sidewalk. There was no pavement. In summer the alley was thick with dust, and in winter it was well nigh impassable with mud. Still the shop persisted year after year, like a plant that is able to defy soil and climate in the desert, or among the mountain rocks.

Sometimes, the curious said, not a person was seen to enter the shop from the alley for day after day. And if anyone entered to investigate, the shopkeeper was found to be a little withered man, hunched in a coat vastly too big for him, and frayed to rags at the wrists. He had a pair of pathetic, feeble eyes that turned up with the innocence of a child when he spoke, and women, at least, rarely had the heart to bargain with him when he named a price.

There was, however, another entrance to this little shop of the pawnbroker, and this was concealed behind two or three sheds that the owner of the shop used for the storage of junk of various sorts, chiefly agricultural tools like mowing machines and plows and rakes, an inextricable tangle of iron in all stages of rust.

Through this blind entrance to the shop came Geraldi. There was a blind door on the side of the wall, but that door he found, and through the slit he picked the lock and turned it. Coming up the dark passage within — lighting it with a few pin rays from his electric torch — he reached a second door, massive, of wood without, but of ponderous sheet steel within. This, also, had a lock, and, having a lock, it was vulnerable to Geraldi.

It opened in turn, and Geraldi with his cat-like step went on through the shop, swerving past tables loaded with all manner of household gimcracks, from pottery to tin statues. In this manner he reached a little office in a corner of the shop, with the wall mostly of glass, and that glass curtained. Inside glowed a light.

Upon the door to this small place, Geraldi worked with infinite patience. There were small sounds within, from time to time — the clearing of a throat, a sigh, a yawn, and then the stirring of papers, the creak of a chair. With each of these noises, Geraldi moved his bit of flat steel inside the lock. At length, the lock gave noiselessly, but still he waited. It was not until a chair scraped that he pushed the door quietly open and stood in the entrance.

It was a little square chamber hardly seven or eight feet in width, and not an inch higher than Geraldi's head. The walls were hung about with old watches, beads, and other gear. In the corner farthest from the door there was a little desk, and at this sat the proprietor of the shop on a high stool, bunched over, his feet wrapped around the legs of the stool in absurd likeness to the position of a child at his studies.

At that moment, the little man was engaged in lifting from a ring the diamond that made it valuable. Now he took it in the palm of his hand and rolled it gently about, to enjoy the play of lights on the facets and fires inside. In the middle of that amiable play, the pawnbroker stopped short and his claw-like fingers froze over the jewel. By degrees and in little jerks, he turned his head, until at last his eyes looked up, dim and wide and frightened, like the eyes of a child, into the face of Geraldi.

The latter smiled pleasantly down — that flashing smile which seemed sometimes filled with joy, and at other times had the brightness of a sword.

The pawnbroker seemed to feel the sharpness of the edge, at that moment. For he shrank suddenly on his stool and began to shudder violently.

"How . . . how . . . ?" he began.

"I simply dropped in," said Geraldi. "I hope you don't mind."

"But," said the little man, "didn't the front door bell ring when you came in? And . . . did I leave this door open?"

"The front door I didn't bother," said Geraldi. "And as for this door, it's never closed against me by such an old friend as that lock."

The little man gaped. "Ah," he said at last, and clasped his bloodless hands together. He peered at Geraldi in greater fear than ever, at the same time nodding his head continually as though great and greater understanding constantly was entering his head.

"You understand?" murmured Geraldi.

"I understand," said the pawnbroker.

"In fact," said Geraldi, "it wouldn't do for me to appear . . . even in back alleys. So I came by the quieter way."

The pawnbroker moistened his lips. "You're Geraldi," he said.

"You know me, then?"

"I know everyone," said the pawnbroker. "Have you something for me?"

"Nothing except a little money," said Geraldi.

"And what do you want?"

"Only to buy."

"Good," said the little man without enthusiasm. "What do you wish to buy?"

"I wish," said Geraldi, "to buy the face of a young man with long yellow hair, and a short yellow mustache. Also, I want other clothes. The clothes of a cowpuncher . . . the young son of a rich rancher, suppose we say."

"Who sent you to me?" asked the pawnbroker, his voice sharp.

"I found my way, as you observe," said Geraldi.

"You can find your way out again," snapped the little man on the stool. "You'll buy nothing from me."

"Do I have to help myself?" sighed Geraldi.

"Not unless you're a fool. It's easy to come in, eh? But you'll find it harder to get out, James Geraldi. Every door is watched now with guns!"

Chapter Twenty-Three

WHITE ROOSTERS AND BLACK

There was not exactly triumph in the voice of the pawnbroker, so much as calm content, and he smiled with a childish placidity at the other.

"You've rung a bell?" suggested Geraldi.

"A light," answered the other. "Very sharp ears may be able to hear a bell, you know . . . ears that oughtn't to. But a light's safe."

"But it seems to me," said Geraldi, "that you're making a great fuss about a small thing."

"It ain't small at all," answered the little man.

"Tell me why it isn't, then."

"Suppose that I help to turn you loose, what would Chalmers say to me?"

The younger man smiled a little. "Of course, there's Chalmers to think about," he admitted. Uninvited, he sat down in a chair near the door and lighted a cigarette.

"You have good nerves," said the broker. "I have good nerves, too. But not quite like yours. Not quite." He shook his head at Geraldi, admiring and wondering at him, and even rubbing his hands together, as though the sight of this wealth of courage and youthful vitality enraptured him, as much as a miser looking at heaped gold. "But," he continued, "no matter how long you think, no matter how long you sit there, you'll never be able to come at more than one way of getting out of this place."

"And what way is that?" asked Geraldi.

"Think as if you were in my place . . . the owner of the trap, you see. What would you do?"

"I can't think myself into your place," said Geraldi a little dryly. "Suppose you tell me what terms you'll make."

"Let me see," said the other, bringing the fingers of both hands to a point together. "Let me see . . . let me see. Of course, I know what they want."

"My scalp?"

"Oh, yes!" He said it so cheerfully, looking up with such a bright acquiescence, that a slight chill ran through the iron nerves of the youth. He began to feel as though he were locked in with an inhuman madman.

"They want your scalp . . . perhaps they'll have it," went on the pawnbroker. "But, you see, there's a difficulty."

"Is there?"

"The fact that you're locked in the shop . . . with *me!*"

"I thought of that some time ago," replied Geraldi, breathing smoke toward the ceiling. He added instantly: "Don't do it . . . don't try it, my friend. Don't even make such a motion again, or I'll have to put a hole in that wise old head of yours, and then trust to my luck to get out of this place."

All that the other had done was to lean a little forward in his chair. The chief alteration had been in his expression, but even that change had been slight enough. Now, however, he leaned back once more and shook his head in honest enthusiasm.

"Ah, what eyes you have," he said. "What an equipment. What a perfect outfitting for your work. A foot softer than the wing of an owl . . . a hand faster than the striking head of a snake and more subtle than the paw of a cat. And strength, too . . . perfect strength! Ah, not the strength of Hercules . . . vast, bulky, brutal. Rather the strength of Hermes, or Phoebus. A great charge of electric energy ready to be flashed into instant use by nerves that are fine copper wires, or else used in little fits and starts. What a beautiful picture you make, my boy . . . what a beautiful thought!" He spoke this softly and rapidly, as though communing with his own judgment at the same time.

"Thank you," said Geraldi. "That's the most thorough-going compliment I've ever received. Thank you. I know that you're a judge."

He smiled a little, and the other shook his head once more.

"Who would think," he said, "that this glorious young tiger cat, this floating hawk of the upper air, should flutter, at last, into the net of poor old Sam Lorenz. Now, who would think of that?"

"And yes," observed Geraldi, "here we seem to be together in the net, as you remarked."

"For the moment, yes. But I can come to terms with you."

"Tell me what they are."

"I'd like to know what you'd expect."

"You'd better put up the price first. Then I'll try to meet it."

"Just as you please. Very well, then. I'll agree that you'll be safe in the hands of Chalmers and the others . . . who want your death. Instead, you'll only have to go to jail to answer the charge for picking a pocket. And that's not a very long term up the river, as you'll agree."

"I go safe from here . . . but into jail?"

"Exactly. I make the great concession, as you see, although there are men who would pay a great price for your head, James Geraldi. Have you any other offer to suggest?"

"There's only one way I could do business and come to an agreement with you," answered Geraldi.

"Then tell me what it is."

"In the first place, you'll give me what I want . . . the perfect disguise, such as you keep in those drawers, yonder."

The pawnbroker started and stretched out his hand — then snatched it back in haste. For an instant, sheer panic had leaped into his eyes. Now he settled back, frowning.

"After that, you'll give me the clothes that I ask for. You'll have a fast horse brought to the rear entrance. Then you'll walk out with me . . . first sending word to your helpers that I am to go safe, but accompanying me to make sure. And you will stay with me until I'm safely out of the whole town."

The pawnbroker pursed his lips, but his whistle made no sound. "Nothing less than that?"

"Nothing less," said Geraldi.

"Then you must prepare to stay here with me until you change your mind."

"Perhaps."

"There is no food," said the pawnbroker.

"None whatever?"

"Not a scrap."

"Ah, but I think that I could find some."

"If you can eat brass and silver . . . yes."

"Something better than that."

"Yes?"

"What do you say to chicken?"

"You may jest, young man. Sometimes laughter makes us fat, I hear."

"Not only a chicken . . . a rooster, let us say."

"Yes, that would be much better," chuckled the pawnbroker.

"A fine rooster . . . what color shall we say?"

"A young color, I hope," smiled the pawnbroker.

"White, then. Let us have a white rooster, Sam Lorenz."

The pawnbroker no longer smiled, but jerked a little on his stool, and then frowned instantly at his younger companion, as though there had been a double meaning in the last words, and a meaning of the greatest importance.

"A white rooster," said Geraldi. "They generally have the most tender flesh, eh? But let it have black legs, by all means."

The pawnbroker openly gaped.

"You see that I'm particular," smiled Geraldi. "A white rooster with black legs is what I want, and a coral red comb, checked with black. . . ."

The pawnbroker, as though he could endure no more, leaped up from his stool. He was trembling. "Who taught you that?" he asked.

"One picks up thoughts . . . about proper cookery . . . here and there, in drifting about the world."

"Let me have a sign," demanded the pawnbroker hoarsely.

"But do you agree to the rooster?"

"Yes, yes!" He actually stamped in his impatience.

"Well, then, we could shake hands on the idea."

The pawnbroker met the hand of Geraldi diffidently, almost as though he expected it to burn like fire.

Hardly had the palms touched, when he snatched his hand away, exclaiming: "You are one of them! You are one of them!"

Geraldi took out another cigarette. "You see for yourself," he observed.

"I am a fool! I am a fool and the father and grandfather of fools," groaned the proprietor of the shop. "I should have known. At least, I should have guessed."

"I really think that you might. Now, then, send the rest of your fellows about their business."

"Unless they could be of use to you?" asked the other anxiously. "I have some very clever men."

"Of course, you have," answered Geraldi, "but not clever enough to suit me, in this affair."

The pawnbroker drew in a great breath, closing his eyes tightly, as if in relief. "And I almost went too far to draw back," he whispered to himself.

"However, you didn't," answered Geraldi. "And now do me a great favor and hurry on with everything that I want. Particularly the horse. You keep some good ones at hand, I believe?"

"I can give you a horse for the desert or a horse for the mountains."

"Give me a horse for both," said Geraldi.

"That is hard to do," said the pawnbroker, somewhat downhearted.

"You have a gray, with black points all around. That will be the horse for me."

Lorenz sighed. "If you know about her, you know about everything," he said. "I'll have her saddled at once."

Chapter Twenty-Four

ANNE

For an hour they worked together. The little corner room of the pawnbroker's shop was littered with wigs, with scraps of hair, with bottles of dye.

At length Geraldi stood before the mirror and viewed himself with care from one side and then from the other. Pale gold was his hair, and swept far down toward his shoulders after a fashion which the Indians had set in the old days and which still was held to now and again, although already it was distinctly past the fashion of the day. A pale, short mustache decorated his upper lip; his eyebrows had been dyed to the same color.

He seemed satisfied with this appearance, and settled on his head, with a sweeping flourish, a sombrero of the high-peaked Mexican fashion, heavily banded with metal work of gold and silver. He wore a Mexican jacket, too, glistening with rich braid, and down his trousers silver *conchas* were sewn in a brilliant row. His gun belt was of white goat's hide, and the holsters of the same leather, with the pearl handles of a pair of expensive revolvers thrusting forth, waiting to catch the sun. Long, spoon-handled spurs on the heels of his handsome boots touched off his costume with the last flourish.

"Will it do?" he said.

The old man regarded him with the half-squinted eyes of a connoisseur. "It's just a little too pretty, to be true," he said. "Wait a moment."

He busied himself for a moment among his bottles, and then made Geraldi take the chair again. For another half hour, painstakingly, he worked, and, when he had finished, Geraldi stood up and looked at a face that was not his own.

A thin seam of a scar traveled from his forehead across his left eye. The lid itself was touched and puckered ever so slightly, and then the scar proceeded down the cheek, broadening and deepening and drawing the flesh more and more until at length it tapered off suddenly toward the chin. It was not so much a deformity as it was a touch of sinister interest to the handsome face of Geraldi.

"Now, smile," said the old man.

Geraldi obeyed, and the cheek muscles

pulled at the newly made scar.

"That's better," decided Lorenz. "You have a smile of your own. And this new grin is just lopsided enough to make a difference. I don't think many will know you unless you talk a great deal."

"I'm a Mexican," answered Geraldi in perfect Spanish. "I haven't the English language except a few words, here and there."

"That should make it perfect," said the pawnbroker. "It ain't the tone of a man's voice that's recognized so often. It's his manner of using his words. It's his phrases and what he says that counts. You are finished, Geraldi. Unless they pass you under a microscope."

"The horse, then?"

Old Sam went grudgingly to the rear of the shop, his companion following, and so they dipped through a side door — although no opening had been visible in the solid wall — and down a passage that opened suddenly into the rear of a barn, sweet with the smell of hay. On the farther side of a high partition were many horses, for Geraldi recognized the location as that of the biggest livery stable in the town. On this side, however, there were only six stalls, and in the middle he saw the horse of his choice.

The old man dropped her headstall and

led her out by the mane. She was richly dappled, the spots seeming to run together at the knees and hocks, for from those points down her legs were polished black. The hoofs, too, were sheer ebony. Her muzzle was black, also, and with it she nuzzled at Lorenz's shoulder. The old man regarded her with a dim eye.

"I know you, Geraldi," he said. "You'll ride like the devil on wings, eh? Burn up a horse a day?"

Geraldi worked the tips of his fingers deeply into her shoulder muscles. They were like strong strips of rubber, stretching and springing back again. And she, feeling the pain, did not wince from it or even toss her head. But, with pricking ears, she turned and regarded him with a steadfast eye. Geraldi passed his hand along the flanks and loins. They were firm as the muscular forearm of a man. So closely was she ribbed-up that he could not lay his hand in the hollow of her flank.

"Stand back and take a look at her," said the old fellow impatiently. "I dunno know how people expect to see a horse when they get right up against it."

Geraldi obeyed meekly. "A saddle will cover that back," he said appreciatively.

"From her withers to her hips," answered

Lorenz. "But look at the ground she stands over."

"She's a little short in front, I take it," suggested Geraldi.

"Short, hell!" snapped the pawnbroker. "That's the heart in her. D'you want more legs than heart?"

"Nevertheless," said Geraldi, "she can't stretch out for much."

"She flattens her belly to the ground, when she runs," declared Lorenz. "She ain't a sprinter. Five miles and up are her distances. If they were any shorter, I'd have her East, on the tracks, and she'd make some of the Thoroughbreds curl up and die. She'd have their heads bobbing like corks."

"You know horses," admitted Geraldi.

"Well, tell me. Did you ever see one like her?"

"I saw a Nejd mare, once," said Geraldi. "She was made as much like this one as two watches out of the hand of the same artist."

"Nejd?"

"Arabia."

"Aye," said the other with enthusiasm. "And that's what she is. Pure Arab. There's not a dash of anything else in her."

"Ah? Where was she foaled?"

"In Arabia, my boy."

"The devil she was! And how did they get

213

her out of the country?"

"That's a story. There was a damn' sheik, or some such creature, that trailed her clear across to this side of the water."

"And then?"

"His trail ended there." Lorenz slipped a forefinger across his throat, and a glint came in his eyes. "Men have died for her, Geraldi," he said, and looked plaintively at the youth.

"I'll bring her back to you," said Geraldi, "as safe and sound as she stands at this moment."

Lorenz shook his head. "You don't know her," he said. "She's as free as the wind to the last stride she can make. She'll carry you like a feather with her tail in the air, until she drops dead."

Geraldi nodded, and Lorenz proceeded disconsolately with the saddling. Two blankets of softest, purest wool he placed on her back. Then he took from the wall a saddle of extraordinary lightness because, as he pointed out, the entire frame of it had been built up of the finest steel, powerful but full of spring. It was not intended to withstand the shocks of roping on the range, but it gave a wonderful comfort, and over this was stretched thin leather of the best quality. So that, completed, the thing had the perfect look of a range saddle, with all its security and a third of its weight. Its supple steel, furthermore, enabled it to give a vital bite to the movement of the horse and the weight of the rider.

Lorenz pointed out the holes in the cinch leathers that should be used — one for the start — another for midday — another for the evening.

"Let her breathe . . . she'll do the rest," he said.

Finally, she opened her mouth for a straight bit of rubber, and over her ears was fitted the lightest of bridles.

"Never touch her with the spurs," said Lorenz. "Speak to her."

"By what name?"

"Anne," said the pawnbroker. "What her original name was, I don't know. But she's learned a new one. You can teach her as you'd teach a child."

"You've kept her too fine," suggested Geraldi. "What will she do on desert fare?"

"She'll grow fat on thistles," said the pawnbroker with enthusiasm. "And yet you could stand her at an open bin of oats and she'd never eat too much. She has sense, Geraldi. She has a brain between those ears. Eh, darlin'?"

The mare turned her beautiful head to

him with speech in her eyes, and Geraldi, at last, was satisfied.

"I'll bring her back, he reiterated, "just as she is now, but with a little exercise to fine her down."

"Will you give me your hand on that, Geraldi?"

"There it is."

They shook hands, Lorenz with a lingering grip.

"Man, man," he said, "if you've lied to me, may you burn a thousand extra years in hell's hottest fire."

"Lorenz," answered Geraldi, smiling, "I might break my word to a man . . . under certain conditions . . . but never about a horse, Lorenz. Never about a horse, in a thousand years."

Lorenz grunted, still uncertain.

"But tell me," asked Geraldi, as they left the stable, the pawnbroker still leading the mare, "tell me, what use is this mare to you?"

"To me?" snapped the little man, "why, she's my anchor to windward. And if the worst comes for me, I'll have Anne to snatch me away from them. Half an hour to the mountains . . . and after that, they can break their hearts, but they'll never have me."

Geraldi did not see fit to ask who "they"

might be, but followed on into a narrow alley where there would hardly be room for a rider to move.

"Here's your way," said the broker sullenly. "Take her straight on. The alley widens in a little way. Then you'll cross a big street. But no one is apt to be near you. If you should be recognized, put her at the tall fence straight across the street. It's five feet high. But she'll clear it like a bird. She'll jump anything she can reach with her nose. So long, Geraldi. I hope to God that you have luck!"

Chapter Twenty-Five

A NARROW ESCAPE

The alley wound slowly in and out, but then emerged, as the pawnbroker had declared, upon a broad street where the sudden full light of the day half blinded the rider.

No doubt what Lorenz had said would have been true enough had he, in fact, been filling the saddle. But he was not such a figure as this flashing gallant in gold and silver work, with lofty hat and gaudy Mexican jacket. There was a sudden yell from a group of half a dozen horsemen who, at that moment, had turned the next corner of the street, and with a whoop they rushed upon Geraldi.

He swung the mare toward the tall fence across the road, but then he remembered the goodness of his disguise. If it were worth anything at all, this was the moment to test it thoroughly with these rough and careless cowpunchers.

They came by like a volley, yelling, and waving their hats to excite the horse. But

Anne, the mare, stood like a stone, flicking her ears back once and then jutting them forward again, in disdain of such men, such crude voices. To no such human voices as these had she been accustomed, from the day of her foaling.

Geraldi, praying the rout would let him be, turned her head down the street. Even from that point he could see the brown fields beyond the edge of the town.

The cowpunchers might well have abandoned this victim after the first failure, but they were newly in from a distant range, their spirits were high, the devil was in them. They came back, the hoofs of their spurred horses volleying through the dust, and one, as they passed, screeching, stooped from the saddle, picked up a handful of dust, and tossed it into the face of Geraldi.

The patience of Geraldi almost snapped. There was not the strength of a spider thread in resistance left to him, but he managed to control his temper by a fierce effort, and calmly wiped the dust from his face with a handkerchief.

The rushing riders were reining up in the distance, hooting, laughing. Another loudly laughing voice approached from the rear. There was something familiar about it, and Geraldi, watching from the corner of his eye, saw none other than big Chalmers cantering down the street to join in the fun. It was like his brutal nature to take advantage of every opportunity to play the bully. He introduced, as was also his nature, a heavier touch. For, sweeping by the gay figure of Geraldi, he struck the latter violently on the back with the flat of his hand. The impact jerked back the head of Geraldi, and his sombrero sailed to the street.

He reined the mare to the side and picked it up deftly. His teeth were hard-set, now, and his fingers were itching for action.

"He ain't a man, he's a picture," declared Chalmers, swinging back to confront Geraldi, and drawing his horse squarely across the street. "Let's ask him where he comes from, boys. We never had anything so pretty as this in Sankeytown, before."

And, in another instant, the 'punchers were pooled about their victim. They had made enough noise, now, to draw further attention. Women, children, idling men appeared. Windows slammed up; doors crashed open. Laughter began to sweep up and down the street.

There were shouted bits of advice to take him to the watering trough in front of the hotel and dip him — to see if the colors would run. Geraldi began to see that he had blundered into a great peril.

"It ain't a half bad idea," said Chalmers. "Kid, where d'you blow in from?"

"*Señor*," answered Geraldi gently, "I have not the English."

"He ain't got the English, Chalmers."

"We might get some for him," grinned Chalmers. "Who speaks Spanish? Look! He's a blond beauty, ain't he? I never knew greasers to turn that color."

"You've scared him pale," answered one of the 'punchers.

Another added: "Sure. That's Castile. That blond hair."

"Castile what?"

"Soap!" shouted a third.

And they yelled again.

They meant no harm, but Geraldi looked a fair victim, and it would be hard if they did not find more pranks to practice on him.

"You come along, kid," said Chalmers, laying his hand on the arm of Geraldi. "We wanna know all about you. Name of your pa and ma and everything. Come along to my hotel. Understand? *Vamoose*, greaser!"

The tightly compressed mouth of Geraldi twitched with fury.

"He's getting mad," said one of the cowpunchers. "Look out, Chalmers!"

"Me? The yalla rat," said Chalmers. "I eat

greasers, boy. I breakfast and lunch on 'em . . . they ain't enough to 'em to make a man-sized dinner! You! *Vamoose!* You can understand that, you white-faced young fool! Get! *Vamoose!*"

He waved Geraldi to the right about, and, to emphasize his scorn and his contempt of any danger from this stripling, flicked him across the face with the back of his hand.

The limit of Geraldi's endurance already had been more than reached. Only by a wild effort had he been able to control himself to this point. Now, as though a string were cut and a strong spring released, his left arm shot forward, and Chalmers pitched heavily backwards in the saddle.

From the hand of a nearby 'puncher, Geraldi plucked the loaded quirt, and before Chalmers, bellowing with fury, could scramble erect in the saddle, a slash of the whip sent his horse lurching forward, squatting with the effort to get into full stride. That sudden start finished the discomfiture of the hotel proprietor. He toppled, clutched wildly for mane or pommel, and then tipped into the street, where he rolled over and over, catching at the ground and throwing up a huge cloud of dust.

"Hey, what the hell!" shouted the 'puncher from whom the quirt had been taken. "You . . . you damn' greaser!" And he reached for the gun.

It should have contented Geraldi. Already he had done enough to relieve his fury, but it chanced, by ill luck, that this was the very 'puncher who had flung the dust in his face, a moment before. Therefore, the quirt whirled again, swift as a sword, and slashed the man straight across the mouth, cutting the skin and well into the flesh — a mark that never would out.

The blinding pain brought a yell from the 'puncher. He caught at his face with both hands, and a roar of fury came from his companions.

Geraldi, cursing himself for his impatience, thought of flight.

"Zuleikha!" he yelled.

And at that forgotten name the mare bounded beneath him. Perhaps that sound, half dimmed by time, brought rushing back upon her mind the pictures of the desert, the tang of sand in the air, the voices of the men, softened for her ears as for the ears of a woman beloved, the sweet smell of dates, the odor of freshly roasting coffee, the heavy scent of the camels, kneeling in the dust. So she leaped under Geraldi as though a spur had been driven deeply into her flesh.

He swung her head toward the high board

223

fence at the side of the road, seeing as he did so the form of Chalmers rushing through the dust cloud of his own raising, with the gleam of a gun in either hand — Chalmers shouting and raging, half mad with shame and scorn and rage and most certainly bent on murder to revenge himself for that fall. He saw the cowpunchers, too, swarming at him, but they had not counted on the desert mare. Like a cat she bounded to full speed, swerved past the nose of one cow pony and past the tail of another.

"Zuleikha!" cried Geraldi again. *"Doos yá lellee! Doos yá lellee!"*

And the familiar words made her bound beneath him again, sweeping instantly into full speed. She was at the fence with never a falter. There was no need to prime her for that work, or settle her at the jump, or take a tight hold on her head. She flew at the fence as though it were an old familiar barrier and rose to it like a bird.

Geraldi, rising to the height of the vault, saw the tumbled surface of an empty lot before him, littered with tin cans, fallen wires, and rusting junk of all kinds. Then guns crashed behind him. He felt a sharp tug beneath his right armpit; the revolver bullet had cut through cleanly, and without touching the skin.

Now he was within, the tall fence sheltering him as he dipped low along the mare. She landed as though wings were breaking the shock, and now, with gathering speed, she swerved across the entangled surface of the ground, picking every footfall with an unerring cunning.

In the rear, big Chalmers was gibbering with fury — gibbering in a scream, the words blended, as he rushed at the fence and flung himself over it.

But already Zuleikha was across the open lot. The rear fence she topped like the other and dropped lightly into a narrow lane beyond it. There would be no pursuit, Geraldi felt sure. Those cowpunchers had seen what the mare could do, and they would not burn out their own ponies for nothing. So he kept her down to a gentle canter, and that pace she maintained with her head turned a little, as though her great, bright eye were considering him, wondering over him, who had spoken her own speech in this far land.

He leaned and stroked her neck, and she lengthened her stride a little. He spoke, and she slowed until her gallop was like the soft rocking of a chair. The reins of her bridle were unneeded; the voice alone could control her perfectly. For she was no common animal. She had been trained as a battle

225

charger in the far-away land, to rush into the charge and leave her master free of both hands, to do as he chose.

Geraldi, with eyes that gleamed with pleasure, turned her out from the final edge of the town. The long brown swells of the hills at once received them.

Chapter Twenty-Six

TO THE CAPITAL

Cousin Edgar loved music. When he found a little time to spare from his duties at the desk — for he maintained a copious and minute correspondence — he always sat down at the piano in the front room of the Asprey house. Sometimes he played from memory. Sometimes he took the new compositions and read them off with a truly wonderful facility. But most of the time he would sit down and improvise.

Mrs. Asprey best enjoyed seeing him at such times, when his head was raised so high that it inclined back a little, fulfilling the noble line of the throat, as though song were about to rise. In those moments the mobile features of Cousin Edgar became extraordinarily expressive. Sometimes a beatific smile touched his lips; sometimes his brow was darkened with pain, his lips parted. Mrs. Asprey always sat close beside the piano where she could watch him, and often she was so enraptured that she dropped a stitch of her knitting.

On this evening Cousin Edgar was at the piano, when a note was brought in to him.

"A man I must see, dear Olivetta," he said. "Will you permit me to see him alone in this room? Or shall I take him to the library . . . and disturb Louise?"

Mrs. Asprey left the room, and shrank in the hallway as she passed the grim face of Renney. Then the latter entered, hesitating in the doorway. Cousin Edgar stood by the piano — which was an upright — resting the flat of his hand on top of it. He smiled at Renney, and his smile was not a pleasant thing to see.

"He's been here, has he?" asked Renney, interpreting in the broadest sense.

"He's been here," answered the big man, and tapped the piano with his soft hand, waiting.

"No horse can win every start," answered Renney, without particular sullenness. "I thought I had this race in my pocket. I slacked up . . . and Geraldi passed me at the wire. That's all."

"He overtook you, eh?"

"He did that."

"Where?"

"At Asprey's house."

Cousin Edgar's face turned dark, indeed.

228

However, he mastered the fury that swelled in his throat. He began to walk up and down in his silent stride.

Renney stood braced for the shock, feet well apart, head jutting forward. He had a strong dash of bulldog in him, and he would not flinch. He simply stated: "Well, I came back to report. I suppose that's about all?"

Cousin Edgar could not answer for a moment. He sat down at the piano and rumbled a few chords, thinking, head bowed. Then he turned on the stool. "Come here!"

Renney approached.

"What happened?"

"I had Asprey spread out with a gun at his head. The kid was a dead man down the railway line, I thought. Well, he wasn't dead. He come to the doorway behind me and shot the gun out of my hand." He extended his right hand, removing a handkerchief in which it was swathed. Between the thumb and the forefinger the flesh was torn, and there was a bruise that showed red and purple on the back of the hand.

"You can't handle a gun, now," remarked Edgar Asprey.

"Me?" grinned Renney. "That's killed one man before this, partner. My left is as good as my right." He proved his point by flicking a gun from somewhere into his left hand and instantly dropping it out of sight again. "Took time and practice to do that," he observed.

Cousin Edgar watched, and made good note. "Renney," he said, "confess that you made a fool of yourself by underestimating this man, Geraldi."

"Underestimate your hat," replied the other. "I knew he was hot stuff. Not so hot as all that, but hot enough. Well, he simply slipped past me. I worked on him like I never worked on any man. I thought I had shot him off the top of a train. I seen him roll and fall off. God knows what more than that a gent can do. Before that, I'd landed him in a jail. But jails ain't made to hold him. It would take all hell to do that, it seems."

Cousin Edgar listened, and weighed, and was reassured. "Renney," he said, "there are some men who never excuse failure. I'm not one of them. As a matter of fact, I think that I can trust you further from this moment than I could before."

"Governor," said Renney slowly, "I dunno how to put it in words. But if I could get Geraldi, I'd take my share of what's coming in the next second." There was a calm fervor in this speech that was utterly convincing.

Edgar Asprey nodded. "You want that

trail, then?" he asked.

"I want nothin' but that."

"Then I can tell you how to cross it. The two of them undoubtedly are heading for the governor."

"They are? Then I'll nail them there."

"If you ride night and day. A horse is faster than a train to get you to the capital from here. I'll give you the horse . . . and a letter."

"I'll start now," urged Renney.

"Wait. Suppose that you meet Geraldi, Renney. What could you do with him?"

"Kill him, chief, as sure as God made little apples!"

"Are you that sure?"

Renney paused. After all, there was no reason why he should show over-confidence. "No," he admitted finally. "I don't know. I'm willing to take my chances with him. That's all. How it would turn out, I couldn't guess. I think I have an even break."

"I like to hear you talk like that," replied Asprey. "Boasting is a fool's game. Then, if you're not surer than that, we need a second man."

"Sure," agreed Renney. "Two would be better."

"Do you know gunfighters who can be hired?"

"I know plenty," replied Renney. "But not

boys that could figure in a game like this."

"Why not, man? Why not? Is Geraldi made of iron? Isn't he vulnerable to leaden bullets?"

"Maybe he is. I dunno. But I tell you this . . . any big ham that you throw into the ring ain't gonna connect with him. The easiest thing in the world is to fight a crowd."

"Very well, then. What do you suggest?"

"I'll think it over. What can I pay?"

"What do you think is needed?"

"For a thousand I could turn the trick with any man I know, if we went in on my side."

"You can have that much."

"There's nothing but the horse between me and a start, governor."

"There's something else to wait for. That's a message I have to give you."

"I'm waiting."

"You've been in the capital?"

"Sure. I lived there for two years."

"You know the politicians?"

"All of 'em."

"You were Bill Sandy Johnson's man, for a while?"

"I was."

"Now, Renney, this is a thing that would make or break me. Do you hear? It's a message that I can't put into the mail. It's word that has to go by messenger."

"You've got your bet on me, chief," replied Renney. "Carry on with it."

"In the capital, who's the biggest of the crew?"

"The governor," answered Renney.

"He is. Is there any one behind the governor?"

"Aye. There's a pal of his."

"Name him."

"Smiling Joe Green."

"You know the Smiler?"

"Like a book. I got a page turned down in him, now."

"Then go to Smiling Joe Green and tell him that you've come from me."

"Will that mean anything?"

"So much," said Asprey calmly, "that you won't have to pay cash. My promise will be enough."

"That sounds real."

"You can tell Joe Green that Robert Asprey is on the way to see the governor to get a pardon for the killing of Frank Lopaz, five years ago. You know that killing?"

"All about it."

"Tell Green that, if he can block that pardon, he'll have a fat check out of me. Do you know him well enough to know his price?"

"It's high."

"Of course, it is, for this sort of thing. Now, Renney, I'll put my figure in your hands. I can pay fifty thousand spot cash the moment I know that the governor has refused to review the case of Robert Asprey. Make your own bargain with Green. If you can get him for less, you have the extra change."

Renney blinked and swallowed. "I hear you," he said. "What security have I got, governor?"

"Security, man? Security?" cried Asprey softly. "Man, you already know enough to wreck me with a word."

Renney nodded.

"Go straight to the capital and see Green. My cousin may have reached the town before you, but, if you ride hard, you'll be there before anything definite is done. Work on Green."

"Can Green handle the governor? Is the governor a crook, too?"

"The governor is as straight as a broom handle. A fool who won't line his own nest. But Green went to school with him. He believes in Green as though Smiling Joe were his brother. Is that clear?"

"Clear as day," grinned Renney.

"Go down to the place of Sam Lorenz. I'll meet you there, and we'll arrange about a horse."

Chapter Twenty-Seven

PLAYING THE GAME

Many a fine horse had Geraldi bestrode in his wild ways around the world, but never another like Zuleikha. She held through the hills as steadily as the wind, seeming to watch her rider as much as she watched the way, and Geraldi let her go on at high speed. He had in mind the warning that the little pawnbroker had given him concerning her willingness, but he was himself no mean judge of the powers of a horse to continue. Moreover, he needed speed. Robert Asprey had headed straight on from the mountains for the capital of the state, and although his way was rougher than that of Geraldi, it was the shorter of the two, and he was most likely to arrive at the town first.

In that case, he had appointed a rendezvous, but he was not to wait there for any extended period, but to press on and strive to make contact with the governor. Ten minutes' conversation with that strong and honest man might change everything and place the game in the hands of Robert Asprey no matter what Cousin Edgar attempted. But it was highly necessary that the meeting and its result should be kept secret. Otherwise, Edgar Asprey, frightened by the first report, might abscond with most of the fortune of his cousin in his pockets. For all of these reasons speed, secrecy, cleverness were needed, and although Geraldi was willing to trust a great deal to the downright force and courage of his ally, still he wished to be on the spot when the troubled waters were reached.

So he went on at a great rate and found that the miles were slipping away behind him with incredible ease and quickness. Twice, crossing small mountain courses, he stopped the mare and breathed her and rubbed her down. Then he went on.

The sun was turning gold in the west, as it sloped rapidly down the sky. They had climbed across two ridges, and the third rose tall above them, and dark with great trees. Up this they worked, abandoning the trail and taking the straightest cut — Zuleikha figuring out her footholds with human wisdom, and more. And in the dusk of the day they reached the crest. The sun was down, and the sky was rimmed with such bright colors that the mountains all around, against such a background, seemed to be pressing in toward the center at which Geraldi found himself.

A hundred yards farther and he left the forest and came upon a broad road. Along this he made good speed, for the slope was dipping down, and at last he came on a shoulder, with a crossroads hotel to the right and, to the left, a view of the city in the hollow beneath. It was spread out in a perfect pattern of lights. The yellow rays gleamed far across the still surface of the lake that bordered the town. There was the final goal, but here was the rendezvous. He was not familiar with the place, but Robert Asprey, knowing it by heart, had appointed this spot. A tall grove of spruce just ahead was the meeting ground. Whoever arrived first was to wait an hour, and, in case it were Geraldi, if he failed to find his companion, he was to linger on and keep coming to the grove at intervals of less than an hour. He rode on among the trees, therefore, and gave the appointed signal of three short whistles. When he had no response, he waited and tried again, but still he had no answer except for a startled squirrel that chattered loudly on a branch just above his head, and then was silent again.

So Geraldi turned back to the hotel. For

himself he did not care, but the mare was dripping, and he yearned to have her walked cool, and then fed and stalled in comfort. After such treatment as that, she would be as good as new.

It was a big, sprawling, comfort-breathing hotel. Here the politicians came from the heat of the little capital town beneath in the hollow and abandoned themselves to the chill mountain winds. They were abandoning themselves at that moment, in fact. Loud voices rolled out from the windows of a private dining room, as Geraldi rode into the yard behind the building.

The stable promised to be equally commodious. He took off the saddle, obtained a heavy blanket that he spread over Zuleikha, and then he began to walk her around and around, she following like a dog, pausing when he paused, starting on when he started, so that the leading rope never could become taut. She was not like a lumbering horse, rather she seemed to have a human intelligence in that lovely head of hers.

The air was sharp and dry, with a stir of wind — just cold enough to make it necessary to walk her fast, so that her armed hoofs rang a continual chant on the cobblestones of the courtyard. A stable boy offered to lead her. He was refused and returned to the group that gossiped about the stable door where a single lantern burned, dimly revealing the interior, out of which stampings of horses were heard and the rustle of hay as they nosed it in their mangers.

A newcomer came out from the hotel. He was filled with excitement. "There's hell loose!" he said.

"Where?" asked one of the stable group.

"Where? Where Smiling Joe is."

"Is Colonel Green up tonight?"

"Sure. Come half an hour ago."

"I didn't see his team."

"He come up with Mister Loftus."

"That crook?"

"Two crooks . . . that's a pair," said another of the stable boys, chuckling.

"And I'll raise that," announced the boy who was newly from the hotel. "They got another pair of crooks from the East along with them. And it's East against West!"

"Are they card-sharks, too, the Eastern gents?"

"Them? They look smoother than oil. They'd pick your pockets while you was saying good morning."

"What's happening?"

"There'll be plenty happening as soon as they can get started on a game."

"What keeps 'em back?"

"They want a fifth man to hold a hand."

"God help that gent that sits in."

"God? God couldn't do a thing with the four of them."

"They all got money?"

"You know Green and Loftus. Then I seen the two Easterners with their fingers twitching. They had to sit down and play a few rounds of seven-up. A hundred bucks every time they turned around. I'm gonna go back and watch the fun. The roof'll rise pretty soon."

Geraldi came to a pause. He surrendered Zuleikha to the stable boy and strolled idly out in front of the hotel. His heart was thoroughly committed to this affair of Robert Asprey and his daughter; there was nothing that he wanted so much as to fling forward in the work. Yet this mention of four rich men, all eager for a game, all spending money like water, was a sad temptation to Geraldi.

After all, he had walked the path of virtue for several days, and virtue for its own sake never had attracted him. However, with a deep sigh he went on past the front of the hotel and reached the spruce woods again. Once more he whistled. Once more the woods gave back to him mere emptiness, and Geraldi walked away. He did not want to approach the hotel. He wanted, above all, to keep away from it, but, as he walked up and down, with every traverse he found himself nearer and nearer to the big building, drawn toward it by a magnetic attraction.

He was drifting past an open window, then, when a loud voice boomed within: "Charlie, can't you and Smiling Joe go and beg or borrow or steal a man? We've waited long enough, and my tongue's hanging out."

It was too much for Geraldi. He hurried to the bar of the hotel, entered, and quickly found his way to the reading room, at one end of which, in a small compartment, he heard the booming voices of the expectant players. Geraldi found a newspaper, thumbed its pages carelessly, tilted back in his chair, and yawned. And as he tilted back, the wallet in his inside coat pocket was allowed to thrust forth a little, easily visible to any who cared to look for particulars.

And there were those who cared to look. He had not been seated for five minutes before a swelling man in clothes that could not accommodate his grossness of body, with a many-folded neck bulging over his white collar, stood before him.

"Young man," he said, "are you yawnin'

because you're homesick, or because you got nothin' to do?"

"Because," smiled Geraldi innocently, "I have to spend a night at the end of the world, here."

"Ah," said the fat man, "and what if you found out that it wasn't quite at the end of the world, my son?"

"Then," said Geraldi, "there's no falling off place, if this isn't around the corner from it."

"In there," said the other, "is three men and myself. All dyin' for lack of a fifth man to play poker with us. A four-handed game ain't good enough. Are you number five?"

"Well," said Geraldi, "I've played the game."

"Of course, you have. And what about to-night?"

"If no word of it gets back to my father," said Geraldi hopefully. "He says that I spend more on cards than would keep another ranch."

The fat man winked. "I'm Joe Green," he said. "If you've ever heard of me, you've heard that I know how to keep my mouth shut." And he fairly carried Geraldi into the next chamber.

Chapter Twenty-Eight

WHO WINS?

Geraldi lost two hundred dollars before he was well settled into his chair. The pace was fast and furious, and it was apparent that every pocket at that table was loaded with money. They were of two types. Joe Green and Daniel Loftus were as alike as twin brothers; Ned Oliver and Charles Lane, the Eastern representatives, likewise, were similar enough to have come from one family. They were like two pale cats with expressionless, agate eyes. They could not smile without forethought. They had gambled so much that every expression of the face and the voice must be preordered; otherwise, they were two masks.

But, once settled, Geraldi played without consciousness of time. He had stepped by accident into his very element. They were no mean foes. When Charles Lane passed the cards to him to be cut, he found a crimp near the top, missed that, found a second, and had to work very deep to ensure an honest deal. Even then it was not too honest. He had not been ten minutes at the table before he detected markings, delicately made with an accurate and sharp fingernail. He called for a new pack. Ten minutes later he detected tiny red smudges on the backs of the cards. They were delicately made and delicately placed by a master hand. Again he called for new cards.

He was reasonably sure that the Easterners were guilty of these shady tricks of the trade, while the other two Westerners contented themselves with manipulating the pack. They were excellent players of the crooked variety, all four, but Geraldi rejoiced in them. They were exactly of the type which he preferred to trim.

Before long, he began to win. Before the first hour was out, he had won something over a thousand dollars — he could not be sure exactly how much. In half that time, he then doubled his stakes. He could see that concern was growing on the faces of all four. They had meant to pick a child; they had found a Tartar; and, in the meantime, the Tartar was scalping them regularly.

Once or twice his conscience pricked him. He should have been out long before this to visit the grove again. But he told himself that big Robert Asprey already must have gone down to the town. The morning would be time enough for the next step in that game.

Money flowed in, and the tension grew. He had five thousand before him. He pocketed three of the five and made the remaining two grow again. The betting grew higher. Smiling Joe Green still smiled, but, instead of a pink spot, there was a streak of pallor in either cheek.

The door was closed. Only the waiter came in from time to time, bringing drinks. Geraldi clung to water. He wanted a clear head for this work. Then he noticed that there was a new waiter serving them. He had the face of a bulldog, and he was clumsy with the tray. That was enough for Geraldi. He put down the new waiter simply as a gunman in the employ of one of the four. He was sure of it, when Smiling Joe Green told the waiter to remain in the room. "Then we won't have to be getting up to punch the bell every five minutes."

The "waiter" sat down in a corner chair, and the corner he chose was behind Geraldi. The thing became patent. His winnings mounted from five toward ten thousand, but now it was apparent that the interest of the others was divided between him and some exterior source of excitement. They depended upon something else to win for them, and their eyes lifted repeatedly from the cards — to glance at the black windows, or at one another.

"It's twelve," said Joe Green suddenly, "and I've had enough."

The head of Geraldi was turned just enough for the corner of his eye to have a sense of what the waiter was doing. Now that bulldog worthy rose softly and quickly to his feet and stepped forward as Geraldi took his winnings from the table. Calmly he took them, expressing a gentle regret that the luck should have favored him so entirely. Then, as the others listened with tense faces and faint smiles in their eyes, he kicked the table over and whirled to his feet.

The crash of the table took down Lane and Loftus with it. Something was knocked from the hand of Joe Green and fell heavily upon the floor. Edward Oliver alone was not touched, but he was sufficiently bothered by what followed. The waiter had made his draw, but, not expecting what happened, the gun was barely clear of his pocket, when Geraldi jammed a Colt into his ribs and with another weapon covered Oliver and the rest.

"Sorry, gentlemen," said Geraldi, "but I always like to harvest what I sow! You might put your hands up . . . up with them quickly

". . . and you . . . drop your gun!"

The last was to the hired gunman who, with a still bewildered face, did as he was ordered. The rest obeyed, except Joe Green. He merely shoved his hands in his pockets and grinned.

"Versatile," he said. "Damn' versatile the kid is. Cowpuncher, crooked gambler . . . and gunman, too, it seems."

Loftus was pushing himself from the floor with a grunt. Every man was totally calm and self-possessed.

"Damned if I understand yet how he got the five of us cold in that shape!" he said.

There was no pretense, no sham. They chuckled frankly.

"I want those hands up," said Geraldi coldly to Joe Green.

The latter paid no attention, merely saying to the waiter: "You poor ham! When did you ever earn your money?"

"You signaled a fall guy to me," whined the gunman. "And here's a red-hot one, instead. I didn't know. I wasn't figgering on anything like him."

"You've figgered your last time with me," snapped Joe Green. "Get out of here!"

"Stand quiet," countermanded Geraldi. "You, Green . . . do you think that I'm joking?"

"Of course, I do," said Joe Green. "What d'you expect to make out of this new deal?"

"A getaway," answered Geraldi frankly. "Before you have half a dozen more waiters in here to hold me up."

Smiling, Joe chuckled again. "All among friends," he insisted. "Kick that fool's gun, will you?"

Geraldi touched it with his foot, curiously.

"Empty, ain't it?" asked Green.

"It is," admitted Geraldi, puzzled.

"Bluff, kid. We were all planning a little touch of old lady bluff. That's all. D'you feel better, now?"

Geraldi glanced hastily at the others.

There was no doubt that they agreed with Green.

"We ain't the Forty Thieves," went on Joe Green.

"No," said Geraldi, "only four of them."

Joe Green accepted the nomination with a perfectly open laugh. "Sit down, kid," he said. "Now that we know you, you're as safe with us as in the bosom of your family. Sit down and make yourself at home."

"You pulled a gun, also," suggested Geraldi.

"As empty as my father's barn," said the politician, kicking the weapon toward him.

Suddenly Geraldi put up his two Colts.

He was at least half convinced. But he warned them softly: "I hate trouble, my friends. I love peace. But I hope that none of you will make a mistake about me again."

"Impossible, kid," said Loftus.

Lane and Ned Oliver exchanged vast grins of acquiescence.

"I don't know what you want," asked Geraldi. "Do you want to continue the game?"

"Me? Not in a thousand years," declared the cheerful Joe Green. "I've burned all the skin off my fingers already."

"I'm through," said Charlie Lane with a twisted smile. "I'm going to give up cards and go to school again."

"But who are you?" asked Loftus.

"A friend to the poor," said Geraldi, smiling frankly.

There was a heavy knock at the door.

"Who's there," boomed Joe Green.

The door opened a little.

"Man to see you, Colonel Green."

"Damn the man to see me. I'm busy."

"He's in a great hurry, sir."

"Who's that?"

"Harry Goodman, Colonel."

"Does he look important, Harry?"

"Yes. Dead in earnest."

"Had I better see him?"

"I think so, sir."

"What name did he give you?"

"Name of Renney, sir."

Colonel Green turned up his eyes to the ceiling.

"Renney," said Loftus. "Don't go near him. That's a snake, and he's deadly poison, too. I know about Renney."

"So do I," said the Colonel. "And I know he's a bad dream. But . . . I think I'd better see him. Sit down, my friend," he added to Geraldi. "Take that corner chair where you can watch all of us, if you wish to. I want to talk to you some more." He left the room in haste.

Geraldi hesitated. Too much suspicion shown on his part might be the forerunner of much trouble for him. On the other hand, he saw that much might be gained from this circle. He had heard of Joe Green before and knew that he was considered, by many, as the most influential of the bosses. Through him, as a matter of fact, it might be possible to bring Robert Asprey in touch with the governor — a task that, otherwise, might baffle them both.

"It's all right, kid," Loftus was assuring him. "I'd pay money to know what you did to those cards."

Geraldi sat down.

Chapter Twenty-Nine

THE NEED FOR HASTE

Renney believed in coming straight to the point ordinarily, but, this evening, he was playing partly for a point and partly to put money in his pocket and partly to sharpen his wits against the defense of another. So, when Joe Green came into the room — a little semi-private sitting room of the hotel — he stood up and nodded in friendly fashion.

"How are you, governor," said Renney, and extended his hard claw.

The loose hand of the politician squashed over it.

"Not governor," he corrected a little sharply.

"Sure you ain't," grinned Renney. "What's the use of the name to you?"

Mr. Green stood on his guard. The first principle of his boss-ship was to remain in the background, to a certain extent. He must appear only to pull wires, not to be absolute. It increased the price of his favors.

"You want something," judged Green.

"So do you," remarked the grinning Renney.

Joe Green frowned. He was a familiar fellow, but there were limits beyond which he did not allow familiarity to proceed. Besides, he had recently been a good deal upset by the loss of thirty-five hundred dollars and the failure of a elaborate bluff to regain that sum.

"I'm a busy man," he remarked.

"Too busy to make money?" asked Renney confidently.

In fact, the rigidity of the politician diminished at once. "Money is a good cause . . . I'm a lawyer, you know," he admitted more genially.

"Sure you are," said Renney.

"Suppose we get to business, then. You're in trouble?"

"Me? Not a bit."

"A friend, then?"

"Aye, a friend."

"Shot someone, Renney?"

Renney looked up from under his brows and sighed. "How well do you know me?" he asked.

"Everybody knows you, Renney," said the fat man.

"They do," sighed Renney. "I gotta find a new range. There ain't any chance for me to work any surprises."

"Who did he shoot?"

"Put it like this," said Renney. "A gent wants to get a pardon. And he. . . ."

"Ah, that's a difficult business," broke in Joe Green, rolling his eyes. "I don't know that I want any part with that. These pardons . . . you gotta fix too many all along the line. I don't know that I'm interested, Renney."

"You are, though," Renney assured him. "Wait till I tell you some more about it."

"Loosen up, then."

"It's like this. Suppose that a gent wants a pardon, and we want to block him?"

"The devil! How could that interest you? Are you afraid of somebody?"

"Me? Hell, no," answered Renney with warmth. "Only, I wanted jist to ask you . . . supposing."

"I never suppose," the fat man assured him. "Tell me the facts, and then maybe I'll do what I can."

"You gotta have the names?"

"Yes. Absolutely."

"There was a killing down in Sankeytown. Frank Lopaz. He was killed by Robert Asprey five years back."

"I know about that."

"That's the job."

"And you, Renney? What have you to do with this?"

"What difference does that make? The point is that Robert Asprey is gonna make a deadline for the governor, and the governor already has promised Asprey's daughter that, if her father comes and talks to him, he'll do what he can."

"That's the point," admitted the other, "but what lies behind the point is always what I try to get at, first of all. Now, then, who wants this job done?"

"I do."

"You do. And why?"

Renney scowled.

Suddenly Green said gently, soothingly: "The fact is that my old friend Edgar Asprey wants that pardon blocked, and I think that's about the truth. Am I right?"

The face of Renney was under good control, but he could not keep his eyes from widening a little. "Suppose we let it go at that," he said.

Joe Green nodded. Then he turned to the door, opened it a crack, as though to make sure that no one was there, and finally closed and locked it. He even went so far as to drop the key into his pocket. "Sit down," he said.

Renney sat.

Opposite him, Joe Green took up his place and began to prepare a cigar for smoking, paring away one end and then notching it with precision. All the time his eyes flashed up from his work to the ceiling, as though grave thoughts were mustering in his mind. "It's Edgar Asprey, is it?" he murmured. He lighted the cigar, and with the first large puff of smoke he blew forth the words: "Then he'll have to pay like hell!"

Renney winced. He had hoped to put thirty out of the fifty thousand into his own pocket. He shrank his hopes to fifteen thousand on the instant.

"Why so hot?" he asked.

"Oh, I don't mind telling you," responded Smiling Joe. "A lawyer or a doctor . . . he works out his fee according to the money that his client makes every year. That's the way with me in my work."

"Percentage, eh?"

"That's it."

"I doubt that this Edgar Asprey's so rich."

"He ain't," said the politician exactly. "He hasn't got a bean. But the property he's handling is worth a lot, and he's about ready to swallow it. Bob Asprey had ten or twenty thousand in Saint Louis-Modock. That jumped twenty-five to six hundred and something. That's only one item. That boy knew how to pick his stocks. He was foresighted, and damned if he wasn't. Now his cousin is all ready to skim off the cream. I say that he'll have to pay damned high."

"How high is damned?" asked Renney anxiously.

"Wait a minute. Lemme remember that killing. By name of Frank Lopaz was the boy that went out?"

"That's it."

"Did you know Lopaz?"

"Like myself."

"Tell me about him, because I only partly remember."

"He was a half-breed skunk. That's all."

"It can't be all. What was his game?"

"Anything from stabbing in the back to crooked cards."

"You knew him, eh?"

"Sure I did."

"Family?"

"Aw, he had a wife and a few kids. Every greaser has."

"Children, eh?"

"Yes. A flock."

"Politics?"

"How d'you mean?"

"Did he know anybody?"

"Around gambling houses, a few."

"Friends?"

"Nobody."

"Even among his own people?"

"Listen," said Renney slowly, "I said this bird was a skunk. I meant it. He was a sneak thief, a poisoner, a gunman in the dark, a dirty card player. He was a coward and a bully. There wasn't anything good about him, except that he was too foxy to get drunk very often."

"I follow that, at last," said the politician. "And you want to keep Robert Asprey from getting pardoned after he killed a man of that kind?"

Renney saw that he had committed himself too deeply. He felt that his margin of profit was being whittled down to the bone, and he silently bit his lip and scowled at the floor.

"I say it will cost Edgar Asprey quite a sum. I'm not at all sure that I could turn the trick for him. Fellows like that Lopaz ought to be poisoned at birth. I know it, and you know it, and so does the governor."

Renney shifted in his chair, but, in spite of himself, he could think of nothing to say. At last he blurted out: "Well, let's have your figure."

Joe Green looked at the ceiling and puffed smoke forth slowly. An expression of pain began to contract his fleshy brow. It was obvious that he was deep in figures. "Very well," he said. "You have the power to represent Edgar Asprey to me, have you?"

"Did I ride here all this way to throw a bluff?" Renney asked sourly. "I got a gelding back there in the stable that'll never put one foot in front of another so long as it lives."

"It gets better and better," decided Joe Green. "The thing needs doing so bad that you've nearly killed a horse getting to me." He lay back in his chair and smiled complacently.

Renney leaped to his feet. "Ah, hell," he cried. "Everything that I say is wrong!"

"Oh, no, not at all," said the politician. "But I should say that you are not a trained diplomat. What a hurry Edgar must have been in to send you on. What a hurry!" He made a clucking sound of commiseration.

"Shut up and let's have it!" exclaimed Renney, tormented beyond endurance.

"A case that requires much speed, eh? He's apt to be at the governor at any time."

"Hell and fire," cried Renney. "He's standing in front of the governor now, talkin' for his life."

"Ah?" said Joe Green. "Then suppose we say . . . let me see . . . about seventy-five thousand dollars to cover everything."

Chapter Thirty

FIGHT FIRE WITH FIRE

It was, to the little gunman, like the twitching of a fortune from his hand. He saw ten or fifteen thousand dollars jerked from his pocket and tossed out the window — into the lap of this fat man. Pale green grew his eyes as he stared at the politician. Then: "Unlock the door," he said. "I'm gonna go." He waited, furious, certain that this would call the bluff. To his amazement, Joe Green deliberately went to the door and unlocked it, waving the gunman out.

"Sorry we couldn't do business," he said.

Not often in his life had Renney been so impressed. He stalked from the chamber, but at the door he whirled again and shook his fist at Smiling Joe.

"You poor sap," he cried, "fifty thousand was his top figure, and he was a fool for offering that much."

"Fifty thousand," said Joe Green. "Very well. We'll close at that."

Renney, hanging at the doorway, could

not believe his ears.

"I simply wanted to be sure of his top notch," said Smiling Joe. "It would have been foolish of me to throw good money away, wouldn't it?"

Something about the fox-like brightness of his eyes made Renney turn black with disappointment and with hate. He even felt fear. He saw that he had been overreached from every side.

"I never knew before how you could run this here state by the gift of gab," he admitted sullenly, coming back into the room. "I see now. You never throw away no tricks."

"Very few, I hope," said Joe Green. "I was raised in a thrifty home, Renney. I was a seventh child of a poor widow, and I have to bless her for the training that she gave me."

"Aw, hell," growled the disgusted Renney. "Save that for the election, will you? I ain't a voter."

"On the contrary," said Smiling Joe. "You're a big voter, and I believe that you've cast every one of the fifty thousand votes you control in my favor."

"I wish that I'd cut my throat sooner," protested the other.

"Of course, you do! Of course, you do," said Smiling Joe. "At the same time, you may forget that I'm the man who never goes back on a friend. Once inside the door you may stay in my house forever, my boy. And I think that this evening ought to make you my friend."

Slowly, with a wrench, Renney stepped to the other side of the fence. He could cease scowling. This connection, for all he knew, might be the saving of his neck more than once. And of late he had been having apprehensions of an early downfall. The champion pugilist stretched on the floor by a despised amateur could not have felt worse than Renney had felt when he was so completely outplayed by Geraldi. So he looked upon Joe Green with a greater favor and even was able to smile a little.

"Maybe we better call it that," he suggested.

"Maybe we better," admitted Smiling Joe. "And now suppose that we clean up the details."

"What in hell can you get out o' me now?" asked Renney in some alarm.

"Don't worry, my boy. I never bleed a friend. Let me tell you something more. If this deal goes through, the minute the cash is paid to me, five thousand of it goes straight back to you for a commission."

Renney opened his eyes very wide. "By God!" he gasped.

"I know a friend," repeated Joe Green, clinching his point. "You're going to be one of us, my boy. I'm going to hold you up, if you break."

In fact, Smiling Joe began to grow mellow. He was seeing the disposition of that money as a farmer sees a growing crop. Three thousand to Mullaley, who was yammering for more coin. Ten thousand into the fund. Five thousand for the new wing he had been promising his wife to add to the house. Eight thousand to Jermin, the editor, because Jermin was a good fellow whose editorialized newspapers almost carried the state in their own weight. Then he could throw a comfortable ten thousand into his checking account, and there would still be nearly ten thousand left for secret and private disposal. He could afford to give Renney the five. Besides, his active mind saw the places where he could fit in just such a servant of the machine — a man to be called on once in five years — where a vacancy in the opposition would be most welcome. All of this ground had been covered in his rapid thoughts. He saw that he had Renney in the palm of his hand. Now he went on to prepare for the work.

"You know about that killing?"

"Yes."

"Was Robert Asprey drunk that night?"

"He'd had a few drinks."

"Was he drunk?"

"Hell, no. He shot too straight for that."

"Very well. He shot too straight for that. What had the Mexican been doing?"

"Cheating at cards, of course."

"Why was Asprey playing with such a sneak?"

"He made a fifth hand."

Smiling Joe winced. He, also, had invited in a fifth hand that very evening.

"And then?"

"He tried a raw job."

"How raw?"

"Aces out."

"Not that!"

"He did. He could palm them. He was slick."

"And Asprey?"

"Asprey found it out."

"And went for him?"

"No, the little snake, when he was caught, went at Asprey like poison in the eyes."

"And then?"

"Asprey knocked him away and shot him dead."

Smiling Joe closed his eyes. "For doing that," he said at length, "he ought to have had a statue of himself put up in the town square."

"Sure he should," agreed Renney, "but there wouldn't have been anything in that for us."

"No sooner said than done," remarked the genial Joe Green. "I have this case, now. How did they ever get Robert Asprey in the first place, for this job?"

"They tried railroading him. But they might have failed. Probably they would have. But he got worried and broke jail."

Smiling Joe whistled through fat lips. "Well, well, well," he said. "And if this man Bob Asprey gets to the governor. . . . What shape is he in now?"

"Looks to me like he was built of rock. He's all man."

"Sour and mean?"

"Him? No, open-handed as a baby. He oughta been a banker. He's that sympathetic."

"Let's have all this from the beginning. How do you figure in?"

"I was to mop out Bob Asprey."

"And?"

"I had him under my gun, when a damned young cat of a man come in between me and him."

"Somebody beat you, Renney?"

"From behind."

"And he's still in the way?"

"He's still in the way."

"Worries you, my boy?"

Renney paused. He considered Joe Green gravely, and decided that the man was too important to be fed with a lie.

"Him and Asprey between them. They're a handful."

"Why don't you get help?"

"Nothing but a top-notcher would be any use to me," Renney admitted sadly.

"And you haven't any on hand?"

"Six months is an old friend for me," admitted Renney with a sour grin. "Gents get moldy on me, pretty quick."

Mr. Green thought again, deeply. "What's the name of this fellow?"

"Him? Geraldi. He's a panther."

"He would rather crowd the stage," observed Joe Green. "He might even get on our tracks?"

"Him? He can smell out a trail a hundred miles away. Listen. He followed me on the train. I dropped off in a gorge. Middle of the night. Backtrailed to the next town. He was there! I got him jailed, took another train. He was there. I shot him off the top of that train and saw him drop over the side. He must've hooked into a window. Anyway, when I got to Asprey, he was there with me. That's the story of him. He reads the mind of a lock, and he . . . shot the gun out of my hand."

"Intentionally?"

"In-tentionally!" insisted the other.

Smiling Joe no longer smiled, and his face turned severe. But illumination came to him suddenly.

"I have a little thought," he said. "What's the best way to fight fire?"

"With fire," said the crook.

"Is this Geraldi fire?"

"Nothing but."

"Well, my lad, come along with me. I've got another of Geraldi's kind. He's in the next room. The slipperiest young devil that ever walked, and the smoothest, and he talks a gun out of thin air. Come along and meet him. He'll make your running mate."

So it was that Geraldi saw the door of his room opened a moment later, and the fat Joe Green entered and, behind him, the familiar cat-like form of Renney.

From the midst of a careless, friendly game of twenty-one he observed Renney, and Renney observed him. He saw the gunman stiffen, like a cat at the sight of a dog. But then the hand of Renney rose, empty. He scratched his chin.

"Hey, kid," said Smiling Joe. "I want you to meet an old friend of mine. This is Dick Renney!"

Chapter Thirty-One

POLITICIAN IN THE MAKING

Governor Thomas Fuller was the son of a rich man, but he was determined that this accident of life should not destroy his activities. He was keenly ambitious. His ambitions drew him in two ways: toward his library and toward the speaker's platform. As a matter of fact most of his waking hours always had been spent among his books. He rose early; he labored late. He dressed without vanity; his table was frugal; his manners were simple. And he was proud to say that his millions had not kept him from living on equal terms with his poorer neighbors. He rubbed shoulders willingly with anyone. He was fond of speaking of the brotherhood of man. He endowed an orphan's home. He contributed to the establishment of a hospital. Constantly his purse was opened privately, secretly, to succor the distressed. He looked upon himself as a man of the people.

Of course, as always happens in such cases, the simplicity of his manners simply made more apparent the gulf between him and the majority of the other citizens in his state. He was simple from philosophical conviction; they were simple because they had spent most of their years punching cows, digging in mines, cutting timber. His very vocabulary, thrice refined toward the golden end of simplicity, was so pure that other men were touched with awe. The people who crossed the threshold of his home caught their breath. They knew that Thomas Fuller had fifteen millions in unassailable bonds and lands. No matter what he did, they were determined to see a difference.

He was gentle, kind, and good. He never had injured any man. He labored with all his might to stand merely on a level with his fellows. Because of the very honesty of that ambition, wolves fell upon him.

At first he wanted to be a member of no party, but merely to throw his weight behind good government, no matter who represented it. But the instant that he appeared in support of a candidate — it was merely for mayor of the town — the opposition press attacked him savagely.

They called him "idle rich," "cold-blooded aristocrat," "cunning, and plausible corrupter of the legislative body," "the representative of big business, crushing smaller people." They cartooned him; they lampooned him. They searched into his past and coined lies about him.

Because he was a faultless man, the attack was all the more bitter. We hate those whom we have harmed, and every man who lifted a hand against Thomas Fuller knew that he was wrong, that he lied. Therefore, their bitterness knew no bound.

Thomas Fuller took these attacks seriously to heart. He used to sit in the evening in his library with a desk piled with papers and, with compressed lips and an aching heart, read every diatribe. He tried to be just and reasonable, and, with a humble spirit, seek for truth in the voices of his detractors. There was never one pile of papers. There always were two. The first was the press that assailed him. The second represented those who supported his side.

Furiously as the enemy attacked him, just so furiously his friendly journals defended him. The enemy dreaded the weight of his name, his wealth; the other party that he had happened to advocate in that first petty election prized him for exactly the same reasons. It was his fifteen millions that made the difference.

Because of these millions his single

speech to a meeting in the town hall placed him in the center of the political stage. He had wanted to belong to no party. But after two weeks, the conservatives had burned him with gas, with fire, and with acid, so that he never could approach them as a friend. And after two weeks, the liberals had salved his hurts and bandaged his wounds so thoroughly that ever to have left them would, to the sensitive soul of Thomas Fuller, have been something akin to black treason. He withdrew from politics. That is to say, he tried to withdraw. But the two parties would not let him. The liberals had won, therefore the conservatives would not cease their attacks. And the liberals dared not abandon their defense.

Presently his name was known to every far corner of the state, and people began to ask questions. Every liberal loved the name of Thomas Fuller without knowing why. Every conservative hated him, and did not know why. The liberals pointed to his charities. The conservatives shouted: "Hypocrite!"

In the meantime, he read the papers and bled inwardly, and inwardly was healed. They begged him to run for the state Senate. He accepted from curiosity rather than from eagerness. For four years he sat quietly and listened to scurrilous debates. He was denounced on the floor. Foaming politicians shook their fists at him. On the other hand fiery liberals rose and defended him, eulogized him.

He spoke only five times in four years. Every word he uttered made a headline, not because it was important but because he was a keenly interesting political personality. He was at home every day of every session.

Finally, he could not help feeling that the conservatives were a little mad and a little wicked. And he could not help feeling that liberals were kind and true. Also, he was led naturally to the belief that his political sagacity was beyond that of other men. Seriously — when he saw all his speeches thrashed out in detail in the papers — he felt that there was something in his thoughts. And that led him, almost reluctantly, to the conclusion that he owed his time and his mind to the state. The instant that his conscience was entrapped, the thing was done. He gave the rest of his days to the service of politics.

Twice he toured the state and made speeches. He never was eloquent. But his slow sentences, his simple words, his gentle manner delighted the liberals. He had become so well known that they were sure he must be brilliant. He could not smile without making the audience shout with laughter. He could not raise his hand without reducing them to stark, expectant silence.

The conservatives were just as violent against him. Four times they raided his house and broke up his meetings. And this made his importance grow greater. The conservative press and all its adjectives on one side, the liberal press began to compare him with Solon and Alfred the Great and Washington. They declared that he had a silver tongue and a golden heart. Nothing was too much.

And Thomas Fuller believed them — just a little.

A time came when the liberals were in distress for a candidate for governor. The last man they had in office had been frankly corrupt, a machine politician. Another of the same stamp would be buried in an election. So they decided to take a last desperate chance. They felt that Thomas Fuller was incorruptible, and most of the political bosses were far from wanting an incorruptible in the office. Nevertheless, the party was desperate. They nominated Thomas Fuller.

Every liberal voted for him furiously.

Every conservative voted furiously against him. Between the two extremes lay a small body of honest, comparatively indifferent people. They, also, voted for Fuller, and he was elected by the thinnest of margins. By the thinnest of margins his party controlled the Assembly; its hold in the Senate was equally small, but, nevertheless, the control of the government was in his hands.

Then the party consulted. It would not do to let him have full sway. Otherwise, in a year he could spend every penny in the treasury, building schools and roads and hospitals, or in reclaiming arid lands, or in other schemes that did not line political pockets fast enough to suit the rank and file of the bosses.

Then Smiling Joe Green remembered that he had gone to school with the governor. It was in the East, a school that Joe had hated. His career had been infamous in the classroom, and glorious on the football field. Now he proposed to recall himself to the governor's attention — and perhaps. . . .

It succeeded better than he could have dreamed. The governor greeted an old school fellow with rapture. Because Joe was a liberal, he was sure in the first place that he was a good fellow, and, before he had conversed with him an hour, he was sure that Joe was a genius.

Colonel Green knew nearly half the voters in the state by name; he knew every town, village, and crossroads hotel. And for this knowledge, it came to pass that the governor looked upon him as a man of immense ability. He could not have dreamed that this knowledge had been compiled merely for the sake of lining the colonel's pockets with political loot. Thomas Fuller was so honest that he could not imagine another man being crooked. Unless he were a conservative.

He began to ask the advice of Joe Green. Joe Green gave it without seeming to. He had a mind like a moving picture. Whatever had come to his attention was his forever. He had only to turn back to the right film. Whenever he wanted to make a point, he reminded the governor of something that gentle man had said in a speech or in an article. He always seemed to be suggesting what the governor already had determined upon.

Finally Thomas Fuller was convinced that the only purpose of these conversations with Colonel Green was for the clearing of his own mind. As a matter of fact, he had delivered himself into the hands of an unscrupulous grafter. In a few quarters, it became known. When something was needed, men approached Joe Green. He began to grow fat in the purse. Whatever he wanted was done, and all the time. Thomas Fuller's hands were as clean as snow, and his self-confidence was increasing. The opposition began to speak of his graft administration. He merely smiled, because he knew himself. They began to rage at his brazen face. It was only the brazen face of utter innocence.

All of this must be understood before we step with Smiling Joe Green through the front door of the governor's home on the bright morning of the next day, and watch him saunter down the hall, and see him tap on the door of the governor's study.

Three quick taps, a pause, and a louder one.

"Come in, Joe Green!" called the governor. "Come in, Joe. How happy I always am to hear your knock."

Chapter Thirty-Two

JOE GREEN EARNS HIS MONEY

The morning was so warm that the governor sat between two open windows. A broad shaft of sun fell through one and made the floor almost as bright as a surface of amber water. By contrast, the governor was a shadow among shadows, except that there was a glint of silver, which was his hair.

"Sit down, Joe. I have to tell you about an adventure."

Smiling Joe had cloaked his face in gloom; he now, apparently, forced a smile of interest.

"Every day's an adventure in your office," he suggested.

"A nocturnal adventure," smiled the governor. "A man, in fact, forced his way into my house."

"They've hired another gunman, then!" exclaimed Smiling Joe.

"Hired one? No."

"Forced his way in," went on Smiling Joe in great excitement. "By heaven, that watchman! I never have liked the look of him!"

"I'm sure it was not the fault of the watch-man."

"You never will place the blame on anyone," said Smiling Joe. "But you must remember, sir, that you don't belong to yourself. You're state property. If you'll let me find you a really fighting man. . . ."

"I wouldn't displace poor Bender," said the governor. "Besides, he's not to blame. This man who broke in was a very resolute fellow. You may have heard of Robert Asprey?"

"The murderer!" exclaimed Smiling Joe, with force and with horror. "The murderer, Asprey?"

"Come, come," murmured Thomas Fuller. "That's a very harsh word, isn't it?"

"Ah," nodded Green, "he played the honest man with you, did he?"

"*Played* the honest man?" repeated the governor.

"He can do that, too," replied Green. "I know all about him."

The governor sighed. "I hope I haven't made a mistake," he said.

"Not about Asprey," Green said earnestly. "That would be a serious matter. There's not a more dangerous man in the state, I should say."

Thomas Fuller sighed again. "I know that

he's the father of a charming girl . . . I know that he built a respectable home, Joe. Surely those things are in his favor."

Smiling Joe nodded. "He's put his best foot forward with you, I see," he said. "No doubt he talked about political enemies . . . railroading . . . and such things?"

"As a matter of fact," admitted the governor, "that's exactly what he said. But if you'd heard the conviction and the manner of his speaking. . . ." His voice trailed away a little. He wanted for Green to speak, but the latter remained discreetly silent. At length the governor added rather weakly: "I've promised him a pardon."

"Good God!" broke out Green.

"Ah?" queried the governor.

"I beg your pardon," muttered Green, and frowned at the floor.

"My dear Joe, you seem quite cut up over this."

"I? Well . . . it will be rather ugly. And we can't afford to throw away many votes, can we?"

"I should think," answered Fuller, "that this is the very sort of thing that would be popular."

"Pardons usually are," said the other. "But, of course, people are a little tired of seeing the gunmen go free. There was

Chandler, last month, too."

The governor bit his lip. "I have taken an oath," he said, "to do my duty as I see it before me."

"And, of course, you do it," replied Green. "I hope, sir, that I'm not the man to doubt that."

"Don't 'sir' me, Joe."

"It slips out of me, Tom. I've formed a habit of looking up to you, I suppose."

"Tush," said the governor, smiling with pleasure in spite of himself. "Well, well, well . . . but, really, I take Robert Asprey to be as honest a man as I've ever talked with in my life. I saw his daughter not long ago and liked her. Now I've seen the father. . . . And I've given him my promise."

Joe Green drew a great breath, but he was silent.

"Why do you take it so very seriously?" asked Fuller with a touch of impatience.

"Perhaps you're right," said Green. "You're a better judge of human nature than I am, of course."

"I don't think that I am," said the governor in haste. "I don't think that's at all true. Besides, I don't know anything about the story . . . except a vague recollection."

"Asprey told you, I suppose?"

"Yes."

"He made it out . . . what?"

"According to him, it was a simple affair. The Mexican was a known gambler, and a crooked one. I believe he palmed an ace, and Asprey caught him out. After that, he flew at Asprey's throat, and the man fired in self-defense."

Joe Green shook his head, smiling his doubt. Then he began to nod, as though he were seeing through the matter.

"It's plain that you don't like this," said Thomas Fuller.

"Sorry, sir," said Green.

"Do come out in the open with me, Joe."

"I was simply remembering that Robert Asprey ran away from prison. He wouldn't even wait for the verdict of the jury."

"He explained that. There was a great deal of enmity toward him at the time."

"Wasn't the trial in his own home town?"

"I believe so. Yes."

"So many enemies in his own town? That sounds rather bad, doesn't it?"

"Ah, Joe," answered Fuller, "think of the number of enemies I have in this very city."

"There's a difference between a man of your caliber and his, I hope," Green said angrily. "I tell you, Tom, you do wrong by taking every man for what he ought to be rather than for what he is. By heavens, that you should calmly sit there and compare yourself with a drunken, brawling, murdering. . . ." He stopped short and pressed one hand over his mouth. "I'm sorry that I went so far, Tom."

The governor interlocked his fingers and leaned back in his chair. "Talk as if you were in my place, Joe," he said. "Suppose that I'm Robert Asprey. I've come into this room where you, the governor, sit. I've asked you to give me another chance to prove to the world that I'm an honest man."

Joe Green hesitated. "I think that I could answer best out of your own mouth, Tom."

"My own mouth?"

"I remember the speech that you made at Bentley Crossing two years ago."

"That was after the fight at the mines."

"Right. It was your speech that day which ended the rioting even more effectually than if you'd called out the militia."

"No, no," smiled the pleased governor. "As a matter of fact. . . ."

"I know what you're talking about," said Joe Green. "That day you said . . . the words still ring in my ear, by God! . . . 'The law is no man's private possession. A man may put a revolver into his pocket, and yet he cannot put the law into his pocket. There will be no peace and there will be no order in this country until the citizens realize that justice must not be left for courtrooms only . . . it must walk the streets and our men must have empty hands.' " Joe Green paused and shook his head in admiration. "Do you remember how they cheered when you said that?"

"Did they? Did they cheer, Joe?" murmured the governor, blushing like a girl.

"They split the roof wide open," Joe Green responded untruthfully. "And they had reason to. They were listening to a man talk, that day. And I tell you, Tom, it hurts me. Damn it, it hurts me most terribly to think of you falling beneath yourself, beneath what you can be! It hurts me still more when I think of how the yellow press will yell at you. They've never had anything to go on before except blind malice. But now they can shout about inconsistency, and, of course, they'll be sure that you were bribed to do the thing."

The governor caught his breath. "I hadn't thought of that," he said faintly.

"Because your heart is so pure. . . ."

"No, no!"

"Your hands are too clean and your soul. . . ."

"Come, come, Joe."

"And your mercy too ready."

"Joe, don't talk up to me. I'm just a fellow like yourself, and not a whit better."

"Like me? If you were like me, do you think that cowardly murderer, that red-handed sneak, would have dared to come into this house and suggest that I pardon him? No, but he knew that he could take advantage of you. He knew that you have no memory even for crimes against yourself, and, therefore, you wouldn't have the full story at the end of your fingers. You would not know about the wife and the children of the poor fellow Asprey murdered."

"Children?" said the governor, touched and excited.

"Five children," said Joe Green. He added, absently: "Of course, this would cost us every Mexican vote in the place. But let them go. I'd rather see the conservatives come in and smash all the work we've tried to do these last few years . . . I'd rather see that happen, than to ask you to change your mind, unless you see good and honest reason of changing it."

"Reason?" cried the governor. "Good heavens, my dear lad, what more reason do I want than this? When he comes back tonight, I'll denounce him to his face and send him off!"

Chapter Thirty-Three

THE TRAP IS SET

Smiling Joe did not linger in the house of the governor. He had other work on hand, and, therefore, he left and drove his span of fast-stepping bays down the street to the telegraph office. There he sent to Edgar Asprey a telegram consisting of a single word: **Arranged.** He signed the telegram: **Joe.** Such a document would be slender evidence in any court — even supposing that Asprey was not wise enough to destroy it. In the meantime, it should prove enough to start fifty thousand dollars on its way toward him.

No wonder Smiling Joe was living up to his nickname when he walked out of the telegraph office and stood for a moment at the edge of the gutter, rubbing his hands together, and regarding life in a wholly favorable manner. Then he climbed to the seat of his buggy and sent the bays rattling out of the town and spinning down the boulevard that fringed the lake. It was not well paved, and it was bordered by more lank, brown fields than by houses. Nevertheless, he looked upon it complacently, for he told himself that before many years the city would have grown out here and then this naked land would have hundred-fold value. The point of his vision was that he owned most of those brown fields. That would be the time for him to retire — when these fields came into the market as tidy city lots. Meanwhile, he had two deadly weapons cached in the hills beyond the lake. He saw a fit employment for them at once.

So he gave his horses the whip, and they sped rapidly around the edge of the little lake, over the ridge across the creek, and then fell to a walk as they worked up the steeper slope beyond. The mind of the fat man was not seeing that dusty highway, but a sheet of well-graded, sweeping macadam that, in time, would pierce the heart of the mountains and double and redouble the population of the capital city.

For he loved that little city by the lake with a greater love than he himself understood, and always, when he had spare moments — when he lay stretched in his bed at night, and when he opened his eyes in the morning — he was turning the bright, dim pages of the future and reading glowing words into them about the town. If he had found a mountain of gold, he would have given half of it, perhaps, to the city.

He turned the horses from the main highway and drove, still at a walk, down a little lane that was hardly more than a cattle trail, faintly marked on either side by wheels, and trampled in the center by the passage of hoofs. But wild grass sprang up in between.

A sudden chatter of guns, ahead of him, made him draw in his reins. However, if there were gun work, he was not the object of it. He reached under the seat, and raised to the place beside him a sawed-off shotgun. He was no marksman, but that gun needed no marksmanship. Anyone who could hit a lawn with a stream of water from a hose could hit a mark with that spray of terrible lead. He passed through a high hedge of brush; below him he saw a horseman galloping at full speed.

It was Renney on a plunging horse, gun in hand, and, in a moment, the gun began to speak. Six times he fired, then he reined in his horse and hastened to examine a small tree that had been his target. The new-found ally of Renney, the splendid young Mexican rancher/card-player/gunman, went along, and the politician heard them announce the result. Out of six bullets, fired at almost full speed, Renney actually had driven two into the mark, and there was a scratch on the bark that, after argument, was not allowed.

Smiling Joe regarded this display with a shuddering horror, for it was uncanny skill. Doubtless every one of the six shots, even if they had not cut through the small trunk, would have passed through a human body.

The young Mexican now whirled his gray mare. A word to her, spoken in a strange language, and she shot across the sloping meadow, and, as she fled, the rider fired rapidly. One explosion followed veritably on the heels of another. And, when the examination was made, four bullets were found to have whipped straight through the trunk of the sapling. A gust of wind caught at its branches during the examination, and so closely had the bullets of the last rider been bunched, that the young tree snapped loudly and fell with a *whish*.

"Kid," said Renney with grudging admiration, "you got the trick. You got it! Damned if I ain't out of practice!"

"There's luck in every deal like this," replied the other carelessly.

Big Joe Green hailed them.

They came to him with a whoop and a rush. Renney was plainly eager; the Mexican showed perfect indifference in his scarred face.

"Bob Asprey won't be pardoned, boys," said Smiling Joe with a broad grin. "There ain't any chance of that, but there is a chance of something else. He's due to come to the governor's house tonight at ten. Well, there ain't any reason why the pair of you shouldn't be there, is there?"

"What sort of a lay is the governor's house?" asked Renney.

"Easy, kid. Easy. There's a garden in front, and an alley behind. The alley for your horses. The garden for you. You sit out there in the cool and wait for your man."

"Ain't there a watchman, or something like that?"

"The watchman will be fixed by me. Besides, he's an old fool who's half blind. Renney, I think I've put him in your hands."

Renney asked curiously: "Will you tell me, chief, what makes you so keen about Bob Asprey?"

"Thorough is my word, son," answered the politician. "And dead men don't vote. I guess that's all." He turned his horses, the tire of the near front wheel scraping with a screech against the guard iron. Then down the road he trotted his span. Soon he disappeared, and left only an occasionally rising wisp of dust above the green.

Then Renney turned to his younger companion. "There's a slick one, kid. Slick for any country."

"In my land," said Geraldi, "we would make him a general."

"Sure," answered Renney, "because in your country the generals get the loot. What time is it?"

"Nearly twelve."

"Do you know the town?"

"A little."

"Then take care of yourself. I'm going in past the lake. You better go in on the far side. I'll meet you in the alley behind the governor's house at nine. We'll plant the job then. So long, kid."

"*Adiós*," said Geraldi.

He was glad to be rid of the gunman, but, when Renney was out of sight, he did not ride down toward the town. Instead, he turned up across the high land, pointing straight toward the hotel, and on the way he entered the lofty grove of spruce. There he halted, whistled three times, and almost instantly had a brisk answer.

Robert Asprey stepped out from among the trees and waved a hand in cordial greeting. He was smoking a pipe; utter content was in his eye.

"You're kind of late and tardy, my boy," said Asprey. "I've waited here all morning for a sight of you."

"I've been with Renney," answered Geraldi.

"Renney!" cried the other. "Did you . . . was there a fight, Geraldi?"

"We're friends . . . we're working together," answered Geraldi.

The other simply stared.

"He got twenty thousand for killing you," said Geraldi. "The political boss, Smiling Joe Green. . . ."

"Colonel Green?"

"That's the man. He gets fifty thousand for stopping your pardon."

"He can't," said Robert Asprey with thorough content. "I have the governor's word for it."

"Is it fixed and final?"

"It will be tonight at ten."

"Green has seen the governor in the meantime and changed his mind."

"Impossible!"

"I've just heard him say so."

Robert Asprey reached for a tree and steadied himself. His teeth were set and his nostrils flaring so that, for the moment, he looked a dangerous man, indeed.

"A damned weak-hearted scoundrel,

then. Is that what I have to think of Tom Fuller?"

"Think what you please," said Geraldi. "At ten o'clock tonight, I'm to be waiting in the garden in front of the governor's house with Renney, and you're to be our meat. Is that clear?"

"Nothing could be clearer," said Robert Asprey. "I'm beaten, then. What did they do? Bribe the governor? How could they bribe a man as rich as he is?"

"Green talked him over, probably. But that's all I can tell you. Now what's the next move?"

"I don't know," Asprey replied sadly. "I haven't the least idea. Fuller has fallen down on me."

"We could try this," said Geraldi. "Go down at ten. I'll be there with Renney, and, when he makes a move, I'll take him under my wing and go in behind you. We'll stand him up in front of Fuller and tell him the straight story, so far as we know it, about what Joe Green has done. I don't know. Perhaps that might win for us."

"It might win. It *has* to win," declared Robert Asprey. "But tell me first . . . does Edgar Asprey furnish all the money that's being spent on this affair?"

"Every penny . . . from your money."

"Money," groaned the other. "Money is in the veins of these people, instead of blood. Geraldi, I don't see how we can win, but up yonder in the mountains I lived a long time alone, and I've learned to trust something to God."

Chapter Thirty-Four

CHALMERS JOINS IN

At nine o'clock, Geraldi rode Zuleikha into the entrance of the alley behind the governor's house. He dismounted, left her standing, and walked slowly ahead — slowly, because the surface of the alley was sadly pitted and rutted, and the narrow way was lost in almost total darkness. Something shifted among the shadows before him, and Geraldi stepped under the shadow of a tree.

"Hello, kid!" called a cautious voice before him.

"Renney?"

The latter came up hastily. "You're on time," he said.

"A shade ahead," said Geraldi.

"I've got a third man coming."

Geraldi bit his lip in the darkness. "You'll spoil things with a crowd," he said.

"You're handy with a gun, kid," admitted Renney, "but besides Asprey there's apt to be along a real hell-devil. That's the Geraldi that I've been telling you about. I got a third man to help out."

"Who is he?"

"Somebody you never seen, probably. But don't worry about that. He's a game fellow, and he shoots straight . . . and quick!" He chuckled a little. "He went straight, a few years ago. Ever since then, he's been hankering for some of the good old times. He couldn't be held, when I asked him for this job. Think of it, old son. He's coming for the fun of it!" He chuckled again. Then he added: "Where's your horse?"

"Down the alley."

"You better get her in closer."

"Very well." Geraldi whistled softly with a peculiar flare to the tone. The mare trotted to him instantly.

"You got her so that she can talk back to you," said the gunfighter in admiration. "Come as far as she hears your whistle?"

"Yes. That far."

"She's worth her price."

"There's someone coming down the alley," whispered Geraldi.

They shrank back against the fence.

"You got ears," commented the gunfighter.

The stranger approached closer, coming slowly and more slowly. At length he called gently: "Dick?"

"It's all right," called Renney in answer.

The figure strode on toward them. He loomed a big fellow before the eyes of Geraldi. "Is everything set?" he asked in a rumbling bass voice that was very familiar to Geraldi.

"Everything," answered Renney.

"Where's your friend?"

"Here with me. This is Chalmers of Sankeytown, kid. Chalmers, this is the kid."

Their hands fumbled and found one another in the darkness.

"What's your name?" asked Chalmers.

Geraldi was silent. He disliked very much having to speak. Renney would not suspect; he had seen Geraldi by day, in the new guise. He was already convinced that this was a friend. But the other was very different, and, hearing that voice, he might hark straight back to the true identity of the speaker.

"He don't wear a name except on Sundays," explained Renney. "He's a good kid, Chalmers. I'll vouch for that."

"Now," said Chalmers, passing over the subject of Geraldi, "let's get to our places."

"Where's your horse?"

"Down the alley."

"You better get it closer."

Chalmers disappeared in haste into the darkness, and Renney added: "He's pretty short when he talks, but he don't mean no harm. Lately he's been upset by this same devil of a Geraldi. He ain't got much temper left with him, but give him plenty of rope and you can handle him right enough."

Geraldi made no answer. He liked this affair less and less. Renney alone was enough trouble for the day. To have the formidable bull, Chalmers, added to the fight, made it tenfold more difficult. But there was nothing to do except to lie low and wait. He must make his decisions about action at the last instant.

In the meantime, his plan with Robert Asprey was that the latter was to approach the house closer to nine-thirty than ten, the time of the original appointment. In this manner, he would have a chance of slipping through unseen. Once he could face the governor, it seemed assured that honest Thomas Fuller must change his mind a second time. In that case, there would be no trouble in the garden. Asprey could exit when he chose, after impatience had driven the watchers away.

Chalmers came back, leading a powerful horse, a great-headed creature that no sooner came near the gray mare than it began to lash out. Zuleikha backed away with a snort, tossing her head, and Geraldi had to run after her and quiet her, speaking rapidly in Arabic.

He came again, leading her back, only to receive a shaft of white light in his face. He side-stepped from that light. It flickered after and found him again. Then it snapped out.

"Go easy! Go easy!" Renney was snarling in a complaining voice.

"I like to look at the gent that I'm gonna do business with," said Chalmers in explanation. "It rests me a lot to know the face of him that's gonna fight along the side of me."

Geraldi said nothing. But he was on edge with nervousness.

"Go through the gate, there," said Renney. "Go into the garden, kid, and make a round of the house and see if the watchman is hanging around. Green said that he'd fix that."

There was nothing for it but to obey. Geraldi passed obediently through the gate, but, having done so, he raised himself noiselessly into the lower fork of an apple tree. In this manner his head was brought above the top of the board fence and hedge that outlined the rear of the governor's ground. Incidentally, he could hear the conversation of the two in the alley. He was enormously relieved to find that they were not talking about him, but about the work that lay before them.

So, feeling safer, he lowered himself to the ground once more, and then proceeded through the garden as he had been directed. He had secured some description of the place from Robert Asprey earlier in the day, but by night all was altered. He had to feel his way forward until he became sure of the paths, often stopping to squint close along the ground, for in this manner one takes the greatest advantage of light at night.

He worked to the rear of the house. Through the kitchen window he saw the cook cleaning pans at her sink. Then he circled to the side and paused in an arbor from which he could see the front of the house. He scratched a match, and, covertly shielding the flame, he glanced at his watch and saw that it was close to half-past nine. He had barely dropped the match, when a big shadow loomed through the darkness and turned straight in from the sidewalk toward the house.

It was Robert Asprey. It made Geraldi smile a little to think how characteristic this bold approach was, in spite of the danger that might be lurking for him, and of which he had been forewarned. So he slipped through the shadows and called in a whisper. Asprey stopped and whirled with the gloom of steel in his hand.

"It's I," Geraldi said, and came close.

Asprey chuckled. "I thought you might be one of them," he said, even his softened voice having a distinctly thunderous rumble.

"Do you expect any warning from them?" asked Geraldi.

"Even a snake rattles before it strikes," said Asprey.

"Not snakes of this breed," answered Geraldi. "But they're behind the house. They don't expect you this early. Maybe the governor doesn't, either. Can you get in?"

"I'll ring."

"We'll see, then."

Asprey mounted the front steps, with Geraldi behind him. In answer to the ring, a servant appeared who took Asprey's name and then shook his head. The governor, he said, had given orders that he was unable to see Mr. Asprey that night. He had left a message that he had changed his mind about the matter between them. The door closed.

Asprey turned with a faint groan. "They've done my business for me," he said sadly. "I can't even have a chance to talk for myself."

"Are you going to let it go at that?" asked Geraldi.

"What can I do?"

"Break into the house and force yourself on Fuller."

"I know Tom Fuller. You can't frighten him."

"You don't want to. You only want to talk with him."

"I'll try a window, then."

"Try this door. Wait a moment."

Only a moment Geraldi leaned before it. Then it gave way, with a muffled click of the turned lock, and Geraldi pushed the door wide.

"Go on into his library," murmured Geraldi. "I think that you'll be apt to find him there. He's a book lover, people say. Go in there and talk for your life, man."

Asprey dropped a great hand on the shoulder of his friend. "You've shown me the way in," he said. "God help me if I can't talk myself into that pardon now."

So he passed in, and pressed the door softly shut behind him. Geraldi descended to the ground like a shadow and skirted back around the house.

He was close to the rear gate when he saw the two companions coming in toward him.

"How's everything, kid?" asked the voice of Chalmers.

"All well," said Geraldi.

"Well," grunted Renney. "You've kept us here, long enough." His manner and tone had altered suddenly.

"Go on ahead," said Chalmers. "Walk on, kid. We'll come behind."

"Just a moment," said Geraldi. "I have a loose spur. It's jingling, and I have to tighten it." He dropped on one knee to the ground, but although he seemed to be fumbling at the spur, his eyes were constantly peering up at the others.

Suddenly Chalmers snarled: "You sneaking traitor. . . ." — and his hand made a convulsive movement.

Chapter Thirty-Five

GERALDI BLAMED FOR MURDER

So complete was Chalmers's advantage of position that he should have been able to drive his bullet straight down between the shoulders of the kneeling Geraldi, but the first word had not left his lips before Geraldi drew. It was a flashing movement into his open coat and out again, and he fired with the outward snap of his hand.

Big Chalmers staggered back. The gesture that had drawn his own gun merely cast it far away, and his out-flung hand crashed into Renney just as the latter was firing his own weapon. Then, as the gun of Geraldi flashed again, Renney and Chalmers dropped in a heap. The killer leaped to them and stooped over them.

Chalmers was shot through the head. There was a broad, wet stain on the forehead of Renney.

"Both," murmured Geraldi. He stood up and looked quietly around him. The rear door of the house opened with a slam, and a shaft of feeble yellow light poured forth. Down the steps ran two men servants and hurried toward the place, but Geraldi slipped back among the trees. He paused by the gate to look back, and he saw the servants reach the two fallen men. Their outcry resounded blocks away, and Geraldi hurried on into the alley behind the grounds.

At his first whistle, the mare came to him. He mounted and rode down to the mouth of the alley, but there he waited for a moment, slipping two fresh changes into the revolver he had used, and wondering what would become of Robert Asprey. Whatever caution should have urged him to do, there was little doubt as to what he would try, and that was to break from the house and, like a good soldier, run straight for the sound of the firing. After that?

So Geraldi waited, turning the affair slowly in his mind. No doubt Chalmers had recognized his voice, and, when he was alone with Renney, they had planned between them the action that followed. It hardly seemed possible that, in an instant, by a gesture, as it were, they had made the final exit.

In the meantime, noise was rising in a louder and louder wave from the grounds of the governor's house. He looked back, and at that instant half a dozen men swarmed up from the shadows and stood about him, every man armed.

"Who are you?" they asked.

Another said: "I'll do the talking."

"Very well, Captain."

"Who are you? What in hell do you sit on a horse here for?"

"You ask the governor," Geraldi said calmly. "He'll tell you why I'm here. And take your hand from the reins of my horse or I'll drill you."

"Why, you fool," said the officer, "we're six against you."

"I don't care if you're a thousand," said Geraldi. "I have the governor's orders behind me."

This bluff seemed to have some weight with them.

"Go back down the alley, Smith and Wilson . . . hold on, I'll go with you. The rest of you watch this fellow. He's a suspicious character, I take it. We'll find out if the governor really has posted a man here."

The three hurried off, but three remained, grouping themselves closely about Geraldi.

"Who are you, bucko?" asked one of the curious.

"A working man," answered Geraldi. "Who are you?"

"A loafer," chuckled the other. "Has the old man put you out here?"

"He has."

"What for?"

"I don't see that you rate an answer to that."

"Keep it to yourself, then. They're raising a row, back there. Now they're through with it, though."

In the garden, silence suddenly followed the clamor. So clear was the silence that they could hear a single man's voice speaking.

"That's Governor Fuller now," murmured one of the six. "What happened, I wonder?"

A wild shout burst from the distance. There was a clamor. Two shots followed, one on the heels of the other. Then a scattering fusillade, like thunder after the quiet. Then, loud and high from the heart of the alley: "Stop him, boys! Jenkinson . . . Spinder . . . Marks . . . stop that rider that's coming!"

The crash of hoofs beat on deep echoes down the lane. They smashed loudly over gravel; they passed on, thudding more softly through thick dust. The three soldiers instantly turned their attention from Geraldi.

He made no movement to escape, however, but, swinging low in the saddle so that his eye would be beneath the line of the hedges and fences on either side, he strained his eyes and made out a big man, very bulky across the shoulders, plunging down the alleyway, but sitting bolt upright in the saddle in spite of the danger into which he was riding.

There was a continual shouting from the rear, but no guns were fired at the fugitive, perhaps for the fear of striking some of the three who were guarding the mouth of the alley. In fact, they seemed to be a sure enough net to capture the solitary horseman.

One of them had dropped on his knee to take aim. The other two each had a rifle at the shoulder when Geraldi made up his mind that it was time for him to act. Something in the erect position of that rider had made him remember Robert Asprey, and he was willing to take his chance that it was Asprey in fact.

A word was enough for the Arab mare. Now he gave her both a shout and the spur, and she leaped straight ahead into the group of the militia. Perhaps in the old days she had been taught similar tricks by her owner.

At any rate, she made nothing of charging down the trio and left them rolling helplessly in the dust while Geraldi swung her about again and rated her alongside the fugitive. It was Robert Asprey, indeed, and he gave Geraldi a ringing cry of — "Well done, lad!" — as they shot away side by side into the dusk.

They spoke no more, merely laying their horses straight and true for the edge of town, and then rounding onto the long boulevard beside the lake. Here, since there was no immediate pursuit, they drew back to a milder pace. They could talk at last.

"Nothing gained . . . everything lost," said Asprey briefly. "Someone has convinced the governor that I'm a cowardly murderer and that Frank Lopaz was a fine man and a good father of a family."

"He refused you?"

"He stood up and gave me a lecture. He said that he'd be glad to see me in prison waiting for the extreme penalty. Those were his words. He was white, he was so angry."

"What did you say back? Couldn't you argue?"

"Try to argue with a man who says that you ought to be hanged."

"I *would* have tried," declared Geraldi.

"I had no time. The guns began to roar in

the garden, and he insisted on going out when he heard that there were two dead men." He paused. Then he added: "You did that, of course?"

"I did that," said Geraldi. "Chalmers spotted me. They tried to murder me when my head was turned. It's hard for me to imagine even that the two of them have gone out."

"Wait a minute before you go ahead pitying them. We went out, the governor and I together. We reached the spot where the two were laid out, side by side. A lantern had been brought. It was flashed in their faces. I knew Renney and, of course, I knew Chalmers with the hole through his head. I thought that Renney was gone, too. But then, when he got to his knees. . . ."

"What?"

"He got to his knees and staggered about for a moment. The governor himself caught his shoulder and pointed to Chalmers."

" 'Have you committed that murder?' asked the governor.

" 'I?' says Renney, getting his wits back. 'I? It was Geraldi! It was Geraldi who murdered him . . . the pickpocket, crook, and thug, Geraldi, murdered him!'

" 'Who is this Geraldi? Where can he be found?' says the governor. 'This is an example of the sort of work that you want me to pardon in your own case, but by heaven, I'll deal an even-handed justice in this state! Who knows the man Geraldi?'

"Then Renney gave a gasp and a yell.

" 'He knows him!' he shouts. And pointed at me.

" 'You know him?' says the governor. 'What have you to do with this, Asprey?'

" 'He's behind it!' yells that cur of a Renney. 'He's hired the man who murdered Chalmers from behind and tried to get me, too!'

" 'Gentlemen,' I said, 'will you notice that that bullet was fired from the front of Chalmers?'

"They wouldn't pay any attention to that. The governor was very angry.

" 'You've taken advantage of my kindness to plant death traps around my house, Asprey,' he told me. 'And you're going to suffer for this. I gave you immunity from the crime for this one night, but that immunity doesn't spread to such things as this. Men, secure this fellow and keep him closely guarded.'

"A couple of his servants started for me. What was I to do? Well, I knocked their heads together and started for the alley. I remembered you'd said that your horse would be back there. I got through the gate with bullets flying after me, the governor shouting orders, and Renney screeching like a wildcat, he was in such a fury. Luckily, I managed to find a horse the instant that I got into the dark of the alley, and, as I rode down this way, you know how they yelled behind me.

"But there you came in, Geraldi, and that's the reason why we're riding along beside this lake and wondering what we can do next. But there's little left for me to do, and, for you, there's only one thing."

"And that?"

"Get out of this country as quickly as possible, or they'll catch you and hang you to a tree."

"They've hunted you for five years," said Geraldi.

"That's true."

"And you, old fellow, didn't have Zuleikha."

She lifted her beautiful head in recognition, when she heard the name.

Chapter Thirty-Six

MRS. ASPREY TRIES TO KEEP A SECRET

Cousin Edgar felt that it was time to take a definite act. He had several reasons. The first was that he had received the telegram — **Arranged.** — and by that he knew that the governor had been persuaded to refuse the pardon to Robert Asprey. The second was that he needed much money to pay off his various obligations and, above all, the handsome lump sum of fifty-thousand dollars for which he had bargained. It never occurred even to the slippery soul of Cousin Edgar to refuse to pay that debt. It was, he felt, a matter of honor. Besides, once married to Cousin Olivetta, five minutes after the ceremony he would be able to sign the checks with his own fair hand.

This was such a convincing argument with Cousin Edgar that at once he prepared to move ahead, and he went to his cousin's wife. She blushed with pleasure at the sight of him, and he took both her hands and printed a brotherly kiss upon her brow.

"My dear Olivetta, we must make a decision."

She trembled with excitement.

"We have waited long enough. Today I am going to call in the preacher."

"Good heavens!" she exclaimed.

"Doctor Cornish will be the man, I think," said Cousin Edgar.

"Louise will be furious. She'll never let us!" objected poor Mrs. Asprey.

"Ah, child," he answered, "you are speaking to one who knows no master, except his helpless love for you, my dear."

Mrs. Asprey sat down with a thud in the nearest chair. "What will people say?" she murmured.

"Do we care?"

"I'm not a marriageable age, Edgar."

"I don't think," he said, "that people will gossip long about my wife."

Mrs. Asprey caught her breath. "They wouldn't dare say a word, Edgar, would they?"

"They certainly would not. I'll send for Doctor Cornish. . . ."

"I must tell Louise, first."

"We'll tell her afterwards. When we walk in, man and wife, she will see that talking is useless. Louise is stubborn, but she has sense."

The directness of these suggestions carried Mrs. Asprey lightly before them like a cork before a flood. "But," she went on, "I've always felt that a wedding that isn't in a church. . . ."

"And white veils, my dear?"

"Well, Edgar. . . ."

"You see, that sort of thing might get even us talked about. But a quiet marriage at home . . . that's different. I'll walk down the street and get Cornish. He's a good fellow and will do very well." Cousin Edgar walked from the room.

Mrs. Asprey set about dressing. At least, she felt that she must appear in her best for the wedding, and she had in mind a certain pink dress of taffeta, too rich for ordinary occasions. When she looked through her closets, there was no trace of it. Half dressed, she hurried to her daughter's room and tapped.

"Louise, Louise?"

"Yes, mother?"

"You know my pink taffeta?"

"Of course." Louise opened the door.

"I can't find it anywhere!" said Mrs. Asprey.

"You gave it to me last year," said Louise, "because you decided that it would never do for you again. It was too small in the waist.

Don't you remember?"

"Oh, heavens, " Mrs. Asprey stated. "Of course, I remember. I haven't a scrap of sense."

"What in the world," said Louise, "could make you want the pink taffeta on a day like this?" She pointed toward the window, and Mrs. Asprey remembered that the taffeta had been a very warm dress, indeed. It was a burning summer day. The dusty street glared like white metal.

"I really don't know," said Mrs. Asprey. "I just wanted to see if it needed patching," she finished lamely.

"Didn't you want to put it on?" asked Louise.

Under the calm, steady eye of her daughter, Mrs. Asprey turned pale.

"You're upset about something," said Louise.

"I'll go back to my room and lie down," said the mother, who only wanted to escape.

"You'd better come in here," said Louise. When Cousin Edgar was not near, she knew perfectly well how to direct the scattered wits of her mother. Now she took her arm and escorted her deliberately into the room. "Do you want to lie down or sit in the big chair?"

"I think I'll just sit," Mrs. Asprey muttered. Her voice was shaking with fear and excitement, and in the big chair she took her place, bolt upright, her hands clasped tightly in her lap.

"Poor darling Mother," said the girl, a warmth of affection coming over her. For she knew that of all kind women in the world, none was kinder than her poor mother, none had a better heart; few had more random wits.

"I have a great deal to do," said Mrs. Asprey. "I think that I'd better. . . ."

"A great deal to do?" Louise echoed. "I wonder what you can have to do . . . on such a warm day?"

"I have to get ready . . . ," began Mrs. Asprey, and then stopped, shocked by the confession that she had been about to make.

"For a trip, dear?" asked the girl.

Mrs. Asprey was on the point of starting from the chair and bolting for the door, in order to escape that clear, inquiring eye. She had feared her daughter since Louise was a mere child. She literally dreaded her now.

"In a way . . . that is . . . not exactly. I really must go, Louise."

"Very well," said Louise. "I'll help you, then."

"Oh, no!" Mrs. Asprey snapped.

"But, dear, if you're in a hurry, you know. . . ."

"But this is a secret, Louise."

"A secret?"

"What have I said?" Mrs. Asprey repri-
manded herself.

"That it's a secret. Of course, I don't want
to make you tell me about it."

"Thank you, child." Mrs. Asprey stood up.

"If it's something I shouldn't know," persisted Louise.

Mrs. Asprey began to speak and stopped.
It gave the effect of a gasp. "I don't . . . I
don't dare tell you, Louise!"

"Why don't you, dear?"

"Because you're so critical."

"Not a bit."

"You are, you are! Of me, always."

"Mother dear, what's troubling you? This
secret . . . it won't make you happy, I'm
afraid."

"I knew you'd say that!" cried Mrs.
Asprey. She clasped her jeweled fingers together and gazed sadly at the girl.

"But you seem so close to tears."

"Because you frighten me so, Louise."

"But I'm only trying to take care of you,
Mother."

"I suppose you are," moaned Mrs. Asprey.
"But I don't want you to."

"Did anyone forbid you to tell me the secret?"

"Cousin Edgar would be very angry."

"I suspected that he had something to do with it," said Louise, with the chilliest of smiles.

"You never give him his due," said trembling Mrs. Asprey. "And we both agree that it's right . . . and you're only a child, Louise . . . and you don't know anything about such matters."

"What matters?" said Louise.

"Marriage," Mrs. Asprey answered. Then she caught a hand to her mouth. "Heavens! I've said it!"

Her daughter shrank back to the door and turned the key. "Marriage!" she echoed.

Mrs. Asprey dropped back into the big chair from which she had risen. "Oh, Louise, don't!" she pleaded.

"Marriage?" said the girl in a changed voice.

"Cousin Edgar says that we should," Mrs. Asprey pleaded.

"Cousin Edgar!" echoed the girl bitterly.

"Oh, Louise, you're going to be terrible to me . . . I know you are, and I can't stand it." She began to tremble violently.

"You're going to be married to Cousin Edgar. Today! That's why you wanted the dress? Where are you to be married?"

"Here, Louise."

"In this house?"

"Yes."

"When?"

"Edgar has gone for the clergyman."

"Now?"

"Yes."

There was a sound of steps on the front porch. Then the door closed and sent its heavy jar shivering through the frame house.

"He's come . . . and I'm . . . I'm not even dressed," said Mrs. Asprey. She started up from the chair, and, like a child running in the dark, she rushed toward the door, turned the key, and dashed out and down the hall with a little moan of relief as she left the room.

Louise had slipped to one side and now stood hesitant, uncertain whether or not she should follow.

Chapter Thirty-Seven

INTERRUPTION

Doctor Cornish, the minister, was a very good man, but, also, he was very old. He wore one heavy pair of glasses when he was reading, and he wore two pairs for the great outdoors. Those glasses had been made for him fifteen years before, and in the interim his sight had grown dimmer and dimmer. The good man felt that it was the passage of time and the will of God that handicapped him, and, although sometimes he prayed for more light, he had taught himself to submit to every physical discomfort. On the level ground, as a matter of fact, he did very well. And if there were someone to guide him up and down stairs, he could get on with perfect comfort.

In the library of the Asprey house he stood by the table, resting one hand on its surface to steady himself, but, when he was sure of his place, he took off the outer pair of spectacles and looked down to the wedding service. From that moment he could see nothing but a mist, five feet away from him.

319

In that mist stood one light-colored figure — the woman — one dark colored form — the man.

He had shaken hands with them both and said to Mrs. Asprey: "I have not seen you and your husband lately, Missus Asprey."

She almost fainted, but the minister turned away with his bland and absent-minded smile. He missed Robert Asprey, but he made no connection between that thought and the marriage of Mrs. Asprey on this day. He was very old, indeed. Besides, he was excited. On the way to the house, Edgar Asprey had said something about the building of a new small wing in the church, where a little library could be installed.

Doctor Cornish now closed his eyes and repeated a little speech that he had composed fifty years before and that he always spoke at every marriage ceremony. Sometimes he paused and faltered, but that was not because he was trying to think of new words and phrases; it was merely because he was forgetting the old ones, like an actor who has been too long in one part.

He finished the little speech and got into the preliminary business. Mrs. Asprey had become strangely calm. Presently, in one of the pauses, she whispered: "Edgar, dear, you're trembling."

"Because," said Edgar Asprey, "because, Olivetta, you mean all the world to me. I can't believe that I've come to this happy moment."

Her rather worn face became almost beautiful as she looked up to him in silent response.

Then the voice of the minister began again after the pause. His voice was as uncertain as his step. He moved in waves — a high wave and then a low wave. What he murmured in the first part of this sentence was really not audible, but in the end his voice swelled strongly: "Speak now, or forever hold his peace!"

Something rustled at the end of the room. Edgar Asprey said through his teeth something that sounded to Mrs. Asprey fearfully like: "Damnation!"

"I know a reason why this marriage should not take place," said Louise.

The sound came thin and small as distant bells to the mind of Doctor Cornish. He turned about cumbrously. "Dear me, dear me, dear me!" said the good doctor. "Do you, indeed? And what do you know, my dear little girl?"

She came closer, and the minister, with a start, realized that some dozen years separated the real Louise from his thought of

321

her. She was a woman, not a child.

"Louise," said Edgar Asprey in quivering fury, "if you. . . ." He paused, choked.

"Oh, what is she going to do? What is she going to do?" moaned Mrs. Asprey.

"There's a reason why this marriage cannot take place," said the girl.

"A reason? What reason?" asked Doctor Cornish, leaning forward to peer more closely at her.

"My father is still alive," she said.

Mrs. Asprey screamed. It was not a loud noise, but it seemed to come from her very heart. "I knew that there was something wrong," she cried.

"It's false! It's false!" said Cousin Edgar. "Louise, God forgive you for such a speech!"

"This begins to be confusing," said Doctor Cornish. "Robert Asprey. . . ."

"Has been dead for five years," broke in Edgar Asprey.

"He's living at the moment . . . and you know it very well," answered Louise.

"I don't want to disagree with you, child," said Cousin Edgar, mastering himself, although the effort left his face patched with white and purple. "I simply want you to understand that you must offer a proof. . . ."

"I have a letter from him in my hand this

moment," she said.

It was like a silent explosion, if such a thing can be imagined — a silent moving picture explosion. There was no sound, but all the people in the room were flung back a step or so, staggered. Even Cousin Edgar shrank and crouched a little, and caught at the back of a chair.

"I don't believe it," he managed to say.

"It's true! It's true!" said Mrs. Asprey. "Oh, Edgar, how dreadful! How perfectly terrible! Why did you want me to marry you? What shall I do? What will people say? What will Robert . . . ?"

Quite overcome, she might have fallen, had not Cousin Edgar caught her and placed her in a chair. He laid a hand on her forehead.

"Now be calm and quiet," he said. "I'm going to show you that this is the result of some malicious plot. Louise, I want to see that letter!"

He seemed to have hypnotized Mrs. Asprey. She sat bolt upright, white and still, her eyes fixed vaguely before her.

"I'll never let you put your hands on this letter," said Louise.

"Give it to Doctor Cornish, then."

"Very well. Can you see it, Doctor Cornish? Will you read it aloud?"

The doctor took it and read it aloud. He read it slowly. He made frequent pauses to gasp. Finally, he turned and confronted Edgar Asprey in accusing silence. But by this time Cousin Edgar was quite himself.

He said sadly, without bitterness, to Louise: "I wanted to prepare you for what is coming, but you've drawn it on your own head, my child. Malice will draw down harm, Louise, and most evil and malicious have you been today."

"You despicable hypocrite!" exclaimed the girl. "Oh, how utterly I despise you."

"Handsome is as handsome does," said Cousin Edgar. "Very soon we shall have a chance to look into the motives and into the mind of this girl, my friends. I trust that there will be no great shock to her poor mother. Ah, well, Doctor Cornish, have no fear. This will all come out right, and the experience will be a lesson, I humbly trust, to this bold, rude girl." He turned to Mrs. Asprey. "In that desk are some of Robert's letters, I believe?"

"Yes, Edgar," she said faintly.

"In the left hand drawer?"

"Yes. In the left hand drawer."

"Now you shall see," said Cousin Edgar. He went to the desk and worked open the drawer. From it he took a ragged sheaf of letters. "May I open one?"

"Yes, Edgar," Mrs. Asprey said in the same dead, hopeless voice.

He took it from an envelope and placed it upon the table. "Now, Olivetta, Doctor Cornish, please to consider the two hand-writings side by side."

Louise saw the point at once and turned cold with apprehension. Five years before, her father had carried on a copious correspondence. He had done much written business. Now he had been living in the wilderness. His hands were stiff with labor. Perhaps he had not written a thousand words in all that time. No wonder, if the hand were changed so, that it would have required a great expert to see the similarities.

Mrs. Asprey walked mechanically to the table and stared at the two specimens. Doctor Cornish then murmured: "An extraordinary dissimilarity."

"How dissimilar," said Cousin Edgar, "I think I can show you still better. I think, in fact, that almost anyone could have copied poor dear Robert's hand far better than in this attempt. See this, for instance." He took his pen and wrote with a good deal of rapidity on the sheet of paper that Louise had produced — **Error will be seen at last!**

"A very true sentiment," said Doctor Cornish, pleased.

"Thank you," said Cousin Edgar. "You see that even a careless imitation like mine is really nearer to dear Robert's hand than this rude and clumsy thing."

As a matter of fact, at the first glance it seemed that there was no difference at all, so extremely alike was the hand in which Cousin Edgar had turned off his small maxim to the body of the old letter with which it was compared.

"Ah, ah, ah!" came from Doctor Cornish. "But who can have written this letter from Robert Asprey, then?"

"Doctor Cornish," said Cousin Edgar, "the matter is perfectly plain. You are too good a man to suspect the truth even now. But the truth is that Louise always has opposed me in this house. She always has hated me. By heavens, Doctor Cornish, it is perfectly obvious that she had made this very clumsy forgery and with it tried to ruin me and stop the marriage. But, thank heaven, she has failed." He turned. "Olivetta, I know that *your* faith is not shaken. Let us go straight forward with the ceremony and. . . ."

"I feel rather dizzy, Edgar, I . . . I. . . ."

"Of course, you do. Lean on me. You'll be

quite all right in a moment. The dreadfulness of Louise. . . ."

"Louise," repeated the mother faintly, catching at the word. "I want Louise . . . Louise, where are you?"

The girl was instantly beside her, supporting her with strong young arms.

"Louise, darling, I think I'd better go to bed. Will you help me?"

Chapter Thirty-Eight

A PARTING

In the hills above the capital, Geraldi and Robert Asprey took council. Their plans had come to wreck. The governor was more firmly set against the idea of a pardon than ever, and Edgar Asprey was free to do what he chose.

They sat about a small fire in the dusk of the evening and considered possibilities — Asprey darkly and sadly, Geraldi with the perpetual freshness of a youth. Asprey puffed solemnly at a pipe. Geraldi smoked a cigarette and whiffed the puffs strongly into the air, where the draft above the fire carried them high.

"This job is finished and failed," said Robert Asprey gloomily. "The thing for you to do, my lad, is to go on with your own life."

"Very good," said Geraldi, "and what shall that life be, Asprey?"

"Whatever you choose to make it," said the older man.

"Guess it out for me," suggested Geraldi.

Robert Asprey lifted his head, and the red of

the firelight flickered upon his strong face. "You'll have your days," he remarked.

"Expand that a little. What sort of days?"

"Cards . . . they'll bring you in enough. You have a fat wallet there even now, Geraldi."

"I have," admitted Geraldi. "But a thousand of this goes to pay a debt."

"A debt?"

"To poor Chalmers."

"Why do you call him that? He was always a savage brute, and now he's dead. Interrupted in the midst of an attempted murder."

"That may be true. But I picked a thousand out of his pocket. Well, that was only a forced loan, as you might call it. I never would keep that sort of money."

The thoughts of Robert Asprey lifted from his own affairs, and he considered the youth gravely. "You don't keep that sort of money, Geraldi?"

"Never. I don't live as a sneak thief, either, Asprey." He laughed at the thought. "It was only to help myself around a corner," he continued in explanation.

"Very well," Asprey said, "but tell me the real difference between picking money out of a man's pocket and taking it away from him at cards. Can you do that?"

"Easily," answered the youth. "When I pick the money out of his pocket, I'm taking advantage of him."

"But when you . . . beat him at cards?"

"Cheat him, you meant to say?"

"Call it that, then," said Asprey, smiling at the frankness of his companion.

"The only games in which I sit are those where the players are old-timers . . . frankly crooked. They expect to keep their eyes out for the others. If I can beat them, when their eyes are open, that's the fortune of war."

"You never impose on a helpless greenhorn?"

Geraldi smiled. Then, after a pause in which he considered, he went on: "It's true that I play for a living, but, chiefly, I play for fun."

Asprey nodded. "Suppose that you had a chance to go straight?" he asked.

"I've had a thousand such chances," answered the youth, and shrugged his shoulders.

"Not enough excitement?"

"Suppose that I do . . . what? Work in a bank?"

Asprey grunted. "Handle real estate," he suggested. "That's exciting enough, in its own way."

"Suppose that people came back at me

and blamed me for telling lies about the land that I sold to them?"

"What about the people who come back to reproach you, now?"

"No one comes back. When they find that they're beaten, they chuck up their hands and admit that they've been fools. And there you are. I have no yesterdays in my business. It's all tomorrows."

Asprey laughed, delighted with the novelty of this viewpoint. "Very well," he murmured. "I won't forget. You'll be a free man to the end of your days?"

"Only one thing will stop me," Geraldi stated.

"And that?"

"I'm human. And women are women. I may find one someday who'll make a slave of me."

"Have you ever been very near to slavery, my lad?"

"I am now."

"Ah?"

Geraldi rolled another cigarette, lighted it, and tossed the match far away. "Shall I be frank?"

"That's what I want."

"Well," said Geraldi, "I've had a few glimpses of your daughter. I beg your pardon. I shouldn't speak like this even after you've invited me. But as a matter of fact, I think that I'm in danger from her, Asprey."

The big man frowned, and under his gathered brows he looked fixedly at the fire.

"I don't know," he said slowly, at last. "Our old systems of morality . . . what good are they? Our old law, what good is it? It's driven me into the wilderness for five years. It's robbed me of the cream of my life. Well, I haven't a right to criticize. If Louise should happen to grow fond of you, I'd never throw a straw in your way." He added suddenly: "Because, Geraldi, you're better than you think."

"You don't know me," answered Geraldi. "You've never had a chance to hear what I've done."

"I've gathered enough," said Asprey. "You've picked a lock here, and you've blown a safe there. You've rambled around the world and made it your meat. Well, you had the brains to do it. You were looking for excitement, not crime."

Geraldi smiled. "Never more excitement than here," he admitted. "And what have we come to, Asprey?"

"To what I said before. Run away, my lad. You can't help me here."

"And you?"

"I'm back for the mountains. There I'll sit

out another five years, perhaps, and see what happens to me."

"You've done with this sitting and thinking," answered Geraldi. "You never can get away from them so completely again. From now on, they'll start hounding you and never stop. I know the crew. They'll be after you, as they've been after me."

"You've kept away from them, and so will I."

"You won't," answered Geraldi judiciously. "You're not fast enough afoot. You don't know how to travel except on a horse. And you're not keen enough with a gun. They'll have you inside of six months."

To this, Asprey returned no answer. Finally he got up, picked up a dead branch, that he had broken off in the bushes nearby, and threw it into the flames. The fire rose in a lofty yellow arm and wagged high in the evening shadows.

"You're asking for a quick finish, I see?" Geraldi commented.

Asprey shrugged his shoulders. "You run on and take care of yourself," he said. "I'm handling this affair for myself. And," he added sharply, "I don't need advice." He glowered at Geraldi, and then around him into the shadows.

The youth whistled, and in the circle of

the firelight, instantly, stalked the gray mare, Zuleikha.

"I take you at your word," he said.

"I want you to."

Geraldi stood up and shook hands, and the older man said slowly: "My head is filled with my own troubles, Geraldi. I haven't the ability just now to think for you, or else I should try to show you another side of life. All I can say is . . . of all the men I've met in the world, you've been the straightest, the bravest, and the truest. God bless you, Geraldi, and bring you happiness. Good bye, my lad!"

Geraldi answered slowly: "I could make a longer speech than that. Let me tell you this. You've made up your mind to stand in the way of trouble and throw yourself into the fire. You don't care what happens. Asprey, I'd like to hear you promise me that for three days you'll take care of yourself."

The big man smiled sadly. "How would you have me do that?" he asked.

"Give me every bullet in your belt," Geraldi suggested. "Let me take away every chance you have of doing damage. Will you let me do that?"

Asprey hesitated. Then he answered with gloomily fallen head: "I can't let you, Geraldi."

"I knew it," said the boy. "Old man, I may meet you again in a different time. So long till then."

"Ride for the upper hills," said the veteran. "Ride for them, and keep high. You'll slip through their hands, that way, but, if you keep to the lowlands and the easy trails, they'll have you inside of three days. They're very hot to get you, Geraldi."

The boy nodded. Then, with a wave of the hand, he sprang into the saddle and turned the mare into the hills above them. He rode on until he was well out of sight and out of hearing. Then he swung Zuleikha to the left.

She made a long semicircle through a gorge. Over the left hand brim he climbed her again, and then turned her straight down toward the lights of the capital city. Once more it was spread out well before his eyes, and the long, dim arms of light extended over the surface of the lake. He dropped her down the incline rapidly, and across the boulevard, and so down the first street that pointed toward the heart of the town.

A buckboard jogged by. He hailed it, and it drew up, the noisy rattling of floorboards came to an end.

"D'you know where Colonel Joe Green lives?"

The other answered heartily: "I know

Smiling Joe better'n I know myself. Turn back to the boulevard. It's the second house on the left."

Chapter Thirty-Nine

ON THE ROAD

On every side of the house of Colonel Joe Green stretched broad, naked fields. Before him, the land sloped sharply down to the lake, and all for hundreds of yards on either side was his own. Someday, he told himself, he would sell that property for half a million — unless he chose to spend, here, the days of his retirement. In the meantime, he was hoping to convert the section into a sort of park that would encourage building all around it. He had planted the trees three or four years ago, and now they had grown up into a formidable little wood. That formed the cover under which Geraldi approached the house.

He came from the side and tried the first lighted window. He saw a servant clearing away a dining table. He turned to the front and climbed to another window. There he looked in upon an interesting group: Colonel Smiling Joe and Dick Renney, gunman extraordinary. They were having coffee,

Renney looking rather ill at ease with his coffee cup. He had a broad bandage around his head, gathered to a point above the nose, so that he could look out from either eye. The wind was blowing in strong, rattling gusts, and Geraldi could not hear a thing. Therefore, he took the jimmy from his coat and inserted it in under the window. Thrice, when the wind screamed, he applied leverage. Thrice the window gave upward a little. The third time it opened an inch or two. The lock had been forced apart. Applying his ear to that crack, he heard everything that was said within the room, and there was much of interest.

Smiling Joe was telling a tale of his early days, and then of his hardships undergone when he first came West. He broke off with a glance at his watch.

"You better start, Renney."

"Is it time?"

"You got a half hour to get to the head of the lake."

"How do I know this gent?"

"He'll be on a gray horse. Wait a minute." He took a telegram from his pocket and read: **Messenger with stuff on gray horse, looking white. Coming down at eight, or after. Watch at head of lake.**

Renney grinned suddenly. "Suppose I cop

this stuff and beat it, governor?"

"What good would it do you? It's stock that I can handle, and you won't know how to."

"It's checked, then," asked Renney.

"Absolutely safe."

"All right," sighed Renney. "I'll go and collect that fifty thousand."

"You'd better simply play escort and bring him in to me."

"Suppose that he don't want to follow?"

"You just ride on ahead."

"I don't see the point," answered Renney frankly.

"Of course, you don't. But if we're going to have trouble, I want you to be the vanguard."

Renney grunted vigorously.

"You draw the fire, and the coin comes through safe," grinned Colonel Green.

Geraldi, having heard enough, slipped down from his place of vantage, but not before, with the greatest of care lest it should squeak, he had pushed down the window. He had struck out more or less at random from Robert Asprey, but now he felt that he had made a strike that might be very useful.

He went back through the young trees to the mare, and with her returned at full gallop up the boulevard to the head of the lake. There was no moon, only starlight, but it was sufficiently bright to enable him to identify the form of a gray horse and rider. He passed up around the end of the lake until he was at the side of a hill, steeply and thickly covered with tall young saplings. Among them he drew in and waited.

Impatience urged him to push farther on, but he was afraid lest he should take the wrong trail, and there was a forking only fifty yards to the west. In this manner he waited for a long half hour. Then a rattling of hoofs approached. He looked out and saw a rider whose horse might have been either black or white. For a following wind was carrying a cloud of dust along with him, and the color of the horse failed to show through at all. He let that one pass on, although he was vigorously tempted to ride in pursuit. But hardly had the hoofbeats died in the distance, when he heard another rider coming up fast with the wind.

The air changed. This time there was a naked horse and rider, with a filmy veil hanging shadowy to the rear. And far away the rider seemed mounted on a marble horse in motion. Not gray, but nearly white it appeared. Geraldi gathered the mare under him with a word. He waited until the other was fifty yards away, and then moved onto the road. He held Zuleikha with his knees and his voice. His left hand he lifted to stop the messenger, if it were he. His right hand was ready at his gun, for, if he were stopping the wrong man, assuredly he would be paid with a bullet on the spot. Questions were asked after action, in this part of the world.

The rider was seen, presently, hunching back on the reins. With high-held shoulders he came to a halt, and the cloud of his dust billowed softly forward and enveloped Geraldi with its pungency.

"Who are you?" asked the messenger.

"Who are you, my friend?" answered Geraldi.

"And what the hell business is it of yours?" came the hostile rejoinder.

"I'll tell you why."

"Shoot it, kid."

"You're from Sankeytown."

"What?"

"Sankeytown. You want the name?"

"Wait a minute," said the other. "Lemme have your name, will you?"

"That's not in the bargain," Geraldi stated.

"It sure is," said the other. "I gotta see your face, and know it. Light a match, will you?"

Geraldi paused, troubled. If his face were seen, it would draw a bullet almost surely. He reached in his pocket. "Just a minute," he said. He opened a match box and scratched several matches. Audibly they snapped and produced no light, for the good reason that he was scratching the butts instead of the sulphur heads. "Damned matches no good," complained Geraldi. "But here, kid. You light one and be a lantern for me, will you?"

"I don't mind," chuckled the other. "Do I know you?"

"You'll laugh when you see me," said Geraldi, and rode his horse closer.

The messenger presently occupied both hands with matches, and, as he lighted the first one and cast its blue flame, turning yellow, toward Geraldi, he saw the light shudder along the blue barrel of a Colt. "God A'mighty!" gasped the messenger. "Geraldi!" He thrust his hands suddenly above his head. "Don't kill me, Geraldi," he gasped. "I never done you no harm, old man."

"Where's the stuff?" asked Geraldi.

"Here in the saddlebag . . . here on the left side."

Geraldi pulled the flap of the other's gun belt. His guns rattled heavily to the ground.

"Bring down your hands and light a match," he suggested. "Only mind that I'm watching all the time."

"Trust me," said the other, with a frightened laugh. "I take no chances with you. There ain't money enough in the world to hire me for that."

"Who are you?"

"Wally Dace."

"Who do you belong to?"

"I used to work for Chalmers."

"And then you shifted to Asprey?"

"He wanted this job done."

"Do you know what's in the bag?"

"Papers for Colonel Green."

"Eh?"

"That's all that I was told, and to hoof it along fast."

"Humph!" said Geraldi.

Carefully, making sure that each motion was safely slow, the messenger brought up and opened the saddlebag. Then he took from it a package of papers and held it forth with a lighted match for Geraldi's inspection. There was no question that this was the right messenger.

"Who else started with you?" asked Geraldi, suspicious that there might be more than one.

"I came on alone."

"Dace, will you listen to me?"

"Sure I will, Geraldi."

"I've got this stuff. It's damned valuable. If you go on with the news to Green, he'll jail you for a thief. If you go back to tell Asprey what happened to you, he'll have you skinned alive. What'll you do?"

"Run for the tall grass."

"Here's fifty. Take care of yourself."

"You're square, Geraldi, even if this busts me. So long."

"So long," said Geraldi. "Cut up here, through the woods. And if you come back this way. . . ."

"No fear of that."

"Very well, then. So long."

Wally Dace dipped into the brush. It was heard crackling rapidly under the stride of the horse. Finally that sound diminished, and in its place Geraldi heard the rattling gallop of a horse at full speed up the road.

The rider drew up to a slow trot as he came nearer. As he went by, Geraldi, reining back into the brush, looked out on the familiar outline of Renney against the stars.

Chapter Forty

WHAT YOU PAY FOR

In the office of Chalmers's hotel at Sankey-town was passionate dispute. There his three nephews had gathered. For it was learned that the dead man had left no will, and, accordingly, the estate was to be left to the nearest kin in equal portions — to wit, to each of the three nephews would be given one third. The great question was how the estate should be split up. For it consisted of three bits — land, hotel, and cattle on a nearby ranch. None of the three would be contented with any single portion; none knew which share to pick. They had sat up the night, expecting to reach a solution, but none yet hove on the horizon of their minds.

They had consulted King Alcohol, that great adjuster, and King Alcohol had driven them mad with eager hatred of one another. Now they were snarling like three dogs — three shaggy dogs, hair over their eyes, left hands on whiskey glasses, right hands free for weapons. They did not notice that the gray of dawn was in the windows until the door opened softly and a slender young man stood inside in the shadows.

"You're the heirs of Chalmers, I hear?" he said pleasantly.

"And what the hell do you want?" asked one of the trio.

"I want nothing. I want to give," said the stranger. "I wanted to tell you that I owed your uncle a thousand dollars, and I've come to pay it back." He laid a little packet of money on a table near the door. Then he stepped back into it.

"So that you'll know that I've cleared off the . . . loan," said the stranger, "I'll leave my name with you. I'm Geraldi." He closed the door and turned down the hall as three bullets from three guns smote that door and split it from head to heel. Three charging stalwarts burst into the hallway. There was no Geraldi in sight. One lunged for the front door, and found it locked from the outside. The other two rushed back from the open rear door, and their united shoulders smashed the door open. They lurched onto the front porch, but they found that Geraldi already was out of sight. Only down the street, a stir of dust, faintly visible in the growing morning light, might have told of his passage.

A little after that, certain knocks came at the rear door of Sam Lorenz. The little pawnbroker lifted his head and listened to them in doubt. They were repeated. Two knocks with an interval between. Two light knocks. A heavy one after another interval.

Sam Lorenz, with a gasp, leaped from his bed. He did not wait to put on a bathrobe. He did not wait to shove his feet into slippers, but, regardless of dangerous long splinters of the boot-worn flooring of his shop, regardless of the chill of the air of the early morning, he rushed to the secret rear door of his place and slid back the well-oiled bolts and then thrust the door open with all his might. He recoiled from the sight of Geraldi. Then, with a little cry, he ran past him and took the head of the gray mare in his arms.

"You *have* come back. You *have* come back," said the little man. "Ah, but she's hot."

"Not at all," said Geraldi. "You had her as soft as grass, and I've stripped some of the fat off her. She's in good hard condition, now. She's in the condition that counts. She could run a hundred miles over hills or desert between now and darkness."

"Anyway, she's back," said the pawnbroker, and ran to get on some clothes.

Then he returned and led the way to the small stable, where the horse was put in her former stall. Together they fed her and rubbed her down. Poor Lorenz looked over the saddle and the stirrups with the greatest care, and then examined the mare inch by inch. There was a slightly swollen spot where the cinch had passed around her.

He complained loudly at this, but Geraldi merely replied: "You can't have your cake and eat it. Let's have some breakfast, Jimmy."

Lorenz winced. "Don't use that name," he whispered. "Come along. At least, she's not dead . . . she's back here."

"She'll die of fat, if you keep her the way you've been doing," said Geraldi, as they walked out of the stable.

A soft whinny came from behind them.

"Listen!" Lorenz said, delighted. "She don't want me to go."

"Go back and talk to her," suggested Geraldi.

The little man, nothing loath, hurried back to his pet, but again the whinny sounded.

Two brief words of Arabic were spoken by Geraldi, and the gray became silent.

Sam Lorenz came out into the cold, pale morning with a gloomy look. He turned this on Geraldi, and then went on to his shop with downward eyes, saying nothing. Plainly he did not relish the manner in which the youth had stolen the affections of the horse.

Geraldi followed him. They passed together to the rear of the shop where there was a small kitchen with a table covered with oilcloth from which they could eat. Geraldi set out a battered pair of plates, nicked cups, and an odd assortment of knives and forks and spoons. Over the stove the old man began to rumble.

"Nothing was good enough for her. When they showed me oats, I sifted 'em by hand. I worked her up everyday. Brushed her and rubbed her down. No curry comb ever touched her. She was kept as clean as a whistle. I changed her bedding every day. Nothing but the whitest and driest straw. All she could eat, and the best of everything." He paused and cast another accusing look at Geraldi. "And now what?" he continued. "She's forgot me! Mares and women! Mares and women!"

"I'll take her off your hands," said Geraldi.

The pawnbroker snorted. "I paid fifteen hundred for her," he said, settling that suggestion instantly. "A damn' bad debt . . . and

I took the mare for it."

"I have fifteen hundred in hard cash, ready to count out to you," said Geraldi.

The little man turned and stared. "Fifteen hundred? Would you pay that much?"

"I have it here. Will you take it?"

The pawnbroker writhed and then shook his head. "I have her, and I'll keep her. She's my luck," he said at last. "And now what d'you want, Geraldi? What's brought you back so soon?"

"The mare brought me back," said Geraldi, smiling. "I'll raise that to my top offer, man. Here you have her locked in a stable growing fat, losing her wind. When you ever need a horse, you'll need one that can run and keep on running. I'll give you my top offer at once . . . two thousand for the mare, Lorenz."

"Two . . . thousand . . . dollars?" echoed the pawnbroker.

"Yes," said Geraldi.

The little man moistened his lips. He had grown pale with emotion. "You be damned!" he said suddenly, and turned his back with resolution.

"You miss something, here," said Geraldi. "You've got a mare that's growing older every day. Liable to get diseases, standing cooped up there, like that."

"That's my business," snapped the other.

"I offer you five hundred clean profit. Do you think you could get that from any other person? That's the price for a race horse, and a damned good one, at that." He paused.

Sam Lorenz, for answer, stirred the lids of the stove, coughed, rattled the coffee pot to drown the voice of the tempter.

"Very well," said Geraldi. "I'll give in to you, then. Twenty-five hundred dollars. And here I have it for you." He took a sheaf of bills into his hands.

At this Sam Lorenz whirled and shook his fist at his guest.

"What do you want?" he said. "You're young . . . you're gay. You got everything that you want. I've got nothing but that mare, and now you'll take that away from me."

Geraldi stood at the table, counting. "Fifteen, sixteen, seventeen, eighteen, nineteen . . . two thousand dollars and more to come."

"Damn your money and damn you!" squeaked Sam Lorenz. "Who are you? You come here and give me the word. I take you in. I fix you up. I treat you fine. And then you try to get the mare! You're the devil!"

"Twenty-one," said the inexorable Geraldi, continuing his counting slowly and placing one crisp hundred dollar bill on top of the other. "Twenty-two, twenty-three. . . ."

"Stop it!" cried the pawnbroker. "I don't want your money. Let it choke you! I don't want it!"

"Twenty-four . . . twenty-five. And there you are, Jimmy. Twenty-five hundred dollars."

He stood back and seemed to admire the stack of money. Lorenz stood spellbound, observing it, also. He had been stirring the fire with the poker, and now this tool quivered in his grasp as though he were about to strike the offending pile of money, like a personal enemy.

"That makes a thousand dollars clear profit," said Geraldi, as though the thought had just struck him.

"It's counterfeit," growled Sam Lorenz.

"Look and see, then."

The hand that Lorenz held forth actually quivered with eagerness and with aversion. But at length, he snatched the handful of money and began to finger it. He made as if to replace it, then, convulsively, thrust it into his pocket.

"God give you bad luck with her," he said bitterly. "You've taken the pleasure out of my life, Geraldi."

"Bah," said Geraldi. "You still have your stuff . . . your stuff half bought and half stolen. You have what you pay for, my friend, and so have I. It's time to try that coffee."

Chapter Forty-One

A PROMISE KEPT

Beside the kitchen there was a little room hardly larger than a cubbyhole. There Geraldi lay down and slept after his breakfast. He slept from sunrise to late morning, and then he was wakened by the sound of voices — particularly the sound of one voice, big, rich, booming — the voice of Joe Green.

He was saying to the pawnbroker: "Send up word to Edgar Asprey that I want to see him here, and I want him quick!"

Geraldi rose, drew on his boots, and was still smiling as he buckled on his gun belt. He had hoped that there might be a break in the ranks of the enemy when the fifty thousand dollars had disappeared. He touched a comfortable lump of money in his breast pocket and smiled again.

Another voice took up the tale. It was the harsh snarl of Renney, saying: "Lorenz, I hear that you've given Geraldi the gray mare that he's riding now?"

"He stole it from me," said the pawnbroker, lying with a fervid vigor. "He stole it from me, and damn him for the stealing!"

"She don't run . . . she flies!" Renney shouted. "I never seen such a horse."

"You!" broke out Joe Green with a sudden violence. "You had him in your hands a whole day, and you never took him! Are you blind?"

"You sat and played cards with him," retorted Renney. "Did his make-up look phony to you?"

"How did he get that make-up?" asked Joe Green. "I thought that old Lorenz was the only man who could make up people as good as that."

"I'm to blame for everything, am I?" asked Lorenz dryly. "What's happened to the pair of you. Been beaten by Geraldi?"

"No, by God," answered Renney. "We've beaten him, smart and smooth as he is. We've beaten him in every side of the game. We made a fool of him!"

"Good," said Lorenz. "Where is he now?"

"Running like hell to get out of the way of the law. He's a couple of hundred miles away from here, by this time."

"I hope he rots," said Lorenz. "I hated the slick look of him, the crook!"

"Honest old Sam," sneered Joe Green. "He can't help hating the crooks. Have you seen Edgar Asprey lately?"

"He never did much business with me," answered the pawnbroker.

"Didn't he? He'll be doing business pretty soon, though. He's gonna marry Missus Asprey at six this afternoon."

"He thinks he is," said Renney. "But he talks turkey to us, first."

They talked at random, skipping from point to point, but Geraldi listened gloomily. If that marriage was about to take place, then all the work that he had done had been undone, and the case of Louise Asprey was almost hopelessly lost.

Presently there was a tap at the door. Joe Green answered it, and he came back, furious.

"Edgar Asprey is out of town and won't be back till five. We gotta wait around all day in this rat hole of yours, Lorenz! What you got to amuse us?"

"A pack of cards," suggested the fence genially. "Sit down, my friends, and . . . I'll deal for you."

"You'll be the house?"

"Just to keep you amused."

"You damned old dried up man, you'd give us a square deal, I suppose?" asked Renney. "Leave the cards be. I'm gonna sleep."

"There's no good place," commented Lorenz in some haste.

"Ain't there a layout near the kitchen?"

"There's not much air. . . ."

"Hell, there's enough for me. I'm tired."

Geraldi slipped from the little room, took care to close the door behind him, and glided across the kitchen. He had barely disappeared into the passage beyond, when Renney entered, opened the door of the little side room, and presently growled: "Who's been in here, you double-crossing old sneak? Hey, Lorenz, who's been in here?"

"No one," said Lorenz. "No one except me. I took a nap this morning."

"You lie," said Renney. "You never sleep. You work all day and you stay up all night figuring out crooked deals and counting your money. I know you, you Jew."

"All right," said Lorenz. "You fix it yourself. Now I'm busy. Leave me alone."

For a moment Renney raged on. Then he settled into grumblings, and, finally, Geraldi heard him slump down on the floor.

At that, Geraldi replaced his drawn revolver in the sling beneath the pit of his arm. Still he remained for a moment in the passage, undetermined.

Once Edgar Asprey met the two criminals, there would be a hot discussion — Asprey claiming rightly that he had sent the blood money duly to them, and the others raging with suspicion and avarice. But if Asprey came to terms with them again and submitted to a second bleeding, then what would come of the position of Louise Asprey?

The marriage would next be consummated, the property would pass definitely into the hands of Edgar, and, within six hours, he would have gutted the whole fortune. The instant he had the right to sign checks, nothing could stop him. He would consume everything. So, no matter if Robert Asprey later succeeded in getting the pardon he deserved, his estate would be ruined and the work of his life thrown away.

So Geraldi figured the matter over and told himself, at last, that there was a single ghost of a chance.

He returned to the gray mare in the little secret stable. She had fed, rested, and now was feeding again with a good appetite. When he came in, she tossed up her head and looked at him brightly, with that sparkle in the eyes that means a fresh horse.

He paused not to groom her. Haste was imperative. He saddled and bridled her at once, and then slipped out through the back alley and mounted. He wound down it, crossed the flaring daylight of the broad street beyond, and so came to another alley, and then the open fields.

He had discarded his flaunting costume of the Mexican. That had failed of its purpose. He was simply Geraldi now, and well enough known to be in danger every moment he remained in this region. Yet he could not leave until he had completed certain work. God was with him to let him out of Sankeytown, unseen.

Then across the hills he raced the mare at her steady gallop wherever the way was fairly level. Down steep pitches he sprang from the saddle and ran ahead of her. Up similarly difficult spots, he climbed on foot again. A man's weight kills a horse in ascents and descents, and at high speed. For ordinary going it is no great burden. So he saved her all the way to the crest of the mountain, and then drifted her down rapidly. He straightened her out to high speed beside the lake.

It was afternoon. Brief, brief was the time that lay before him if he was to succeed in his work and return to Sankeytown by five. But that was his determination, and, counting seconds, as he laid his schemes, he set his jaw in resolution. He went straight through the heart of the city and to the house of the governor. It was opened at once as he rang the bell. He gave in a card which had the name of **William Thompson, Thompson Detective Agency** written upon it. Under this he wrote in pencil rapidly: **About the apprehension of Geraldi.**

He was shown into a small room near the door, a little semi-official waiting chamber. No eye of suspicion was cast upon him by the servant. All worked with such smoothness that he began to grow uneasy when he was told that the governor would see him. So he followed into the big library and stood beside the door. The governor told him to be seated.

"I'm taking only one moment of your time," Geraldi explained.

"Then you must be very sure of your man," said Thomas Fuller. "And I've understood that he was not so easily handled."

"I promised to see you about his apprehension," said the youth, stepping farther into the light, "and that should be easy. I am James Geraldi."

The governor smiled. Then he started to his feet and reached for the bell. When he saw that Geraldi did not stir, he withdrew his hand from the bell and waited, frowning, alarmed, but keeping strong control of himself. "I recognize you now, I think," said the governor. "Young man, what business has brought you here?"

"To show you a way out of the dark," Geraldi said.

"You have come to help me?" smiled the governor. A stern smile it was.

"I have come to help you."

"In what way?"

"To find criminals and recognize honest men."

The governor smiled again. "You are a bold young man, Geraldi," he said. "What mischief you intend to do here, I don't know. But I am very busy today. In ten minutes I shall ring this bell. The interim is yours."

"I wish to prove to you," said Geraldi, "that Robert Asprey is an honest man."

The governor shook his head. "I have the word of my most trusted adviser about him."

"Your most trusted adviser I can prove," said Geraldi, "to be a scoundrel, and a grafter."

The governor frowned and slightly shrugged his shoulders. "Of whom are you speaking?"

"Of Colonel Green."

"If you have anything to say against him,"

said Thomas Fuller, "you may wait until he is able to meet you. And that may be difficult for you."

"I still have eight minutes," said Geraldi. "Will you listen to me and try to understand that, although I have lived at the expense of society, I may not be entirely evil?"

"What are you to gain from this, Geraldi?"

"The satisfaction of keeping a promise."

"Sit down," said the governor. "I shall listen with all my heart."

Chapter Forty-Two

THE GOVERNOR RIDES

Governor Thomas Fuller always had felt — in his heart of hearts — that there was that in him which could have made the hero, the man of action. Perhaps it was this vein of his nature that made him so apt to spend more for a horse than the use he was apt to get from the animal. At any rate, there never was a time when half a dozen of the finest were not in the stalls of his stables. And of these he this day took the strongest and the swiftest of all, a mighty bay gelding with the heart of a lion and the pride of an eagle. On this monster he plunged through the city. People thought that he was being run away with. He rushed out onto the boulevard, and there drew rein, wondering how far behind him he had left this strange guide.

Geraldi had told him to look for a gray mare. But as he glanced behind, he saw nothing, and he smiled a little, in satisfaction. But yonder, straight before him, three or four blocks away, was a gray. Knowing it could not be she, but curious, he rode rapidly ahead, and there he found Geraldi.

They flew down the boulevard. They turned into the hills. His gallant bay stormed up the heights, and from the crest, looking back, he saw that Geraldi actually was on foot, straining at the run up the steep slope, while the gray mare jogged like a dog behind him. He paused, certain that the animal must have been lamed, but as they reached the upper level of the top plateau, he saw Geraldi bound into the saddle and come on at the same swimming pace that distinguished the mare's motion.

The governor swung his gelding into a canter beside the other.

"I don't want to cut out too fast a pace," he said. "Of course, I know that I'm not on an ordinary horse."

Geraldi answered, almost with impatience: "Ride on, sir, for God's sake. Trust me, I'll overtake you before you come into Sankeytown. But do you know the shortest way?"

"Overtake me?" echoed the governor. He laughed and added: "I've fairly lived through all my vacations in these mountains, Geraldi. There's no fear of my missing the road. Only . . . do you mean what you say? Overtake me?"

"I have a hundred that says I can," answered Geraldi.

The governor flushed. "Very well," he said. "I've seen enough to know that you're a very capable fellow, Geraldi. But as for your knowledge of horseflesh. . . ." He gave the bay the rein, and the fine fellow leaped away from the mare as though she were standing.

She bowed her neck against the bit in her desire to follow and match paces, but Geraldi was holding her in firmly. Some artifice, the governor had no doubt, but he wondered what the trick could be that would make the little gray mare run ahead of his gelding in the course of that run to Sankeytown.

He forgot the ominous things that Geraldi had promised to reveal to him before that day was over. He concentrated on the work before him, and, having spent a great portion of his life in the saddle, he carried the gelding along cleverly, saving its strength, rating it for the long journey. Besides, in the back of his mind, he formed a cheerful narrative, a gay story of how he, the chief executive of a great Western state, had challenged a famous criminal, a brilliant, man-killing devil of a fellow, and beaten him in a fair match, horse to horse, across the open mountains. That sort of a story, once told, would bring him ten thousand wavering, uncertain votes. It would figure well in his memoirs. It would strike a note of bold, manly relief to the recriminations and accusations of political tales. So the good governor rode with all his might.

He saw the ridges swell before him, and then drop away. He came to the last heights, and far away, beneath him, he saw the valley in which Sankeytown lay, with every window flaring in the westering light of the sun.

Then he looked behind him — and behold! not three hundred yards behind him came the gray mare, trotting like a dog, and at her side was Geraldi, spent with exhaustion, teeth set, face crimson, save where the dust had coated it gray.

The governor looked back in amazement and in fear. He told himself that no man would work like this for the sake of others. Geraldi himself, therefore, had something great to gain by this adventure. But what was more important than that, to the governor's mind at that moment, was that Geraldi was in some likelihood of winning a hundred dollars from him in that race across the mountains. So he sent the gelding ahead with a rush to cover the last long miles of the downward slope. Smoothly and easily the ground fell away, and the drop of the land gave an added reach to the long stride of the bay.

He rode for a half mile and, turning, he saw that the mare was sweeping after him. He put another hard mile behind him, jockeying the good gelding with skill. He looked back again, and the mare was not twenty lengths behind. Still another mile he worked, and then the head of the little gray, darkened with sweat, slipped up beside him, and, with a flaunt of her pricking ears, she turned and looked at the long, bony, snaky head of the gelding.

The governor drew rein with an exclamation that, in fact, was almost an oath. He was very angry. He was filled with wonder.

But Geraldi seemed to have no thought of what had happened in that race. He leaned from his saddle, lightly as a leaf, and called: "Tighten your girths a little, sir. That'll pull him together a shade. He's all abroad and beginning to sprawl."

Sure enough, Thomas Fuller felt that tall bay staggering a little. He drew rein still further. The bay fell into a trot. Even in that pace, he was stumbling. His sides went like bellows. His head bobbed like a cork among waves. It was a very sad thing, indeed, to feel the looseness of those usually mighty limbs beneath the rider.

"You weighed a good bit more than I," Geraldi was saying. "Trade horses and we'll make better time. Every minute counts, sir! Will you take this mare?"

The governor was crimson with humiliation, but he was a game winner and he was also a game loser.

"That's a glorious little mare," he said. "I've never seen her superior."

He dismounted and took the mare. She was strong as a rock beneath him. He watched Geraldi swiftly adjust the girths. He ambled the bay for a moment, and then brought him into a gallop. Half of the weariness seemed to have passed from the gelding. He strode along nobly, but the mare floated like a bubble beside him.

"By heavens," said the governor. "She doesn't seem to be touched!"

"Sir," answered Geraldi, "bear a little easier on her. She's dying on her feet."

"What?" cried Thomas Fuller.

"She's dying on her feet," answered Geraldi. "She's run from Sankeytown to your house already, today."

The governor was crushed. He opened his eyes very wide. He had always prided himself upon his knowledge of horseflesh. Now he felt sure that he always had been a rank novice. And as he thought of that, other possibilities swarmed into the mind of the governor. Before the buildings of Sankeytown loomed in front of him, he was a depressed man, looking with a touch of awe at the face of the young rider who was beside him. It seemed to Thomas Fuller that the bay gelding was actually gaining in strength.

They reached the outskirts.

"Geraldi, what price for this gray?"

"A diamond of her size," answered the youth gravely.

The governor knew he meant it.

Then they were in a twisting alley. They came to the blind wall of a building, dismounted, and Geraldi, fumbling at that blank wall, opened a little door. The governor bowed his tall head and humbly entered. The door was closed. They walked through blackness. Was it a plot, a clever trap for him? Like a fool he had followed a confessed criminal. Yet there was a pure fire of faith in Geraldi beginning to grow up in Thomas Fuller.

Another door opened. He passed into a dimly lighted, small room, and at that instant the loud voice of Colonel Smiling Joe Green boomed from the distance: "We'll have the money now . . . damn you, we'll have it on the spot! Or else we'll have your hide, you cur."

Chapter Forty-Three

THREE MEET

The face of the governor hardened. He never had heard the voice of Green pitched on this note. Geraldi beckoned him forward. They stood beside a door. Through that door the voice of another man answered: "I've sent the money. I give you my word of honor. Fifty thousand in crisp, new banknotes."

"That's Edgar Asprey speaking," whispered Geraldi.

"Damn it, man," shouted Green, "d'you think that I'm a fool to put up with such nonsense? I've talked Fuller into a twist of rope. I've made him refuse a pardon to one of the few honest men in the state. If that's not worth fifty thousand, by God, I'll talk him back again, and make him pardon Robert Asprey. Then what becomes of you, man?"

There was a pause, and a hard, snarling voice broke in, not overloud: "You got me to think of, if you try a double-cross, Asprey!"

"That's Renney, the gunman," Geraldi murmured.

The governor closed his eyes — and clenched his hands.

"I need time to think," said Edgar Asprey. "Let me see what I can do. The estate isn't entirely in my hands until I've married Missus Asprey. You have to admit that it isn't easy to pick up a hundred thousand dollars in a moment. I've already raked up the fifty. I see that you're doubling the price on me."

"You sneaking rat!" growled Renney. "Marry her? You'll pay down the cash to us before you marry her. Marry her? Three hours after that, you'd be on your way out of the country."

Geraldi took a wallet from his pocket and showed the governor that it was wadded thick with notes.

"That's the fifty thousand that was sent," he said. "That's the blood money. Suppose you keep it . . . for Robert Asprey, sir." He dropped it into the coat pocket of the governor, and Thomas Fuller took his glance away from the door and probed deeply the eyes of this youth who was resigning a fortune of that size, as a casual matter of course.

"The thing is impossible," said Edgar Asprey. "As a matter of fact, it can't be done. I can't raise another fifty thousand until after the wedding. It is scheduled for a half hour from this moment, and I have to go now."

A chair scraped.

"If you go," said Joe Green, "I'll have your blood, man. I warn you now. If you double-cross me, I'll have you shot like a dog."

"As for that," answered Edgar Asprey with a touch of lightness, "every man has to die someday."

"Open the door," said the governor suddenly. "I want to see the faces of these villains."

Geraldi, obeying, cast the door wide.

There looked in upon the trio, the tall form and pale, handsome face of the governor of the state. Edgar Asprey had risen already. The other two like crouched dogs seemed about to spring on him, when Asprey said calmly: "Gentlemen, his excellency, the Governor, Mister Thomas Fuller!"

And he, in person, bowed to the governor.

Renney cast a glance over his shoulder and groaned. Smiling Joe turned slowly, and then clutched the back of his chair. He wavered like a reed in the wind, for, in that glance, he saw his happy future smashed; he saw his life work undone, and prison gaping before him. He tried to speak. Blood rushed purple into his face, and he pitched forward senseless. The chair crashed under the impact; he rolled on the floor.

"Pick him up," directed the governor, as Renney and Edgar Asprey disappeared through the farther door. "The scoundrel was once my friend. Ah, Geraldi, this is a sad and humiliating day for me. But by God's help, I am not too late to see justice done!"

Geraldi had leaned and caught hold of the shoulders of the fallen man, when a double report of revolvers roared in the next room.

He and Thomas Fuller ran and cast the door open. On the floor they found Renney writhing in the death agony.

He had only strength to gasp: "Asprey . . . the devil's a gun-shark. God forgive me. So long . . . Geraldi."

Epilogue

In the house of Robert Asprey sat that long-exiled gentleman in person. Beside him was his daughter. On the other side lay his wife on a couch, her hand continually before her face and shudders convulsing her from time to time, as fresh waves of shameful recollections swept over her.

Across the room, giving sanction and permanence to the scene, was the governor of the state.

"Geraldi's nearly half an hour late," said Robert Asprey at length. "It's not like him to be delayed."

"I trust that nothing has happened to him," said Thomas Fuller. "He has many enemies."

"He has," said Asprey. "But I don't know one of them that's able to delay him five minutes, let alone a half hour. You've never seen him at work, sir."

"On the contrary," smiled the governor. "I once rode across from the capital with that very wonderful young man."

Then Louise said slowly: "He won't be here."

"Do you know, honey?" asked her father.

"He . . . he said good bye to me . . . this afternoon," she answered more slowly than before. "He won't be here this evening."

After this, there was a pause.

"Will he come back, ever?" asked Robert Asprey gravely.

"I don't know," said the girl. She raised her eyes and looked dreamily at the fire. "I don't know. And neither does James."

The governor and Robert Asprey exchanged significant glances. But the girl was lost in her contemplation of the fire and the future which she seemed to see in it.

"Wherever he is, wherever he may intend to go," said Thomas Fuller at last, "God give him fortune as good as he has brought to all three of us."

"Amen, by God," said Robert Asprey.

"Amen, amen," sobbed Mrs. Asprey.

But Louise said nothing at all.

Geraldi was far away across the desert. He had started with the dusk of the day, after spending a vigorous hour rubbing down the gray mare.

He had shaken hands with Lorenz. He had made up a small pack of provisions, taken a rifle and ammunition, put on his feet the moccasins of an Indian, and then he went forth secretly from the town.

He did not ride the mare. She was fairly fresh, even after her prodigious work of the day, but Geraldi would not burden her again. He struck out along the southern trail on foot, at a steady jog-trot, such as the Indians use when they have a long journey before them. He kept on without a pause, without a variation in his running. There had been a rain. The sand was firm beneath his feet, but soft enough to hush the sound of the footfall. Like two ghosts he and his mare trotted on until the moonrise.

Then they dipped over a rise and descended into a shallow valley through which ran a meager stream, bordered with willows. Here Geraldi paused for water for himself and the mare, and, as they rested a moment among the low trees, they heard the sound of a strong man's voice singing down the valley.

Geraldi came to the edge of the trees and kept watch. Presently he was aware of a mule, known by the bobbing of its head as it jogged softly along, by the trailing of its heels, and finally by the flopping of its long ears.

The jogging of the animal put a sort of secondary rhythm in the music of the song that was carried on with much strength and sweetness by the singer. He came closer, and Geraldi, smiling with pleasure, heard the words of an old Mexican song, sung long ago when the *conquistadores* first found the empire of the Montezumas and made it their prey. Still closer they came. The moon now was soaring well above the low eastern wall of the little valley, and this light fell in a full flood of silver upon the rider and his tawny mule. Geraldi saw a big man, smoothly fat, his head cheerfully thrown back, a guitar in his hands, and his dexterous fingers striking the chords with much skill.

Edgar Asprey?

A revolver glided into the hand of Geraldi. He was on the point of leaping out into the trail with a shout, ready to fire. But then something held him back, some feeling of respect, perhaps, for the brains and the dauntless cleverness and courage of this heartless rascal.

At any rate, down the valley went the singer. He became a great black silhouette, bobbing up and down. This faded in the moon haze, but still the voice flooded richly back upon Geraldi, sometimes full and strong, sometimes falling to a whisper, until the whisper itself went out and left the wanderer to the desert and the great, silver silence of the moon.

Then Geraldi whistled to the mare. Zuleikha came up the riverbank, treading like a deer softly through the brush. She came to him and laid her head on his shoulder as he looked down the valley in the direction in which Edgar Asprey had disappeared.

Then he himself began to walk forward along the same trail.

About the Author

Max Brand is the best-known pen name of Frederick Faust, creator of Dr. Kildare, Destry, and many other fictional characters popular with readers and viewers worldwide. Faust wrote for a variety of audiences in many genres. His enormous output, totaling approximately thirty million words or the equivalent of 530 ordinary books, covered nearly every field: crime, fantasy, historical romance, espionage, Westerns, science fiction, adventure, animal stories, love, war, and fashionable society, big business and big medicine. Eighty motion pictures have been based on his work along with many radio and television programs. For good measure he also published four volumes of poetry. Perhaps no other author has reached more people in more different ways.

Born in Seattle in 1892, orphaned early, Faust grew up in the rural San Joaquin Valley of California. At Berkeley he became a student rebel and one-man literary movement, contributing prodigiously to all campus publications. Denied a degree because of unconventional conduct, he embarked on a series of adventures culminating in New York City where, after a period of near starvation, he received simultaneous recognition as a serious poet and successful author of fiction. Later, he traveled widely, making his home in New York, then in Florence, and finally in Los Angeles.

Once the United States entered the Second World War, Faust abandoned his lucrative writing career and his work as a screenwriter to serve as a war correspondent with the infantry in Italy, despite his fifty-one years and a bad heart. He was killed during a night attack on a hilltop village held by the German army. New books based on magazine serials or unpublished manuscripts or restored versions continue to appear so that, alive or dead, he has averaged a new book every four months for seventy-five years. Beyond this, some work by him is newly reprinted every week of every year in one or another format somewhere in the world. A great deal more about this author and his work can be found in THE MAX BRAND COMPANION (Greenwood Press, 1997) edited by Jon Tuska and Vicki Piekarski.

The employees of Thorndike Press hope you have enjoyed this Large Print book. All our Large Print titles are designed for easy reading, and all our books are made to last. Other Thorndike Press Large Print books are available at your library, through selected bookstores, or directly from us.

For information about titles, please call:

(800) 223-1244
(800) 223-6121

To share your comments, please write:

Publisher
Thorndike Press
P.O. Box 159
Thorndike, Maine 04986